# A Little Bit of Grace

# A Little Bit of Grace

## Phoebe Fox

BERKLEY
*New York*

BERKLEY
An imprint of Penguin Random House LLC
penguinrandomhouse.com

Copyright © 2020 by Tiffany Yates Martin
Readers Guide copyright © 2020 by Tiffany Yates Martin
Penguin Random House supports copyright. Copyright fuels creativity,
encourages diverse voices, promotes free speech, and creates a vibrant
culture. Thank you for buying an authorized edition of this book and
for complying with copyright laws by not reproducing, scanning, or
distributing any part of it in any form without permission. You are
supporting writers and allowing Penguin Random House to
continue to publish books for every reader.

BERKLEY and the BERKLEY & B colophon are registered
trademarks of Penguin Random House LLC.

Library of Congress Cataloging-in-Publication Data

Names: Fox, Phoebe, author.
Title: A little bit of grace / Phoebe Fox.
Description: First edition. | New York: Berkley, 2020.
Identifiers: LCCN 2020009922 (print) | LCCN 2020009923 (ebook) |
ISBN 9780593098356 (trade paperback) | ISBN 9780593098363 (ebook)
Classification: LCC PS3606.O967 L58 2020 (print) |
LCC PS3606.O967 (ebook) | DDC 813/.6—dc23
LC record available at https://lccn.loc.gov/2020009922
LC ebook record available at https://lccn.loc.gov/2020009923

First Edition: August 2020

Printed in the United States of America
1   3   5   7   9   10   8   6   4   2

Cover art by Claudio Marinesco
Cover design by Rita Frangie

*For all those who have the courage to be who they are.*

*For John Jones, who lived it every day.*

*And for Joel, like everything.*

# One

My mother used to say that when she read me bedtime stories, my favorite time of the evening because I finally had her all to myself, I would stop her midway through and tell her what was going to happen to the characters whose lives she was spinning for me. The stories I guessed correctly I had her read to me over and over. The few that I couldn't I put in the back of the bookshelf, never to come off it again.

Of course, the biggest ending I never saw coming came just over a year ago, the day my husband and business partner—and the love of my life for as long as I could remember—sat me down and told me that although he loved me and always would, he kept thinking there must be something more, for both of us. I deserved better, Brian told me, tears I'd never seen before streaming down his face. I deserved someone who was crazy about me.

Making it heart-twistingly clear, as if he already hadn't, that he wasn't.

So I moved back into my childhood home three doors down from ours to take care of my mother in the final days of her illness, my life coming full circle as Brian and I wound up right back where we'd started—best friends and neighbors, now sharing a family law practice.

I've always been good at endings.

Maybe it was in my blood. My great-grandparents had partnered with Brian's decades ago in founding our estate planning law firm, and for generations my family had concerned itself with the end of things—the only certain, predictable part of life. The one you couldn't prevent, but you could plan for. There was something comforting in helping people do that.

Death—the ultimate ending—was a constant presence in our family's life, as much a daily part of our household as my mother and I were.

Maybe more, after my dad was gone.

Which might have been why I wasn't frightened or horrified or even particularly surprised when I waded through the unshoveled snow on Dorothy Fielding's walkway, grasped the icy wrought-iron knob on her solid-wood front door, and let myself in to find her sitting upright in a faded floral silk armchair, her eyes wide-open and staring at nothing—or perhaps, finally, at everything.

Ignoring the thickly sweet rotten smell that seemed to smother me in the stuffy heat of her house after the chill outside, I walked to Mrs. Fielding and crouched in front of her still form, looked into her glassy eyes, and placed a hand over her cool one clutching the arm of the chair as if she meant to push herself out of it as soon as she caught the breath she'd never draw again.

We'd talked about this chair she was in—a Hepplewhite antique that had been in her family for generations, which she wanted to bequeath to a cousin in Springfield. The silk upholstery was faded and frayed at the edges—she knew it needed to be redone, but hadn't had the chance to save up for the pricey job.

"Besides, I like the flowers," she'd told me in my office—one of the few positive comments she'd ever made. "It reminds me of Flevoland."

Mrs. Fielding, who had terrorized children in our small Missouri town ever since I was one of them by turning her watering hose on any who dared to dip a foot onto her manicured yard, even if we'd only lost our balance on the sidewalk and tripped a little (as I could attest after one thorough shin soaking), confided to me during our estate planning in an unguarded moment that she had dreamed of seeing the bright cups of tulips blanketing five thousand rolling acres in Noordoostpolder at the spring tulip festival but never saved enough to go. She'd had to pay for the care of her brother, who suffered from schizophrenia, after her parents had passed away penniless from the costs of his lifelong treatment and therapy.

"Besides, who would have made sure those lazy nurses at Franklin's home wouldn't leave him to starve to death while I was off gallivanting through the tulip fields in the Netherlands?" she'd griped to me.

Dorothy Fielding was as charitable as she was cheerful.

I knew all of these details about her—as well as others: that her house had been completely paid for until she had had to take out a second mortgage on it, and then a third, for Franklin's continuing care; that she had still somehow managed to save a few dollars here and there—sometimes literally—that sat glacially growing in a certificate of deposit at Sugarberry First National Bank because she didn't trust Wall Street or national chains. Our only local financial institution was run by the Faraday family, who lived in town and so "they know they'd better take good care of my money because Sarabeth Faraday has to look me in the eye every Sunday at church," Mrs. Fielding told me. I knew she'd never touched that account except to salt in her irregular deposits, and that despite its having been started in 1989, the balance was only $3,410.97.

In my line of work in our small town I learned some of the most intimate details of many of the people I'd grown up knowing all my life, but it was a patchwork quilt, as with Mrs. Fielding. Some things people told me I suspected even their dearest friends didn't know—Mrs. Fielding, for instance, had left her house and everything in it (except the chair) to a seeming stranger she had never met who lived in Arizona, and I may have been the only person in Sugarberry who knew that the woman was the daughter Mrs. Fielding had been forced by her parents to give up for adoption when she found herself pregnant at seventeen. Yet I did not know her favorite color, the best day of her life, or the name of her first love, who had fathered the child and then left for college and never returned. Such things rarely came up in my work.

I reached up and gently pressed the woman's crepey eyes closed.

But the one thing I knew most clearly of all was this: Despite the finality of one person's ending, life went on for everyone else. So I would call Ben Ferguson to come and do the official pronouncement of death and take her to the county morgue. I would call her cousin Mandy Yeager, a woman Mrs. Fielding had spoken of often, with a hard glint to her pale green eyes and a smug smile on her creased face that I didn't understand until she gleefully specified the sole bequeathal of the Hepplewhite chair: "Because I told Mandy she could have Grandmother's chair over my dead body, and I'm nothing if not a woman of my word." Mrs. Fielding had taken that vow to the extreme, I reflected, breathing through my mouth as I looked at where her body sat slumped in that same chair, thinking that new upholstery might not be enough to get the smell of her decomposing body out of the antique for Ms. Yeager.

I would also call the group home in St. Louis. Although Franklin Fielding had passed away the previous year, I hoped there might still be people on the staff used to seeing his sister several times a week for so long who might want to take a moment to honor her passing.

Not that I was counting on that.

I'd turn down the thermostat to dissipate the stifling heat that was baking poor Mrs. Fielding like a pie, and then knock on Marbelle Mason's door two houses over and let her know that she had been right about Mrs. Fielding perhaps needing someone to check on her. Mrs. Mason had cornered my cart in the soup aisle at Dierbergs the night before and told me her neighbor's porch light hadn't been turned off for two days running—"And some may say what they like about Dorothy—never me, of course—but one thing she is not is wasteful." Mrs. Mason liked to think she had her finger on the pulse of Sugarberry, and she generally arrowed straight toward me in the eternal hope that I might offer some juicy insights about our clients that she hadn't managed to dig up any other way. She always left with a hurt look of disapproval on her face when I redirected the conversation.

After all that, I would stop at Sweet Stuff Bakery before heading into the office; it was my day to pick up Friday doughnuts.

And then after work I'd rush home and wait for my husband.

Late last night, as I lay in bed waiting for sleep, my phone rang and I lit up as bright as the screen when I saw Brian's name.

"I hope it isn't too late to call." His voice slid over me, soft and warm and comforting as the childhood blanket I still slept under.

"Of course not," I said, cradling the phone to my cheek.

"So, listen, I . . ." Brian cleared his throat, and I could tell he was nervous. "I was hoping we might get together tomorrow evening and . . . talk."

I sat up, feeling a pulse leap in my neck. We hadn't ". . . *talked*" about anything deeper than the day-to-day running of the practice for quite some time, defaulting to a hale cheeriness with each other that felt like skating on plastic. "I'm free tomorrow night." As if there were anything on earth I wouldn't cancel. "What time?"

"How about I knock on your door?"

"Okay," I said, trying to control the tremor in my voice. "I'll be around."

It was too late for Dorothy Fielding to get what she'd always dreamed of.

But maybe not for me.

# Two

I knew what I'd done as soon as I came through the office door and saw Susie, our longtime receptionist.

"I forgot Bavarian crème. I'm so sorry."

I'd been on autopilot at Sweet Stuff, asking for a half dozen mixed and completely forgetting that you had to specially request the upgrade flavor—Susie's favorite.

She took the box from my hands, setting it on the counter. "It's not like I need the sustenance," she said, pulling me into her sizable bosom for a hug. "You had plenty on your mind, Grace. I'm so sorry you had to be the one to find Mrs. Fielding."

I should have known. Susie's son Daniel was the police chief of Sugarberry, and not an accident, crime, or death happened without Chief Smith calling his mama to keep her in the know. It was her primary hobby.

I sank into her pillowy softness, relishing the comfort for just a moment. Mom had gotten so skinny at the end, skin stretched over bones so fragile I'd been afraid to hug her. It was nice to cling to Susie's strong, substantial heft, to breathe in the soothing scent of baby powder to clear away the lingering stench of decay still in my nose from Mrs. Fielding's house. Her passing had left me off balance in a way I wasn't used to, and I couldn't put my finger on why.

"Is Brian in yet?" I asked when she released me.

Susie's face seemed to pull just the slightest bit taut. "Not yet," she said shortly. "Now, I've already fetched Mrs. Fielding's documents and they're on your desk. Coffee will be right in, and I suggest a nice, bracing cake doughnut."

"Thank you, Susie. Yes to coffee, but I'll pass on the doughnut." The thought of eating brought the sights and smells of the morning too viscerally to mind.

Brian was all I really wanted—the same way I always gravitated toward him anytime I was unsettled . . . or worried . . . or happy. No matter what I was feeling, he'd always been the person I used to share everything with.

A flutter of wings in my stomach reminded me that in another eight or nine hours he might be again.

As promised, on my desk was the file folder of documents Mrs. Fielding and I had worked on so diligently. We'd spent hours together, both in my office and at her house, with me having to extract every last detail from the mistrustful woman like an impacted wisdom tooth. I'd begun to suspect she just wanted the company—her will and financial situation and health documents were fairly straightforward, and on most of our visits Mrs. Fielding would wind up telling me in painstaking detail about Tulpenfestival and the Bollenroute and Noordoostpolder's orchid garden. But I didn't mind—it was the only time the hard lines of her face softened, and I was touched by the crusty older woman's enthusiasm for something as delicate as flowers, her wistful plans for the trip she'd never gotten to take. I hoped that all our talking about it had at least given her some measure of the enjoyment she might have gotten from actually going.

While I waited for my computer to boot up I flipped the folder open, reviewing the documents I already knew by heart. The will was simple—a couple of pages. The power of attorney and health power of attorney were moot now; I set them aside. We'd made a list of contact info for her few bequeathals: her cousin's cell phone, email, and address, and her oblivious daughter's name and mailing address—I was under strict instructions not to reveal the reason for the bequeathal, thank goodness. The one part of my job I dreaded was tearing back the curtain on long-kept family secrets, and I didn't need to know how Mrs. Fielding had located the girl—who'd be a middle-aged woman now—from the closed adoption records of the time. The only other thing we'd put in the file was a letter she'd written for the child she'd never claimed, sealed in an envelope, which I hadn't read and didn't intend to.

But now there was another envelope behind that—one I'd never seen. This one had my name on it in Dorothy Fielding's heavy, deliberate handwriting. I pulled it free, frowning at it.

"Susie?" I called out, but she was already standing on my threshold.

"She gave it to me a while ago," she said before I could ask. "Stood in front of my desk badgering me until I practically took an oath to put it in there in the event that . . . well."

"What does it say?"

Susie raised her eyebrows. "You don't really think Dorothy Fielding told a 'glorified typing pool girl' her deepest darkest, do you?"

I sighed, shaking my head. "Sorry about that."

"That woman's sharp tongue is hardly your fault, Grace." She ducked back out of the doorway.

I ran a thumb under the corner and slid out a single sheet of stationery, the words written in dark, blocky ink as if she'd been trying to emboss them into the paper. Something else fluttered out with it, but I ignored it for the moment, too curious about what Mrs. Fielding could possibly have wanted to tell me that she hadn't said in our many hours together.

Grace,
    Do something for yourself with this. Something ridiculous.
    Don't wait.
Dorothy Fielding

I already knew what I'd see even before I leaned down to pick up the thin rectangle of paper from the floor and flipped it over.

A cashier's check. Made out to me. In the amount of $3,410.97.

A SOFT KNOCK on my doorjamb sometime later that morning startled me; Brian was standing in the doorway when I looked up. His dark gray pants were pressed to perfection and closely fitted on his narrow hips, the cobalt color of his tailored button-down shirt bringing out the blue in his eyes—a fact I knew that he was aware of from the lavish shades-of-blue area of his side of the color-coded closet.

"Mind if I interrupt?"

My smile was as beyond my control as a patellar reflex. "You know you're never an interruption. Come on in."

He stepped to my desk, taking a seat on the edge of it, right in the spot that was slightly worn from years of this kind of informal consultation between us, his long legs canting out at acute angles, and for just a moment things were the way they'd always been. "I heard about Dorothy Fielding. Did you suggest Ben drive a stake through her heart before he bagged her up to make sure she actually stays dead?"

I laughed despite myself. "Believe it or not, it was sad."

"Susie said that dotty Dotty must have been a little juicy by the time you found her."

"Yeah, she'd probably been there a couple of days. Alone." The image of her sitting there dead with no one knowing—no one caring—clenched an invisible fist in my midsection. Was there anything sadder than being utterly alone in the world? "I've got most of her paperwork ready to go—I'm just waiting to call her beneficiaries till the police make the official notifications. But she left something strange."

"Stranger than Bob Sheldon's gallbladder?"

One of the time-honored stories at our firm concerned an early client we'd had after Brian and I joined our families' practice, and it was still our gold standard of bizarre bequeathals: a local surgeon whose postmortem instructions had included the endowment of his own removed gallbladder floating in formaldehyde to his ex-wife—"who took everything she could get out of me in life, and might as well have a piece of me after I'm dead."

"Not *that* strange. But I feel a little funny about it, ethically." I reached into my narrow top desk drawer and pulled out Mrs. Fielding's check, already creased from my handling of it as I'd contemplated her final gift several times that morning. Mrs. Fielding hadn't specifically mentioned her bank account in any of our consultations—it would have fallen under the banner of the estate she was leaving to her biological daughter if she hadn't superseded that with the note she'd left me.

Brian reached across to take the check, his hand brushing

mine. That was new—for months we'd kept a careful physical distance from each other too. "Is this a payment?" he asked, frowning at the face of it.

"No. It's everything she had in her savings account. She'd earmarked it for a dream trip she wanted to take. She left this specifically to me in a holographic codicil"—meaning handwritten—"saying I should use it for something impractical."

Brian laughed as he handed me the check back. "Does she know you? You're not exactly going to run out and buy some Manolos."

"Some what?"

He smiled warmly, shaking his head. "Grace . . . you're literally the only woman on earth who's never heard of Manolo Blahniks."

*That's not what "literally" means.* I bit my tongue on the familiar refrain.

"Shoes. I know them," I said, dropping my gaze back down to the check. "So what do I do with it? It's a cashier's check, so it's already drawn from the account; I can't just not cash it."

"Why would you not cash it?"

I flipped the edge of a stack of documents awaiting review with my thumb, listening to the *sssszzzip* of the pages fluttering. "I hardly knew Mrs. Fielding. I don't quite know why she left me this—she has specific beneficiaries for everything else. And I have savings . . . it's not like I need it."

Brian stared at me for a long moment. "Grace . . ." he said. "For God's sake, do something nice for yourself. You deserve it."

Heat rose to my cheeks, and not just from his words. It had been a long time since Brian had looked at me like that. Really looked at me.

"Well, we'll see," I murmured. Maybe I would donate it to

the staff of the assisted-living facility where her brother had lived out so much of his life. The nurses probably deserved a little bonus after decades of Mrs. Fielding breathing down their necks.

"Listen, Grace, I wanted to ask you something." Brian shifted on the edge of my desk, near enough that I had to control the automatic impulse to rest my hand on his thigh. "I hate to ask— I know I've been out of the office a lot lately—but is there any way you can take my meeting with the Kravitzes this afternoon?" His sheepish expression reminded me of the way he used to look when we were kids and he'd caused some kind of mischief he needed my help extricating himself from.

I masked the release of my held breath with a light laugh and nodded. "Sure. Just get me their file so I can prep."

He smiled, and it was like the sun coming out. "You're the best. I'll make it up to you."

Maybe he leaned in for a quick kiss, or maybe he was just pushing to his feet—I was too nervous to find out, and quickly turned to my monitor.

"Hey . . . Grace."

I looked back up to see he'd stopped in my doorway, glancing briefly toward the clacking of Susie's acrylic nails on the keyboard down the hall before stepping back inside and swinging the door closed but for a discreet crack. I slowly straightened in my chair.

"Listen . . ." he said, cupping the back of his neck with a hand the way he did when he was nervous, as if massaging his brain stem. "Well, look, I'll see you at home tonight." That radiant smile broke through the clouds again as he gave a little wave and let himself out, shutting the door behind him.

I automatically got up and went toward it—I kept an open-door policy at the office. But I stood there with my hand on the knob for a long moment, blowing out a slow breath of air to control my pounding heart.

"See you at home, Brian," I repeated softly, then pulled the door back open.

# Three

There were few memories in my life that didn't somehow include Brian McHale.

Sugarberry, Missouri, wasn't a large town—population 6,436 when I was born, which had dwindled now by a couple thousand as the younger generation fled its green pastures for greater opportunities in less rural areas. Between my family and the McHales, we knew most of the ones who stayed—partly because of the estate law practice our two families had run together since long before Brian and I came along.

Our mothers had inherited the practice the same way Brian and I had, and were BFFs decades before the term was invented, growing up three doors down from each other on Garrison Way—inseparable throughout school, roommates in college at the University of Missouri in Columbia, and, when each of them came back home from law school with fiancés in tow, eventually neighbors again in the houses they grew up in.

Brian's mother, Barbara—who had become Bobbie at MU and remained that way to every single person she ever met for the rest of her life—married Richard McHale, Fighting Tigers, baseball and wrestling, and my mom married William Adams, whose accomplishments as a championship runner might have served as a forewarning to her if she hadn't fallen head over heels for the varsity track star—and all four were Mizzou Law.

Mom and Bobbie had gotten married within weeks of each other, and they conceived their first and only children the same way, delivering so close together that for a single day, they actually managed to share a hospital room.

Brian and I might as well have been cousins, as closely as we'd grown up. Our families worked together, socialized together, even celebrated most holidays together. We tore through each other's houses as comfortably as if they were our own, and we felt like we had four parents each.

In school we'd run in separate social circles—Brian was on the debate team, the football team, the student government, and I went to math camp and worked backstage crew with the drama club—but unlike a lot of his crowd he didn't seem to care about social status or popularity. Not that I wasn't popular—but though I felt welcome in most of the high school social cliques, I was always on the periphery, even in drama, where the hard-core acting students bonded together like platelets and the crew floated silently around the fringes, a bunch of quiet kids like me who did their jobs and then drifted into the wings, happy not to be in the spotlight.

But Brian was always there, walking home with me when our schedules coincided, sometimes joining my table for lunch—always coming over when he saw me at my locker, across the hall from his, and leaning beside me for a moment to chat between classes. My childhood playmate had grown into a young man who was kind, focused, openhearted—and tall and handsome.

After the third time beautiful blond Marilyn Martin walked

right in front of me my senior year as if I weren't even there while Brian and I were talking at our lockers—and Brian politely dismissed her—I finally asked why he wasn't interested in the prettiest girl in school when she was so clearly interested in him.

"She's only pretty on the outside," he said with a one-shouldered shrug.

Maybe that was the moment I fell in love with him. Although it was hard to say. I think I might have loved him my whole life.

I was his best friend, Brian said often, a compliment that both warmed and chilled me. I cherished our relationship, our closeness, his trust—but it was always clear that for him, at least, it was never more than that.

But he was loyal. Regardless of the other girls he'd dated throughout high school, it was me on his arm for prom, me who watched with pride beating my heart all the way up into my throat as he was crowned prom king—opposite mean-girl Marilyn, who'd seethed as Brian had stepped away from her as soon as they walked off the dais and come straight to me, laughing good-naturedly about how silly the whole thing was as he playfully put his crown on my head and kissed my cheek.

My good, loyal best friend. It was enough.

But after college, when we'd both come back from separate law schools ready to join the family firm—he was University of Alabama, I was University of Kansas—something had changed.

Brian dated in school—not a lot, I knew from his occasional calls and notes, and not seriously, except for one fellow estate-law student he met during a summer internship in Boston, a woman who came home with him Thanksgiving of our last year, with her slim, dark, varnished beauty that made me feel like a clunky oaf, but disappeared shortly afterward. But when we both came back home after graduation he was different with me. Not more attentive, necessarily—but he paid attention to me *differently*. As if he saw something new he'd never taken the time to notice before.

It wasn't until the third time he took me to dinner that I realized they were actually dates—and only because that time, when he drove me home, he stopped the car, shifted toward me, and leaned his face close, then closer still.

It was so unexpected that I angled my face away to give him better access to my ear, assuming he wanted to tell me some secret, and if he hadn't touched my chin and pulled me back toward him I would have missed his lips meeting mine for an unprecedented kiss on the mouth.

A kiss that sent my heart jackhammering, my blood racing . . . and changed everything.

And at the same time it felt so familiar and comfortable and *right* as we started going out regularly, became known around town as a couple. One frigid winter night I thought Brian slipped on the ice as we came home from an awkwardly fancy steak dinner at Plaza III in Kansas City, but when I leaned over to help him up he stayed down on one knee and held up the ring that his grandmother had worn until her passing the year before, his hands shaking from the cold as much as from nerves.

I burst into tears and fell to my knees beside him, heedless of the snow melting through my fleece tights, my right hand clasped over my mouth to hold in my sobs and my left hand out, steady as the earth, as he slipped the ring over my finger.

Brian McHale could have had any woman he'd ever set his

sights on—any of the many beautiful women who'd set their sights on him all their lives. But he'd chosen *me*.

He'd been my best friend. He became my lover. He'd always been my family.

And ten months after that magical, unexpected night, he finally became my husband.

BY THE TIME I wrapped up with the Kravitzes—our one-hour meeting had ballooned to nearly three when Marsha and Ken Kravitz couldn't agree on how much of their estate would go to his son from his first marriage—the office was quiet, the lights dim. I shut down my computer, which took three tries in my haste.

"You all wrapped up for the night?" Susie said as I walked past the front desk, and I stopped in surprise.

"I didn't realize you were still here, Susie. I'm so sorry—you should have gone home an hour ago."

Her thick-penciled eyebrows were bunched. "I didn't want to leave you to walk out all alone so long after dark." The winter days in Missouri were depressingly short, and most of the time I saw the sun only through the slats of the blinds in my office window. "How'd it go with the War of the Roses in there?"

I smiled ruefully. "I guess you heard the shouting?"

"I think they heard it at the McDonald's on the corner. You managed to broker a cease-fire, though, I noticed—they left holding hands."

"They just needed to find some common ground."

"Well, they're lucky it was you who took their meeting. Come on—I'm about ready to get out of here." Susie tapped a few keys to shut her computer down and reached for her purse in a file drawer.

"I'm so sorry," I said again. "I wish I'd realized you were—"

"No need to keep apologizing, honey—you didn't ask me to stay."

"Can I at least buy you some dinner?" I made the offer reflexively, but my feet itched to bolt out to my car and get home to Brian.

Susie laughed. "Honey, you're wiggling like that time your mama was taking you to Six Flags and you had ants in your pants." One of the hazards of working at a family business in the small town where your family had lived for generations was that no one ever quite saw you as the adult you'd become. "I'm not about to keep you from whatever you're burning to get to. I hope it's something good."

My face broke into a smile I couldn't contain at the bubbling hope that I was headed to something good too. Something very, very good. "Come on," I said. "I'll walk with you—I think there are still patches of ice in the parking lot."

Joining me at the door, Susie looped one ample arm through mine and winked. "I'm hanging on to *you*, honey—maybe that way I can just float to my car."

THE MCHALE FAMILY home Brian and I had moved into after Bobbie and Rich retired and moved to a much smaller townhome in the heart of St. Louis was as familiar to me as the one I grew up in. Tonight it was glowing in the February gloom of early evening in a way I could relate to. Brian hadn't reprogrammed the timers I'd set in each room; I'd always hated to come home to a dark, empty house, especially in winter.

I swung into my own driveway three houses down. My windows cast yellow light over the snow as well, but it didn't seem as welcoming.

I dropped my purse on the table in the back hall where my mom had left hers after work every day of my life as I walked through to the kitchen, tossing the stack of mail to the counter. From the fridge I pulled out a cold bottle of water—not much else in there at the moment besides mostly unused condiments—and a frozen Amy's burrito from the freezer, before immediately putting it back. Brian hadn't said what time he'd be coming over, and I didn't want to ruin my appetite in case he had dinner in mind.

I took a jar of nuts from the cupboard, looking around the kitchen as I opened the lid.

This room had been empty and quiet now for longer than it had once served as the busy heart of my childhood home. When Dad walked out my mother seemed to lose some essential part of herself along with him. She stopped cooking the from-scratch meals I'd grown up on, as if the effort wasn't worth it for just us, and dinner often started with a box from Uncle Ben's or Stove Top or Hamburger Helper. She buried herself in work, staying at the office later and later—"because I have to do the work of two now," she told me over and over after he left to move to L.A. with his new aspiring-actress girlfriend, Nan.

It was the reason I'd come home as soon as I was awarded my law degree and started working in a practice I hadn't yet been ready to join. When I was young I'd dreamed of traveling, seeing the world before I came back to Sugarberry to settle down; despite the wide-open spaces of the Midwest farm country, the borders of our small town had always felt a little constricting.

But there was no question of that once Dad left the practice, and I'd known since middle school what my future held: carrying on the family legacy that was everything to my mother. And by then Brian was there too. To my surprise I wound up loving my job.

When Mom was diagnosed with Parkinson's disease I was extra glad I was home, and by the time she needed constant care a few years later I was on hand to help provide it until her disease finally got the best of her—because by then Brian had dropped the bomb on our marriage.

Our divorce was almost easy—neither one of us wanted to hurt the other, and above all, we both agreed, we wanted to honor and preserve our friendship. In many ways our lives stayed remarkably the same. We still worked together every day in the office, still shared the same affectionate camaraderie, and many evenings we still wound up on the couch together—at my house or his—and watched movies shoulder to shoulder, the same way we had for years.

Really, all that had changed was my address, and only by six digits. If it weren't for climbing into my childhood bed alone every night—I couldn't bear to take over Mom's room after she died—it would almost be just like it was for the duration of our marriage.

*Why* had nothing changed? I thought suddenly as I circled through the bottom floor of the house, taking in the hydrangea-print curtains in the living room that I could remember trying to count the petals of when I was barely as tall as the sill of the front bay windows they bordered, the matching aqua-colored armchairs opposite the twin of the sofa in my office—my parents had bought the set knowing they'd split it up, always frugal—the cocktail table Mom had inherited from Grammy, which had probably sat in this exact spot when my mother was little enough to crawl under it. Even my bedroom upstairs was a pastiche of furniture and linens that someone else had selected—my grandmother, before she and Gramps bought the farm (literally, not figuratively, at least not then) and moved ten miles outside of town; my mother, back when she cared about things like that. Before Dad left and Mom stopped caring about anything.

I passed the large gilt-framed mirror in the entry hall that had been in my family for generations, catching my reflection amid the crackle of its tarnished surface.

I hadn't even put my own stamp on my appearance, I realized, stopping to really look at myself. My long hair, a color between brown and blond that couldn't really be called either, was pulled back in the same easy ponytail I'd worn since I was in elementary school. My face was free of makeup. Even my clothes were as basic as could be, chosen from catalogs based on practicality and size more than style or color or fit.

Why was I always so content to bob along on the path of least resistance? I didn't even fight to keep my marriage intact, to hold on to the husband I still loved, when we hit the first speed bump of marriage a few years ago—just docilely acquiesced as though arguing would be the height of rudeness.

*All* marriages had tough times. All of them went through highs and lows, ebbs and flows—Brian's own parents were proof of that, rock-solid until retirement, when cracks began to show in new periods of irritation and impatience with each other. But they got over it, came through it, and stood stronger than ever together right up until they were hit by a drunk driver on I-35 in 2009 and died as they'd lived: side by side. As long as two people loved each other, were committed to each other, to the family they'd created together, all they had to do was hold on tight during the tough times and weather the storm.

Why hadn't Brian and I realized that?

But maybe he had. Maybe his coming over tonight meant that he'd had the revelation I was only having now: that things didn't have to stay this way. That we could carve out the path we wanted for ourselves, fight for it, grapple our way through the rough patches to stay on the track we chose.

*Do something for yourself. . . . Don't wait*, Mrs. Fielding's note had said.

What I wanted to do was win Brian back. More than anything. And I was ready to fight for that.

When the doorbell rang I nearly leaped off the carpet, my heart galloping in my chest.

Things were going to change.

But as I took a deep, steadying breath and opened the door to a whoosh of frigid air, it wasn't Brian's bright, nervous, hopeful smile that struck me the hardest.

It was the stunningly beautiful and unexpectedly familiar brunette beside him—a woman I hadn't seen in twelve years, since she'd accompanied Brian home from law school and sat almost silently beside him at the Thanksgiving dinner Mom and I always shared with the McHales.

Things *were* going to change, I thought as I gripped the door so hard the ancient wood gave under my fingers.

Just not in the way I'd expected.

# Four

I slammed the door in their faces.

It happened before I could stop the action, before I even realized I'd done it. The iron grip I had on the wood turned into a sudden swing back, forward, and then I let go.

*Wham!*

The sharp clap woke me up out of the trance I'd been in, and as I saw the two silhouettes shifting uncertainly through the frosted beveled glass insert in the door—which I was somewhat shocked hadn't shattered with the force—my mind raced. I reached for the brass door handle and swung it open, my soothing work smile in place.

"I'm so sorry," I said. "My hand slipped. Come in—we've met, haven't we?" I said to the brunette, as slim and varnished as I remembered. Had the woman even aged in the years since I'd met her? I thought of the face I'd just been examining in the mirror, the lines threading across it.

They were from the tarnish spidering across the silver surface, I reminded myself. Not from wrinkles.

The woman glanced at Brian, who gestured her in before following, and I somewhat woodenly led them to the front sitting area. She sank like a ballerina to the floral sofa, Brian settling a few inches away, while I took one of the turquoise armchairs, dropping into the sprung seat. I scooted forward to the edge, my back rigid, hands clasped over my knees, eyebrows nailed upward, the mechanical smile fixed to my face like a glue-stick collage.

"I can't believe you remember Angelica," Brian said.

Angelica. Of course. It couldn't have been Olga or Bertha or Gertrude.

"It's been a long time," I said, my gaze meeting the other woman's. Big dark Cleopatra eyes glinted out from eyelashes so long they looked practically bovine against her glowing skin and glossed lips. Everything about the woman was shiny, from her liquid-looking shoulder-length dark hair that seemed to bounce back the yellow light of the lamps to her silky fitted blouse to the reflective gleam of her polished patent-leather pumps. I felt like a black hole. "Thanksgiving of 2006," my voice said.

Oh, for God's sake—even the woman's perfect white teeth reflected light into the room as she smiled. "You're as smart as Brian said. I can't believe you remember that."

Because people tended to forget the first time their lifelong love finally got serious enough with someone to bring her home, and it turned out she was a goddess. Because *that* wasn't a life-altering dream crusher or anything.

But I was *smart*. Smart enough not to say any of that, at least.

"So . . . you two have reconnected?" I said instead. "How nice."

"Grace, I could never lie to you, or hide anything from you," he said. "That's why we . . ." He slid a glance to Angelica, who missed it entirely, looking directly at me with what felt uncomfortably like pity. "That's why I wanted to come talk to you. I didn't want you hearing anything from anyone else but me. Angelica and I . . . we couldn't make it work in school because, well, she wasn't ready to think about moving to a town like Sugarberry, away from Boston. But now . . ." He shrugged. "Well, you know how life can change things you never thought were changeable."

*Yes, I can think of an example off the top of my head.*

As if in slow motion I saw him reach across the scant inches that separated his leg—*my* leg, attached to *my* husband, wearing the pants *I* bought for him—from the long, iridescent expanse of Angelica's nylon-clad thigh, saw him take her smooth white hand, cradle it in his own while he brought the other over it as if to shield it from the hot stare I realized I was giving the gesture.

"Well, now that circumstances have changed for both of us . . . Angelica's going to be living here. In Sugarberry." His voice had grown softer and gentler on each word, as if wrapping them in gauze would cushion the blows. Angelica was watching me carefully, as if I were a volatile material.

"How . . . completely . . . marvelous." My smile felt like Silly Putty pulled taut between my ears.

"Really?" Brian said. "It's . . . you're okay?"

"I want the best for you. And *look* at her!" I said, waving a vague hand in the air. "If that's not the best specimen of womanhood I've ever seen, I have no idea what is."

Brian's forehead crinkled. "Grace . . ."

Angelica had leaned back as if waiting to see whether a coiled rattler were going to spring, and I swung my gaze to her. "You're obviously everything any man could want. Certainly everything this one does!"

I looked at the two of them sitting beside each other, genetically superior beings who had just beamed themselves to the galaxy of primitive man, looking on with indulgent, pitying smiles as he tried to impress them with how he could make fire. I remembered my breathless determination to fight to make my husband love me again and felt foolish shame rise up in my throat.

My laughter tore into the room like bullets. "If he doesn't snap you up, I just might, and I'm not even gay. Ha, ha, ha!" The sound I was making went on and on, leaking out of me like a sitcom laugh track that had glitched into a loop, while the beautiful couple in front of me looked on poker-faced, apparently not getting the joke at all.


AFTER THEY LEFT—mercifully soon after my incontinent giggling—I stood in the upstairs bathroom, again examining myself in a mirror.

I pulled the scrunchy from my hair and shook it out across my back, shrugged out of my suit jacket and laid it on the counter, smoothed the brushed white cotton of my blouse. *The hell with it*—I unbuttoned the top button.

I wanted to see what Brian saw when he looked at me. What the exquisite Angelica had seen.

No wonder she had seemed so confident.

I turned out the light.

# Five

By six thirty the next morning, the inside of my kitchen was a match for the view outside its window: drifts of white covered nearly every surface—a blanket of snow in the backyard over the browned grass I hadn't seen for weeks, a scattering of flour and sugar on the counters inside.

The coffee cake that baked in the oven was starting to pillow up at the edges, the smell of cinnamon swirling through the house. The family recipe was one I remembered making with Mom from the time I was old enough to climb onto a plastic step stool she kept in the kitchen pantry so I could stand beside her and help her cook, always in the same battered metal rectangular pan, but it had been a long time since the sour cream kuchen's familiar scents had filled this kitchen.

While it finished baking I took a quick shower and dressed, then polished off the pot of coffee while I watched the kuchen cool on the counter. Mom always said it was best served exactly fifteen minutes after baking, when it was hot and tender and crumbly. Dad and I would gather eagerly around the yellow kitchen table as Mom set the pan in the center and cut us each a still-steaming square. He'd slather the already-buttery cake with even more fresh butter and let it melt into the crevices while Mom rolled her eyes and smiled . . . every single time.

The family memory brought an ache to my eyelids. There weren't many good ones.

I had to wait a little longer so I could transport the pan without burning my fingers, and realized it was far too early for a neighborly visit anyway, baked peace offering or not.

I filled the time by shoveling the fresh sprinkling of snow off the front walk—as quietly as possible, so as not to disturb Mrs. Aronson, the widow who'd lived alone next door all my life. Temperatures were supposed to warm up near the forties today before plunging again tonight, and I didn't want to have to chisel a sheet of ice up tomorrow if I let it melt to the concrete. With that in mind I shoveled hers as well.

After that I read the St. Louis paper—all of it, including every single obituary by force of habit. Pulled up my email and answered a few questions from clients. Watched twelve minutes of some crudely animated show with what looked like a paper-cutout tiger farting rainbows. I remembered weekends being a lot more fun when I was a kid.

Or when I was married.

Finally a little after ten I pulled on a coat and hat and walked down the street carrying my tribute. *Kuchen makes* everything *better*, Brian used to marvel when we were kids and he'd shovel a fist-sized hunk into his mouth whenever he saw the signature pan sitting on the counter.

Let's hope that applied to mortifying social faux pas with your ex and his new girlfriend.

At Brian's, I balanced the pan in one hand while I gave a muffled knock with gloved knuckles. The air chilled my lungs as I sucked too much of it in, trying to calm my tripping heart.

When the red wooden door swung inward, I was grateful it was Brian who answered. I didn't think I could face the beautiful Angelica opening my old front door.

He looked startled to see me, but then his face quickly warmed into a smile.

"Grace . . . hey."

I lifted the pan on my fingertips like a pizza deliveryman. "I brought you something," I said with a smile that stretched my frozen cheeks.

"Is that what I think it is?"

"Have you ever seen anything else come out of this pan?" I shot back. Brian laughed, and for just a moment we were us again.

"Come on in," he said, opening the door wider. "Have some of it with me."

*With me.* Breath trapped in my lungs siphoned out of me. She wasn't here. She hadn't spent the night. Maybe she didn't even exist. Maybe last night had been just some nightmare I'd had that seemed unusually real.

But as soon as I stamped the snow off my boots and stepped across the threshold, Angelica glided down the stairway, her glossed lips smiling, and my chest seized up again.

She should have looked more human in the light of day, less luminescent, but even in faded skinny jeans with ankle boots and a fitted plaid flannel button-down she looked stylish, like Hollywood's idea of a sexy female lumberjack.

Had she just come down from the bedroom—our old bedroom? Rolled out of Brian's arms in our center-dipped queen-sized mattress and into our shower where the water always pooled along the back edge because when Brian's dad redid the bathroom himself eighteen years ago, he didn't remember to slope it? Were the clothes from her suitcase hanging on the side of the closet where mine used to be, her no doubt silky delicate underthings folded into the drawer where my practical cotton panties were once crammed in?

"Grace," she said, flashing that dental-ad smile and yanking me out of the thoughts making me feel queasy. "What a . . . nice surprise to have you visit first thing on a Saturday."

"First thing"? At practically lunchtime? "Visit" the house where I'd never even had to *knock* my entire life? I stumbled over the petty words I didn't say: "Is it . . . Oh—I'm sorry. I thought it was . . . I waited, but I guess I should have called—"

"It's fine." Brian patted my shoulder, turning toward Angelica so I couldn't see his expression. "Grace was thoughtful enough to bring over one of my favorite things—wait till you try her kuchen."

"Kuchen?"

"German for cake," I said. "It was my grandmother's recipe, and that's what she always called it."

"It's literally the greatest cake ever made." Brian had lifted the foil while I still held the pan (and my tongue) and was inhaling the warm sweet smells it released, his eyes closed. "Ohhhh, it's like I'm twelve again and all is right with the world."

Wouldn't it be fantastic if Grammy's kuchen could actually magically take us back there, when everything *was* right in our world? I could go back and start over, knowing what I knew now, and somehow prevent us from winding up here: me standing awkwardly opposite the love of my life in the foyer where we'd once stood shoulder to shoulder to greet our own guests. As Brian took the first bite we'd be swept back in time, and this go-round I'd try a little harder, be a little more vigilant . . . make myself a little prettier, I added, glancing at Angelica's perfect profile.

I whipped the knit hat off my head, realizing too late that static would send my frizzy hair into a crazy halo. I tried to smooth it down with the hand holding the hat, still balancing the pan in the other, but that just made it crackle more.

"Well . . . I guess I can just leave this with you guys . . . ?" I said, holding it out again stiffly.

Angelica stepped forward, but she didn't take the pan. Instead she set her slim fingers gently on the edge of it and pushed ever so slightly toward me. "It was such a sweet thought, but why don't you keep it for yourself, Grace?"

"Oh . . . well, I—"

"Are you crazy, Angel?" Brian said. "This thing is literally heaven on earth."

His nickname for her was so perfect it made me want to puke.

"Honey . . . all that sugar," she said sotto voce, as if I might not hear sounds in a lower register even spoken thirty inches away from me. "It's hard on the digestion," she said, patting her flat stomach delicately. "For both of us." She made meaningful eyes at Brian.

Was she really going to monitor not only what she chose to eat, but what *he* could? I had a sudden urge to upend the cake right into her perfectly made-up face.

Angelica must have seen my reaction, but she misinterpreted it. Her hand flew to her chest and her expression turned crestfallen. "Oh, my gosh, Grace, I'm being horribly rude. I'm so sorry. I don't know what I was thinking." She lifted the pan from my still-extended hand—*finally*—and took a cautious sniff as the knot in my stomach started to uncoil. "Wow, Brian's right—this smells like nirvana." She beamed that smile directly at me, and a wash of relief came with it that I'd misjudged her. Brian hadn't abandoned me for a monster.

"This is perfect—now we'll have something to offer the movers this afternoon when they get here with my things."

Later I would realize that the residual snow clinging to the rubber soles of my boots had melted into a puddle in the entryway, which was why, as I took an involuntary step backward, I slipped on the wet tile.

But at the time it felt as if Angelica's casual announcement that she was not just moving to Sugarberry, but moving *in*—here, with Brian, into our old house—slammed me like a fist, and I went down.

*Six*

I hit my head hard enough to send me to the emergency room for fear of concussion. Angelica had to wait for her movers to arrive, but Brian accompanied me in the ambulance to make sure I was okay. "She'll be fine—the EMTs are professionals," "Angel" assured him. At which he'd shrugged her restraining hand off his arm and insisted that I not be alone.

In the exam room, seeing me lying pale and bleeding in a hospital bed, Brian realized how he might have lost me forever. How fragile and impermanent life is. Not to be wasted on frivolous whims, like shiny new playthings, but to be spent strengthening already meaningful, deep connections. He laid his palm alongside my cheek, leaned close so I could hear him over the clattering chaos on the other side of the curtain, and said—

"Hey! Did someone order a pizza or what?"

The muffled words jolted me awake. I didn't realize I'd dozed off on the floral sofa in the living room, and I sat up, my heart pounding.

The other end of me started pounding too as soon as I did— instead of the tragi-romantic knock to my head at Brian's I'd been dreaming about, in reality I fell flat on my butt, my tailbone hitting the slate of the foyer so hard that tears sprang to my eyes. I was going to have a strange-looking bruise blooming out the top of my underwear for a while.

Luckily there was no danger anyone would see it.

The loud clattering from my dream came again, right outside my front door, along with the same voice: "Hey! You want your pizza or not?"

I lumbered to my feet, wincing at the pain every step brought, and opened the door to see a skinny guy with an insulated food carrier in one hand, a set of keys in the other, which he'd been using to bang on my door. His face was red from the cold and the wind that came swirling around my feet with a smattering of snow, his eyes watering.

"Please don't do that," I said, turning to the entry table for my wallet. "You might break the glass."

"Thought you weren't home. You got no idea how many kids think it's hilarious to call for pizza delivery to the wrong address. Like I got nothing better to do than stand out here freezing my ass off for ten minutes." He spoke with a jaded, tired air despite being barely more than a kid himself. I wondered how long it would be before he got tired of his thankless job and followed so many others out of Sugarberry to career opportunities greater than pizza delivery. Or whether he'd wind up like me, watching all his friends slip out of town one by one.

"I'm sorry. I didn't hear you. I was"—*napping* sounded too pathetic at seven p.m. on a Saturday night—"using a band saw," I finished inanely.

He looked at me strangely. "Yeah. That's twelve fifty."

I handed him a twenty. "Keep it."

After the door had shut behind him, I shuffled into the

kitchen with my small pepperoni—because, sure, kids pulling pranks placed sad little orders like that—and slid it to the counter beside the pile of mail I'd grabbed from the box earlier and hadn't bothered to sift through. I got out a single plate and a single napkin and opened the lid of the box. I hadn't eaten since breakfast, but either the kid had been telling the truth about how long he'd been out there or I needed to find a new pizza delivery place, because the congealed mess the pie had become in its thirty-degree commute made any appetite I thought I'd had flee. I closed it up again and put it in the refrigerator, reaching to the cabinet to the right of the sink where we kept medicine. Mom's prescription bottles were still huddled together where I hadn't yet gotten around to cleaning them out, and I pushed them to one side. Two Advils and the glass of water I washed it down with would be dinner.

I stood staring out into the blackness of the backyard, the sun having set hours before. Winter days were short in Sugarberry, the nights long.

Perfect for lovers.

I pictured Brian and Angelica wound around each other's bodies, naked on the floor under a bearskin blanket in front of a roaring fire, murmuring endearments to each other as they made love all night long in the cozy warmth of the house against the frigid night outside.

Some part of me registered that I was casting them in a Hallmark movie, or a Nicholas Sparks film—I really needed to do something else in the evenings than sit in front of the TV—but I couldn't stop the images, even when I pressed my cold hands into my eyeballs till kaleidoscope colors swirled behind them.

After a horrified Brian had helped me off the floor of his foyer, Angelica looking on with a troubled (but still astonishingly attractive) expression, I'd brushed off their concern and quickly let myself out the front door, limping back up the street to my parents' house. Shame had heated my face to what I knew would be a telltale red, and showing them the visible evidence of my embarrassment would have added insult to injury—not just my bruised tailbone, but my pride.

Twice now—in less than twelve hours—I'd acted like a complete fool in front of Brian. In front of the woman he was apparently serious enough about to have move into his house—*our* house—at a dead run.

Or so it seemed to me. For all I knew they'd been seeing each other for a while.

Maybe a long while.

The thought clamped a fist around my heart. We'd been divorced for almost eight months, separated—by three houses—for over a year. And yet for me our marriage still felt so recent, close enough that sometimes I thought I could rewind the clock just a little bit and pretend none of the last year had ever happened.

But maybe Brian had been over it even before it was actually over. Maybe he'd wasted no time calling his old flame and rekindling the fire.

Or maybe, when he had told me I deserved someone who was "crazy about me," he was already thinking of someone else he felt that way about.

That thought knocked the air out of me, and I leaned over, bracing myself on the counter, trying to remember how to breathe.

*In. Out. In. Out,* I coached myself silently as I stared without seeing at the Formica. *Suck it in. Push it out.* Oxygen got into my bloodstream, but it didn't wash away the images still playing in my head.

Brian had taken an extended trip right after we decided to separate. "I need to get my head straight," he'd told me. "And it would be too hard on both of us for me to see you moving out."

It wasn't as though I needed his help for the move—knowing I was headed to Mom's, I didn't take much. I didn't want to clutter up her ordered household with furniture she didn't need, so I simply packed my clothes and toiletries and carried them in suitcases up the street.

Later, while I'd nursed my mom through the final stages of her illness, Brian left again for nearly two weeks, and he came back looking easier, comfortable in his own skin for the first time in months.

I'd thought it was a good sign—that the vacation had done him good. That perhaps now that his head was starting to clear and he was seeming like himself again, maybe soon he'd be ready to work on *us*. I only needed to be patient.

And I was—while he took several more trips in the next months, I held down the fort at work. I sat with Mom in the evenings, read to her, brought her the food she could eat, and, once she couldn't manage to get it to her mouth anymore, fed it to her.

As the weeks and then months went on, I was almost grateful to Brian for his timing, however unexpected—at least I could be there for Mom. And as much care as she increasingly needed, I wasn't left with a lot of time to wallow in self-pity.

But the downside of that, I could see now, was that I'd delayed processing what had happened to us. It was as if Brian and I were on hold while I dealt with the crisis at hand—I'd compartmentalized the dissolution of our marriage as something I would cope with later. Meanwhile he'd apparently been working through whatever grief and mourning there was over our divorce . . . and moved on.

And "later" for me was apparently now.

A blink cleared my vision and made me realize it had been blurred by self-pitying tears. I blinked again . . . again . . . till finally what I was looking at came into sharp focus.

A turquoise beach. Crystal-white sand. Blue, blue sky. The image was so achingly beautiful and opposite the cold monochrome winter world I was living in that it almost seemed like a mirage. *Everything's Perfect on Cypress Key!* the caption said in a jaunty font.

It was a postcard, tucked in among the other envelopes and junk-mail flyers that had fanned out across the counter where I'd tossed them.

Who sent postcards anymore?

And who on earth did I know in a tropical paradise like this?

I swiped my eyes and stood up, reaching for the card and flipping it over.

*Dear Tricia.*

It was jolting enough to see a handwritten personal note addressed to my mother, who'd been gone for nearly a year. Stranger still that I had no idea who might have an intimate enough connection with her to call my mom "Tricia," a nickname I'd never heard anyone else use, even my dad. I kept reading.

*The sun is warm here and the sea soothes all ills. I know we have had a difficult past, but as I get older, I realize more and more what matters most: the people we love.*

*We are all we have left, my dear. Let's let the sea wash away*
*old wounds and enjoy the present while we have it. Please come.*
*I have never stopped loving you.*
M

I stared at the words as if they were written in another language. It was signed with only the single initial—*M*—and underneath was a phone number with a 239 area code. Where was that?

I flipped the card back to the front, the paradisiacal image
instantly uncoiling something wound tight inside me, just as
the note had said. *Everything's perfect on Cypress Key!*

*I know we have had a difficult past. . . . Let's let the sea wash*
*away old wounds. . . .*

Who was this person? I quickly flipped the card again, investigating the handwriting for clues, but it told me nothing: a
neat, elegant cursive that could have come from the hand of either gender.

My father left my freshman year of high school, when I was
fourteen. Mom would have been young enough to not want to
spend the rest of her life alone. Why wouldn't she have been
open to loving someone else?

But I remembered the shell of a person she had become after
Dad and Nan, his too-young, overdone girlfriend I could only
think of as *nubile*, moved out west. It was as if Mom's life had
simply frozen in that frame, only a two-dimensional static picture of who she had been remaining.

I couldn't imagine the woman she had become looking for or
embracing new love. Or anything, for that matter. It always
seemed to me that when my father had so harshly stopped caring about her, so did she.

*I realize more and more what matters most: the people we love.*

But who was this person who had loved my mother when Mom seemed to have stopped loving herself?

And why did my mother seemingly reject their relationship, whatever it was?

The insistent peal of the doorbell sliced into my thoughts, startling me, and I fumbled the card back to the counter. Did I forget to tip the pizza boy?

It rang again.

"I'm coming! *Please* be patient."

But it wasn't the skinny kid with the short temper.

It was Brian.

# Seven

He'd come over without a jacket, and he stood on the porch in the same red flannel shirt he'd had on that morning, huddled in on himself against the cold and wet snowfall with crossed arms and fingers jammed into his armpits.

"Good Lord, come inside!"

I took a step back and he wasted no time following my instruction. "Your bulb's blown in the doorbell," he said, stamping the snow off his shoes on the mat and rubbing his hands along his forearms to friction-warm them. I battled my instinct to take them and chafe them between mine, like I would a child. "I can fix that for you this week."

"You're freezing," I said, ignoring the offer.

He looked at me from under the fall of hair over his eyes with his familiar grin. "I forgot I'm not twelve and coated in baby fat."

I shook my head, trying not to smile and failing. How many times had we stood here just like this when we were young, running back and forth to each other's houses without bothering with coats or sometimes even shoes, regardless of the weather?

"You're crazy. We're not kids anymore."

His face sobered and the spell was broken. "I know we're not, Grace."

We stood there in an awkward silence.

"Do you . . . want some hot chocolate?" I finally said.

"Yes! That would be perfect!" he said too enthusiastically. "Adams-style, right?"

"Of course."

My mom made hot chocolate from scratch on the stove, and Brian and I would always head here after playing in the snow to warm our fingers and our insides with mugs of the thick, spicy, intensely chocolatey beverage that was nothing like the watery powdered kind his mom served at their house. Neither he nor I would be caught dead drinking cocoa from an envelope with oily, sickly sweet reconstituted marshmallows bobbing on top.

I broke squares of baking chocolate into a saucepan on the stove and added the milk and sugar and vanilla, feeling Brian's eyes on me the whole time, grateful to have something to occupy my hands and my attention.

Why was he here?

And where was "Angel"?

But I said nothing, just let the silence sit between us, knowing that when he was ready he'd talk. I sprinkled into the pan a dash of cayenne and grated in fresh cinnamon and nutmeg, poured the thick concoction into two of the squat, chunky mugs my mom always served the drink in, and set them on the kitchen island, taking the stool beside him.

"Grace . . . I'm so sorry," he said down into the rising steam.

*For what?* I wanted to ask. *For Angelica? For our divorce? For forgetting the life we built together? For not having an absorbent doormat in your foyer?* But I simply took a sip from my mug with a slight nod. Brian always had to talk till he found his way to what he was trying to say.

"I didn't . . ." He trailed off, wrapping both his reddened hands around the mug, and I imagined the warmth I'd created seeping into his chilled skin. "How's your heinie?" He gave a cockeyed grin and tipped his head toward where the body part in question was perched on the stool.

I wiggled slightly, trying not to wince. "Almost good as new. Well, at least as good as it was before I went down like the *Titanic* in our . . . in your foyer."

I meant to make him laugh, but neither one of us did.

"You could have cracked your head open, Grace. You could've . . ." He stopped, took another sip, and I heard the evidence of his throat closing up in the audible sound of his swallow.

"It was just a stumble, Brian," I said softly. "It wasn't your fault."

"Grace . . ." His eyes lingered on mine. "How did things get so totally screwed up?"

Well, I had a few ideas on that one, chief among them the human disco ball sitting back at the house we'd started our marriage in. I gripped my own mug, pressed my lips shut against the urge to blurt out that I forgave him, that we could get past this, that all he had to do was send Angelica away and give us a fresh start.

He stared down into his cup of chocolate as if whatever words he was looking for might rear up from the murky depths like the Loch Ness Monster.

"Angelica's pregnant."

I'd just taken my first careful sip when his mumbled words caused my hand to jerk. I leaped to my feet, bending over, clutching the counter as a thick slosh of burning liquid clung to my tongue and the roof of my mouth, my eyes watering. Finally I risked swallowing, the chocolate blazing fire down my throat.

"What did you say?" I immediately wished I could unsay it—the last thing I wanted was to hear the awful words repeated.

"I'm so sorry, Grace. I wanted to tell you . . . I kept trying." He looked like he was going to cry. "But there never was a right time—I mean, you know why."

I knew why. Of course.

When our fertility specialist had finally told us that it was unlikely I'd ever conceive, thanks to the reproductive double whammy of "poor-quality eggs" and a childhood infection that had caused "destruction of the endometrial lining," it was Brian who'd taken the news as a full-body blow. "I always thought I'd have kids," he'd murmured, his knees on his elbows in Dr. Atman's office, his head hanging into his hands.

I'd imagined it too—but as something that might happen in the future, down the line. As one possibility among many. I hadn't realized until that moment that for Brian it was a mandate.

"Brian, it's okay . . . if we want children we can adopt," I suggested, rubbing a slow circle on his lower back, as if I could soothe this away as easily as I did his tight muscles after a workout.

"No, *real* kids," he said into his cupped hands. "*Our* kids."

I hadn't known what to say to that, how to comfort him, my hand falling back to my lap as the doctor suggested giving ourselves a chance to process the news before discussing our options.

After a silent walk through the parking lot afterward, we sat in the car, me staring at Brian with his hands tight to the wheel,

Brian staring at the dashboard. I kept quiet, my hands clenched on my thighs as if his bunched shoulders and biceps made him too brittle to touch. What could I say?

"Everyone thinks it's the woman who has the hardest time with news like this," Dr. Atman had murmured kindly when I hung back after Brian charged out of the exam room. "You'd be surprised how often it's the man. Just give him time."

On one level Dr. Atman was right. Even before we got home, Brian loosed one hand's grip on the wheel and reached for mine, holding it so tightly my fingers collapsed in his and grew numb, but the connection told me we'd get through this.

And we did. Though there were nights when he retreated to his home office after I'd gone to bed, as weeks turned into months our lives finally began to feel normal again. We went to movies, we worked together on home improvement projects, he went back to the gym and rejoined weekend pickup games with his friends, and Brian's smile slowly returned.

I thought a lot about our future, the family we'd always assumed we'd create together, and Brian's clear desire for children of his own. And so one night when he'd come to bed long after I had, as I lay on my back watching the ceiling fan swirl and felt his side of the bed dip, heard the slide of his legs against the sheets, the uneven sound of his breaths telling me he wasn't sleeping either, I spoke into the darkness: "Brian . . . I'd be okay with a donor. And a surrogate. It would still be our child."

For a long time he didn't answer, and I wondered whether he'd fallen asleep or was pretending to. Finally the bed shifted and he rolled over to face me, propping a hand under his head and looking at me for a long, silent moment I couldn't read in the fuzzy dark. "It's okay, Grace," his voice finally rumbled into the night. "We'll play the hand we were dealt." He reached over and touched my face, leaned down, and pressed soft lips to my temple.

The tender gesture was the first time he'd reached for me in bed in a while, and hope ballooned in my chest even though he pulled away and lowered himself to his pillow. *Baby steps*, I told myself. We lay side by side, our pinkies linked, for a long time before I finally heard his breathing even out.

It was the last time we'd talked about it.

Still slumped on the bar stool, one elbow propping him up against the breakfast bar, Brian gripped the back of his neck, rubbing like he meant to start a friction fire. "And then I just decided I had to tell you, it wasn't right, so I—"

"That's why you came over here last night. With her." My voice was unrecognizable to me, scratchy and tight, stretched thin like a rubber band.

He nodded. "I told Angelica I can't be happy if you aren't happy."

He'd come over last night, at the eleventh hour, to spring his new girlfriend, their cohabitation, *and* his impending baby on me. All at once. In front of an impossibly glossy total stranger.

I had a sudden flash to this morning, Angelica rubbing her perfectly flat belly and saying sugar was bad for *both* of them. It wasn't Brian she'd been talking about. She'd wanted me to know.

My stomach churned, blood surging in my veins like hot lava.

"You want me to be happy," I said, my tone flat and dead as roadkill. But something was building in me. Something terrible.

He had the good grace to look at least slightly ashamed. "I do. You're my best friend, Grace. I can't stand hurting you—it's literally killing me."

"That is *not* what 'literally' means!" The words were loud, shrill, and they startled both of us. "If it were *literally* killing you, Brian, you would be dying right now. *Literally*. Like, incinerating from the inside from all your deep, burning pain for hurting me, and crumbling to nothing, like a log disintegrating into ash."

I snarled the words, and Brian was staring at me with wide eyes and an expression of disbelief.

My head felt tight, pounding, my eyeballs too big for their sockets like the stress doll my father used to squeeze all night long in front of the TV. My nails dug crescents into my palms as I advanced on him like a predator and my tongue kept going in an unstoppable caustic stream.

"But you're *not* dying—see?" I jabbed his arm with one finger, hard enough to leave a bruise, and he scrambled off the stool as if I'd stabbed him. "No crumbling. So don't say stupid things you don't really mean! You want me to be *happy* for you? Are you insane?" The words burned worse than the chocolate, hot with sarcasm and rage.

Brian was frozen in shock and what looked horribly like disgust, but there was no stopping me. The volcano had blown and lava was spewing out.

"'Oh, golly, sure, Brian, of course! Of course I'm happy for you, hyuk-hyuk-hyuk!'" My bad Goofy impersonation included a deranged, stiff Bojangles jig with my arms held out and dangling from the elbows. "'As long as you're happy, then dumb little docile Grace is happy too!'"

"Grace . . . are you okay?"

"No, you moron! I'm not okay! I'm the furthest thing from okay! Are you somehow not *seeing* this, or are you *literally* just that stupid?"

He had one hand over his mouth, the way you look when

watching a natural disaster unfold, but from a safely removed distance. I'd gone too far—much too far, I realized with a sick, choking feeling, and I could see Brian retreating from me even before he took two slow steps away, then turned on his heel and walked out of my house.

THE SECOND I heard my front door close—a soft, controlled click that seemed infinitely worse for some reason than an angry slam—I ran to the front window, peering through the blinds like Boo Radley as I watched Brian walk toward my old house. His steps were sharp, quick, as if he couldn't get back to his pregnant girlfriend fast enough, but even so he paused in his driveway to lay a reverent hand on his car—the beloved Cadillac (blue, of course) he bought brand-new, over my practical objections to the premium price tag, just for the privilege of driving it off the line, and then coddled and babied like the child we'd been unable to have. I'd helped him clean out our garage as soon as I realized the car's symbolism, not uttering a peep when he insisted on buying expensive rubbery flooring to cradle it, all our lawn equipment and garden tools and stored detritus shoved into the other side so that they ran no risk of ever grazing the precious vehicle.

The car was never left out to fall victim to the elements—even if Brian forgot something and ran home to grab it, he opened the garage and snuggled it safely away from the never-ending fall of old needles and bird poop from the unfortunately placed cedars canopying the drive (and constantly blanketing my old Toyota, which had been edged out of the garage—a small price to pay for my substandard eggs and endometrial lining). Why would he have left the car out in tonight's slush and snow, even protected by the custom cover he'd also bought to store in the trunk (for use in questionable parking areas without adequate shelter)?

The answer came almost as soon as the question had: Angelica. Her car must be nestled safe and warm inside the Cadillac's cozy den.

Fury flared up hot again. My car wasn't good enough to merit garage space—*I* wasn't—but of course the perfect Angel's was. Brian could summon reserves of chivalry for *her*. Sacrifice his stupid cosseted Cadillac for *her*. I hoped icicles dropped from the branches overhead and perforated the top. I hoped a tree fell on it. I hoped the sparrows that drove him crazy spent the night shitting all over it.

But hope was for fools and suckers. If you wanted something in this world, you had to grab the bull by the balls.

Maybe I'd failed to take control and go after what I wanted with my marriage—but starting right now, there was at least one thing I could do to make something I wanted happen.

## Eight

By the time it was too hard for my mother to navigate the stairs, I'd moved her bedroom into my father's old office, a new hospital bed replacing his desk, which I'd pushed to a corner, and his plush leather chair repurposed for her reading area by the bay window for some natural light. When she became too unsteady on her feet to trust her balance she spent hours in that chair or sitting up in the adjustable bed, reading. And when she became too shaky to hold the book steady, her greatest—her only—pastime seemed to be looking out over the backyard and watching the starlings and sparrows, blackbirds and orioles and wrens swoop into our feeders, their chatter and squabbles and frenetic energy. It didn't make her smile, exactly, but it eased the drawn lines that had carved themselves into her face.

Determined to keep this last slim pleasure in her life, I'd bought giant sacks of various birdseed from the feed store down on Sycamore and kept all the feeders well stocked for the various species that rotated in with the seasons. The huge bags were heavy—but not so much that I couldn't lift them now from the concrete floor of the garage into the rusted wheelbarrow propped up on one side of Mom's old silver Ford and push the whole thing a few houses down. In my dark jeans and black coat, and under cover of the night, the only thing giving away my steady progress to Brian's driveway was the low squeak of the slightly flat front tire and its soft crunching over the slush.

I didn't worry about finesse—just dumped the contents of each bag all around the vehicle and, once I'd loosened the canvas cover and pulled it off (folding it neatly and laying it near the driver's side, thoughtfully weighted by a rock in case the wind picked up), across the hood, roof, and trunk.

My mother always worried about the birds—how such fragile, delicate creatures managed to survive when the cold and blankets of snow and ice diminished the food supply. Even with our meager efforts to offer sustenance, she marveled at their resilience.

Missouri winters could be brutal.

BY MORNING THE seed would be gone and there would be no evidence left behind except the intestinal contributions of scores of winter sparrows and longspurs and the occasional wren. I congratulated myself on orchestrating the perfect crime—being charitable, even, offering food to hungry creatures in a season of scarcity.

But as I watched from my front window as first a few scouts flitted down to investigate, slowly joined by more and more until the car and its immediate surroundings were a writhing dark mass out of a Hitchcock film, my fury was smothered as if a pressure valve had been closed.

What had come over me?

Mortification swept through me as flashes of my actions played in my head, the way you remember an accident or crime scene snapshotted in the bloodred strobe of police lights.

I sank to the floor and pressed trembling hands to my eyes till I saw fireworks behind them, wishing I could squeeze the images out of my head. Wishing I could take back the last twenty-four hours, rewind and get a do-over, the way Brian and I used to do as kids playing silly games when one of us messed up.

I'd messed up, all right. But I didn't think yelling, "Backsies!" and starting over would erase any of it from his memory. Or "Angel's"—they were probably over there right now discussing exactly how unbalanced I might be.

Or maybe they'd heard what must be a cacophony of chirps and cheeps and screeches from the feeding frenzy in their yard and were even now watching from their front window the way I had been moments ago, weighing whether I posed enough of a danger to myself or others that they needed to call the psych hospital in Kansas City to come cart me off.

At the moment that didn't sound half bad. At least that way I wouldn't have to hunker down here in my house the rest of the weekend to avoid facing Brian, furtively watching from behind my blinds as he and shiny Angelica came out tomorrow morning to see his car desecrated, Brian realizing at once—of course— what I'd done. If I were safely committed to an institution I wouldn't have to watch him finish moving "Angel" into the life that was supposed to be mine. Or face him again in the office on Monday. Or the day after that. Or the day after that.

I squeezed my eyes shut hard behind my fingers, wishing I could make myself disappear.

*Everything's Perfect on Cypress Key!*

I lowered my hands, my mind racing, and hustled over to the

counter, sifting through the scattered mail there. Where was it . . . where *was* it?

A flash of turquoise caught my eye and I fumbled for the edge of the card, yanking it up from the counter. Grabbing my phone, I dialed the numbers scrawled underneath that cryptic signature on the back before I could rethink my actions.

"Hello?"

It was a woman's voice. Questioning but not unfriendly. As if she thought any caller might be some sort of delightful surprise.

*Surprise!* I thought wildly.

Whoever wrote my mother that postcard couldn't have expected to hear from me, a total stranger. And I was about to drop a bomb. Maybe a few bombs.

It was starting to feel like a war zone around here.

"Hel—" My voice cut out on me and I cleared my throat, trying again. "Hello . . . I'm looking for"—"M" seemed entirely too James Bond—"someone who knows Patricia Adams. Patricia Bean Adams," I added quickly, in case this person was from so far back in Mom's past she had known her only by her maiden name.

There was an intake of air, and then silence. And then . . . "Tricia? Is this you?"

"No, this is Grace. Grace Adams McH—" I literally bit down hard on my tongue. "Grace Adams. Her daughter."

"Her . . . Oh, my dear Grace! Hello. Hello, there! It's such a *complete* pleasure to know you."

Easy for her to say. I had to press my lips together to keep an uncontrollable giggle from slipping out, and the effort made my eyes water. There was a house a few doors down she could call whose residents might give her a starkly differing opinion.

"Not to be rude . . . but who *are* you?" I said when I could finally trust myself to speak.

"Oh! I'm, well, I'm Millie. Millie Jenkins. Your mother's . . . aunt."

I stood holding the phone, staring blindly out the kitchen window into the dark backyard, my fingers and face feeling numb.

My mother had an *aunt*?

I was the only child of only children—a lack of fecundity that ran back three generations on my mother's side, and apparently that hose had finally trickled dry with me. That meant there had been no loud and chaotic family holidays with generations of offspring running around underfoot. No sprawling family reunions. No family trees with complex branch structures. It had been me and Mom and Dad and their parents, and that was the extent of the Bean and Adams families.

"Her . . . aunt?" I said in disbelief.

I'd never been close to my father's parents. They lived in Charleston, South Carolina, and spent their retirement years traveling overseas and on long cruises all over the world, visiting us only sporadically and for brief stays. Grandmother Adams, as his mother preferred to be called, always seemed frosty and terrifying to me as a child, her eyes reminding me of the cold gaze of a lizard as it dispassionately watched the world from its rock. Grandfather was of the "children should be seen and not heard" school of thought, so on their rare visits I paid my dutiful respects before ducking happily back into my room to read, usually leaving Dad leaning forward on the sofa talking too eagerly to his father, who sat back impassively in the armchair solely reserved for my dad while Mom bustled in the kitchen, chattering nervously as Grandmother Adams observed with her reptilian eyes from the doorway, arms crossed. I always wished I could take Mom into the safety of my room with me—she didn't seem to enjoy their visits any more than I did.

After my father left with Nancy—who became the much sassier "Nan" when they moved to L.A.—I saw my paternal grandparents as often as I did my dad—which is to say never.

My mother's parents were different. Grammy was warm and soft and cushy, and I loved leaning into her generous girth and sinking into her like a pillow. Gramps spoke few words in a gravelly rumble that scared me when I was little, but as I got older I realized his gruff demeanor hid a tender heart that revealed itself in the little treats he always carried in his pocket for me: a rubber ball swirled with colors, a Werther's butterscotch with its thrilling gold wrapper and tightly twisted ends, a tiny plastic animal—a pink pig or a white lamb or a spotted horse.

Their farm was in Marceline, only a few towns over, so they were regular fixtures in my childhood. But a stroke took Gramps, and heart failure took Grammy not even a year later—in my childish interpretation I always believed her heart just gave up when Gramps died—and they were both gone before I started high school.

Perhaps that was one reason I'd always clung so tightly to Brian and his parents. They made my family feel less finite, our borders broader, especially after Dad walked out and it was only me and Mom in a house that had suddenly gone silent.

If my mother had had an aunt all along, why hadn't I ever heard of her?

"Yes . . ." Now the voice had gone hesitant, cautious. "Do you . . . do you know about me, honey?" Her tone was gentle and kind, as if she were talking to a child, and I wondered whether she knew I was a full-grown adult.

Or maybe she somehow sensed that I was balancing on a very thin edge.

"I . . ." I cleared my throat again. "I don't, no. I never even knew you existed."

"Oh. I see." She sounded so disappointed—hurt—that I wanted to apologize.

But I *didn't* know her, or what had happened between her and the rest of my family. Our family. For all I knew she was a serial killer.

"My mom died," I blurted.

I realized that my blunt words might be a blow, but it was too late to take them back.

A heavy silence met my announcement, and then a slow, shaky sigh. "Oh. Oh, no. Oh, my stars. My dear—Grace—I'm so very sorry. More than I can say." Her voice trembled, and something about this stranger's clear, simple grief loosened the vise around my sternum.

But where had this woman been after my father left us and we were so alone? Or when Mom grew ill, and I was the only one there to take care of her as she battled Parkinson's and I battled the pain of my broken marriage? She could have been here with us then. With *me*, I thought, a sharp, hot flare lancing through me that it took a moment to identify as anger.

"When?" the woman asked.

I told her in short, dispassionate sentences, filling in the cause, leaving out details.

"What a loss. What a terrible, terrible loss." Her voice had lost some of its strength. "That must have broken your heart. How horribly painful for you . . . and so disconcerting."

That was exactly how I'd felt, I realized. Terrible. Heartbroken. In horrible pain.

Disconcerted. Such an odd way to describe it—but precisely right. I was endlessly disconcerted by the loss of first my grandparents, then my dad, then my husband, and then my mother, leaving me alone in the world, a lone branch lopped off our sparse family tree.

"Were you and my mother close?" I asked.

There was a pause, and then: "At one time. Not for many, many years—as you must have figured out." I heard a long sigh. "I'd hoped like hell to fix that before it was too late. I just never imagined it was Tricia it would be too late for. Oh!" Her voice shook again, and I heard the sound of a nose being blown. "What great fools we are. What great and awful fools."

Her words seemed to sink into my skin, into my bones, and I turned over the postcard I still held, the edges now wrinkled and damp in my tight grasp.

*We are all we have left, my dear. Let's let the sea wash away old wounds and enjoy the present while we have it. . . . Please come.*

I knew nothing about this woman—not even if she really was who she claimed to be. And she knew nothing at all about me.

But my mouth made the decision before my mind caught up.

"Millie, you mentioned wanting my mom to come visit . . ." I took a breath. "How would you feel if I came down there instead?"

# Nine

My feet moved almost before I heard the woman's surprised "Oh, Grace, I would adore that!" I flew up the stairs, yanking open the hall closet, pulling out the oversize suitcase I'd bought right before Brian and I got married and had used exactly twice: once for our honeymoon at Niagara Falls (no, really), and once when I moved my things from our house back to my mother's.

I gave Millie Jenkins my email address, asked her to send the relevant info, and told her I'd be there sometime the next day.

Last-minute air travel was ludicrously expensive. I thought of the "mad money" Mrs. Fielding had left me: *Do something for yourself with this.* Fleeing from the sight of Brian and Angelica setting up house together, from my own shame and humiliation, probably wasn't what she had in mind. I booked the first open flight—a weeklong round trip leaving early the next afternoon with a long layover in Atlanta, putting me into the Southwest Florida International Airport at eight thirty p.m. I hoped that wasn't too late for Millie—if she was really my mother's aunt, she had to be at least in her late seventies.

I left a message for Susie asking her to postpone my appointments indefinitely—"I'll call and let you know when to reschedule them," I said on her voice mail. "Or see if Brian can handle them."

I hung up and then immediately called back, feeling bad for being so abrupt.

"I'm sorry about that last message. This one's just for you." I chewed on my lower lip. "Whatever you hear . . . whatever Brian might tell you . . . I want you to know I'm okay. I just had a . . . well, I just have to get out of here for a little while. Don't worry about me, okay?" I started to disconnect but then pulled the phone back to my ear. "And, Susie . . . just . . . thank you. For everything."

For just a moment after I hung up I felt a twinge of guilt for ducking out on my responsibilities, heaping them into Brian's lap when he was probably hoping for a light workweek to help "Angel" settle in—and without even leaving him a call or note.

But I didn't have to let him know my plans. He wasn't my boss and he wasn't my husband anymore. I didn't owe him any explanations.

I threw some clothes into the suitcase, not even sure what, but I did remember the bathing suit I hadn't worn in years. I pictured myself lying in a chaise longue on the palm-studded white sand beach from the postcard on my kitchen counter, losing myself in enough frozen drinks to forget that eventually I would have to come back.

There was nothing left to do—no pets to secure care for, no plants to water, no one else I needed to call.

IT WASN'T UNTIL I was on the first flight the next day—climbing into my middle seat, all that was available, over the woman on the aisle who didn't even look up—that I finally slowed down enough to wonder what the hell I was doing.

I didn't know this woman—I didn't know anything about her. Even if she really was who she said she was, for all I knew she'd done something terrible that forced our family to shut her out. Or maybe she'd been the one to walk away from them—maybe she left them high and dry and never looked back?

What if I was opening a door that should have remained tightly sealed? After all, there was a reason my mom never answered any of the woman's notes she said she'd sent over the years.

And now it was too late for me to do anything about it. Millie Jenkins was planning to pick me up at the Fort Myers airport in about five hours, and I'd be essentially trapped with her.

I couldn't have planned this more irresponsibly.

Then again, I didn't actually plan it at all. And this was why I didn't do impetuous. Good old practical Grace might be dull as coal, but at least she never got herself into ridiculous situations like this one.

The air grew stuffy the moment the plane door swung shut, vacuum-sealing me inside. Twisting open the dial above me sent a warm, stale trickle of a breeze down on my head, and I concentrated on taking steady breaths, trying not to think about the air having been expelled from other lungs moments before.

"First flight?"

The voice belonged to the man sitting to my right smiling directly at me, wearing a dark green polo shirt that strained around his biceps. His groomed hair looked freshly cut, in that inexplicable way that made a man look like some kind of celebrity or cover model, even though you couldn't quite put your finger on exactly how the style was different from what most guys got at their local barbershop.

"No. Why do you ask?"

He dipped his head to my lap, where my hands clutched my purse so hard the skin had whitened. "I figured that or you were worried about pickpockets."

I consciously eased my grip. "Third flight, actually," I admitted.

The first two were on my honeymoon. We had been on our way to Niagara Falls, and Brian knew I was a nervous wreck about flying.

I'd wanted us to go somewhere coastal and exotic: Costa Rica, or the Cinque Terre in Italy, or, if we wanted to be more frugal (and generally I always did), even just a state I'd never been to, which was most of them: the rugged coastline of northern California, or the oyster-studded salt flats of North Carolina's Outer Banks.

But Brian kept insisting on Niagara Falls. "It's our honeymoon! It's traditional!"

*It's clichéd*, I'd wanted to say but didn't, because I loved the way his blue eyes lit up with excitement at the idea of going to the preferred honeymoon destination of grandparents around the country as if it were Rio de Janeiro.

Brian knew I was nervous about the flight, telling me he'd never let anything happen to me, and as he held my hand tightly in his from the moment we checked in—"Do *not* let go except to put my oxygen mask over my hyperventilating face," I'd demanded—I believed him.

He kept hold of my hand once we settled into our seats—me tucked in beside the window with the shade pulled down so I didn't have to see how terrifyingly high our three-hundred-ton tin capsule was climbing—and didn't let go even after we hit altitude, despite how sweaty my palm was making his. As soon as the drinks cart came by he ordered two tiny vodka bottles and a can of OJ. "Keep them coming," he'd told the flight attendant with a grin, then proceeded to pour the contents of both bottles into one cup of ice with the merest splash of juice—all one-handed. "Drink."

I did—and I obeyed him again when the next round came, especially as by then the edges of my fear had started to soften and I had a peaceful, warm, loose feeling blossoming inside me that was making my earlier qualms feel silly to me. So silly they made me giggle . . . and I couldn't stop, and as I doubled over trying to catch my breath and snorting with laughter, Brian started giggling too, until we were both afraid we were making a spectacle of ourselves.

It was one of my favorite memories—sitting pressed against the man I adored, who was somehow miraculously all mine, forever, as we both laughed so hard we couldn't speak, just sat with our hands entwined thirty thousand feet above the rest of the world, alone together in one all our own.

Until we hit turbulence over Detroit and all that alcohol in my stomach came gurgling right back up. I managed to get most of it in the airsickness bag Brian scrambled for as soon as he saw my face take on a greenish tint. He wound up with the rest in his lap, sitting there with orange juice and vodka and bile drying on his pant leg until the captain announced we were through the worst of the turbulence and we could move about the cabin. Brian beelined for the tiny bathroom and came back fifteen minutes later with his pants fairly clean, but soaking wet.

And even with that I'd been so happy, overwhelmed with joy

and my own wonderful good luck. Because he sat down and offered me a piece of gum he'd bummed off another passenger,
and stroked my hair, and told me he loved me even if I couldn't
hold my liquor, making me laugh weakly again. And in the end
Niagara Falls had been lovely: the impossible force of thunder-
ing water, the breathtaking scale of it, the misty rainbows rising
like gaily colored ghosts above the deafening cataracts.

The memory made my eyes sting, and I leaned over to tuck
my purse under the seat in front of me, avoiding the man's gaze.
"I just . . . I guess I'm not really sure about this trip."

"Well, that's why they serve alcohol on board."

"Oh, good God, no—been down *that* road," I blurted.

The man smiled, revealing stunningly straight teeth, and his
fingers rested on my arm as he leaned in as if to tell me a secret.
"I'm with you—that's why I prefer Xanax." He winked.

He was undeniably handsome, and there was something
about the way he was looking intently at me that made me feel
seen, appreciated . . . and gave me an unexpected jolt of savage
pleasure.

Maybe I didn't have glossy hair and perfect skin and long
smooth legs. But there was nothing wrong with me.

A snort came from my other side, and I glanced at the woman
sitting there. She still had her head buried in a magazine. "Way
to work it, Pete. Hit on a woman with your wife sitting one seat
away."

I yanked my arm off the divider.

"Oh, for Jesus' sake. I wasn't hitting on her. It's called being
nice. You might try it sometime, Helen."

"Huh. Maybe I will." She craned her neck, exaggeratedly looking around the plane. "Let's see if *I* can find some poor lonely
single traveler I can pretend to reassure."

I stared into my empty lap as the two bickered across me. *Some poor lonely single traveler . . .*

*My life wasn't supposed to be like this!* I wanted to shout at Helen.

I was supposed to be sitting here beside my best friend whom I'd loved since I was a teenager. Not crammed between a good-looking man who apparently couldn't keep from hitting on any woman within seduction distance, and his long-suffering wife. *I don't want your husband!* I wanted to tell her. I wanted *mine*.

But I couldn't fool myself anymore. He wanted someone else.

# Ten

Millie Jenkins and I hadn't exchanged photos, but I didn't think I'd have any trouble identifying her. My second flight was delayed by a storm that had blown through southwest Florida, the ticket agent in Atlanta had wearily announced, and my layover went from two hours to more than four. An elderly woman waiting alone at baggage claim in a small-town airport at nearly eleven p.m. wouldn't be hard to spot.

But apparently mine wasn't the only delayed flight. As I came down the escalator a sea of people waited at the foot of it, smiles in place, faces expectant—and nearly every head white, silver, or gray.

The middle-aged man on the step below me chuckled and met my eye. "Welcome to Florida—Death's Waiting Room."

"I thought it was supposed to be more *Girls Gone Wild*."

"Maybe at spring break. But it's snowbird season now." He leaned close enough to bump his shoulder conspiratorially into me, like we were BFFs in study hall. I grappled for the rubber handrail to keep my balance. "Don't worry. You'll get used to it. Just make sure to drive defensively. Some of these grandmas can't even see over the dash."

"Right." I let my eyes scan over the crowd, searching for some familiar feature that might suggest which one of the people flocking the end of the escalator like cowbirds was related to me, but it was impossible. How was I supposed to see some evidence of my mom, who'd died so relatively young, in these aged faces?

I didn't realize I was at the end until the collapsing stair served me up to the slick floor like an hors d'oeuvre. I stepped out of the way of the people still coming off behind me, standing as conspicuously as possible in the hopes that the woman would somehow identify me.

One by one the bystanders claimed their loved ones: A grandmotherly type stood scanning the escalator with a warm, expectant smile, her hand resting in the crook of an older man's arm, until they caught sight of a pretty, young blonde waving frantically from the top of the escalator. A Santa Claus look-alike knelt down to catch two young children, who flung themselves into his arms with cries of "Papa!" while their mother waited patiently behind them, a smile on her face. My throat ached. One day this would be Brian, greeting shiny, dark-haired grandchildren who would not be mine.

Three sharp buzzing noises sounded and bags began appearing on the nearest carousel from behind the rubber strips like freshly washed cars.

Suitcases promenaded past me, plucked out of rotation one by one until finally I realized that I'd probably watched my non-descript black bag pass by a dozen times without realizing it was mine. By that point it was almost the last bag from the flight, and I only narrowly beat the airline baggage agent to it.

"Thought this one was going unclaimed," the man said with

a wide grin. "You okay getting where you're heading this late? Want me to help you get a cab?" he asked, indicating the sliding doors and the dark night beyond.

I looked around and saw that the crowd had thinned to nearly nothing, a few people milling about, perhaps waiting for the next incoming flight. But everyone from mine had found the people waiting for them or gone to where they were expected, and only I was still here, alone and apparently forgotten.

I'd called Millie on my layover to let her know of the delay. "Let me get a ride-share," I told her. "Or is there public transportation?" The frugal option was my default setting, but at the moment—tired and lonely and full of second-guessing and doubt—I was thinking that using a little more of Mrs. Fielding's unexpected bequeathal for a limousine and driver would honor the spirit of her gift entirely.

Millie had given a surprisingly full belly laugh. "If you can find a city bus that will drive out here to the hinterlands, I'll suck a duck," she'd said. "Don't you worry—I'll be there to pick you up."

As the plane was further and further delayed I'd called back twice to see whether she'd reconsider, but each time she'd been increasingly insistent. "I won't hear of it. You're family. Family doesn't catch a cab."

But apparently "family" needed to figure out some alternate means of transportation out to "the hinterlands" of Cypress Key, or I'd have to find a place to bunk down in the terminal.

A wash of warm, humid air found its way to me through the sharp chill of the air-conditioning, and I looked up to see that the sliding doors leading outside had swooshed open. A babble of voices, a sea of pastels and bright colors; a horde of elderly people were bursting through the doorway like the Kool-Aid man in that old commercial, and all of them seemed to be talking at once.

"What's she look like?"

"Why didn't you just tell her to wait out front?"

"Hush up, Harold; that's rude."

"She's not gonna fit if she brought too much luggage."

"She might if you lost a few pounds, Adele."

"You don't have to be such a mean old tart, Ruth."

They streamed into the room and fanned out, twisting their heads all around—an elderly reconnaissance troop scoping out the terrain. But my eye went to the woman in point position.

*Vivid* was the only word that popped to mind.

She towered over most of the rest of her group, even the men—although to be fair many of them were stooped into shorter versions of what they may once have been. Part of that was her chunky stacked heels—she wore blue suede boots that came to her knees and gave her an extra inch or two. Part of it was her hair—a thick mass of silver that cascaded down her back and added another two inches above her forehead.

But most of it was simply her *presence*.

She stood like a Broadway star, feet planted apart, arms just a little akimbo with a grace that might have been natural or learned. Her shoulders weren't broad so much as solid and strong-looking, and despite an impressively high chest that would have done a thirty-something proud (certainly I'd have been grateful for it), her slim waist and hips helped her pull off the silver leggings and flowing white top she wore, a sleeveless fuchsia vest trailing from her shoulders to her knees.

She was astonishing. I couldn't take my eyes off her.

And then, just as I realized I was rudely staring, the woman's gaze settled directly on me and her expression lit up like a Roman candle.

She pointed one imperious finger and the entire group suddenly veered in my direction like a school of attacking piranha.

I took an involuntary step back, and then they were upon me, surrounding me as the woman in the lead stopped and one hand flew to her chest, the other to her pink-lipsticked mouth. The handle of my roller bag fell from my grasp and I lunged for it before I realized that one of the men had eased it from my hand just as Millie reached out and took both of mine in hers.

"Oh, you *have* to be Grace! I'd have known you anywhere. I can't believe you're here!"

"Millie?" I said in a squeak I barely recognized as my voice.

The group burst into loud laughter.

The tall woman's face broke into a wide smile and suddenly I saw my mother—not the way I'd grown used to seeing her, but the way I remembered her from my childhood, when her smiles hadn't been so scarce. When she'd stop whatever she was working on whenever I came into the office and throw open her arms with a smile as bright as if she hadn't seen me in weeks, instead of since she'd put me on the bus that morning.

But this woman *wasn't* my mother. Although for one moment I was tempted to close my eyes and pretend she was.

I felt as if I were moving in slow motion, or the rest of the world was operating in fast-forward. Who were all these people, and why had Millie brought them with her?

As if she read my mind, Millie dipped her head to speak into my ear as she led us toward the doors. "Sorry for the unexpected crowd—I'd planned to come get you after I took everyone to the dance, but then your flight was delayed, and . . . well, we're just making some drop-offs on the way home. I hope that's okay."

Her attention shifted to the cluster of men hanging back with my bag in tow. "How we doing, boys?"

The two men exchanged a glance and shook their heads.

"It's not gonna fit . . ." one of them muttered under his breath, woolly eyebrows yanked together in one uninterrupted thicket, and I realized they were right. The group hadn't held still long enough for me to get an accurate count, but there had to be six or seven of them, plus me. Had they come by bus?

"Put a sock in it, Harold," Millie said good-naturedly.

With quick, firm steps she led the group back out the sliding glass doors, and instant warmth rolled over me like an incoming tide. Palm trees rustled in a balmy breeze that felt like midsummer rather than February, their sound like distant applause. Even at this late hour it had to be seventy degrees outside, and I'd dressed for winter—Missouri winter. Under my puffy jacket the wool of my sweater began to adhere to my skin before we'd even cleared the ground transportation lanes.

Without warning the weight of my purse disappeared, and I turned to see Millie holding the strap. "You'll melt if you don't get that coat off, honey."

Before I could I felt it lift from my shoulders, and I craned my head around to see one of the men—balding, with a snow-cap fringe of white hair—easing it off me. I shrugged it the rest of the way off, and he settled the garment over his arm like an attentive butler.

"Thank . . . thank you."

"Who was supposed to remember where we parked?" Millie's wide stride slowed, the rest of the group grinding to a halt behind her in the middle of the blacktop parking lot.

"There wasn't a sign, remember?" replied one of the women,

whose broad head seemed plugged down into her stocky body like a cork in a bottle.

"We had a little mnemonic device . . ." a scrawny man with a friendly death's-head grin said.

Millie looked skyward, as though the car might somehow have been airlifted to heaven.

"Did we color-code this time?" asked Scrawny. "Green van—parked next to green grass?"

I glanced around the parking lot, which was lined around and throughout with landscaped patches of vividly green grass.

"Hope not," Hairy Eyebrows said with a snort.

"How about we split up and look up and down a few of these rows?" Snowcap suggested.

"Well," Millie said, "damn fine idea, Bennie. It'll be like a scavenger hunt." She broke the group into three delegated search parties and they scattered like spooked fish.

"Give a holler, whoever spots it first," Scrawny called out to the others; then he took Eyebrows and the stocky woman by the sleeves and pulled them off down their appointed row.

I was exhausted down to my marrow, the long, wrenching last forty-eight hours catching up with me. I wished I could just lie down right here on the asphalt and wake up again two days ago. Or better yet, two years ago, when everything was normal—when I still had my husband and my mother and some idea what the hell I was doing with my life. Now suddenly everything felt adrift, and I had no solid ground to cling to.

I'd been silly to come down here with some idea of taking refuge with this stranger who claimed to be my mother's aunt, as though I could just magically snap my fingers and create some kind of relationship with Millie that would fill the gaping hole of everything I'd lost, like a little kid who believed in fairy tales.

An arm came around my shoulders. "This must seem a bit overwhelming," Millie said quietly. "And I'm so sorry for all the chaos. It was too late for me to change everyone's plans for tonight, but I simply couldn't bear for you to show up and not have family here to greet you."

I nodded, blinking.

A shout came from the direction the two men had taken.

"Got 'er!" a voice sang out. "Over here!"

As soon as we turned the corner of the next row, I stopped cold. Millie was waving at the two men standing next to . . . an eyesore.

It was an old seventies-style conversion van painted a Day-Glo lime green, the entire thing covered with fat-petaled sherbet-colored flowers, the words *Merry Widows* written in large fluorescent pink letters along the side like the Mystery Machine.

"It's a wonder we lost it, wouldn't you say?" Millie asked brightly. "Come on, Grace."

"Merry Widows?" I was having a hard time making my feet move forward.

"Millie, didn't you tell her about us?" That was the portly woman.

"Well, we've hardly had a chance to chat, Ruth." Millie shot her an arch look.

"Tsk," the woman said. "Poor girl's probably all kinds of confused."

*Yes. All kinds.*

Up close the vehicle was even more vivid. And how were all these people going to cram in there? But one by one everyone disappeared inside like clowns in a Volkswagen. I ended up in the very back row, my knees pushed into the seat in front of me as I fumbled for a seat belt.

"Everyone comfy?" Millie sang out.

"Can't hardly breathe," Eyebrows muttered under his breath, shaking his head.

The stocky woman—Ruth?—craned herself around in the seat and jiggled her eyebrows suggestively at me. "So, how about it, sweetheart—are ya single?"

My heart fisted. "Yes," I said, the word short and sharp.

The entire group burst into chuckles.

"Well, I think you'll like it here just fine."

"Boy, are you in the right hands."

I frowned. "What do you mean?"

The man with the eyebrows turned to look at me, both those hairy caterpillars lifting to his receding hairline. "Don't you know who your aunt is?"

"Who she is . . . ?" I stared from face to face, all of them watching me with some mixture of amusement and surprise and disbelief.

"Now, you all stop," Millie called from the front seat. "Can't you see Grace is worn out?"

"What do they mean, who you are?" I called to the front seat.

"You just relax, Grace—we're just dropping the group off and then we'll get you settled in at home and be able to chat."

I shifted in my seat, trying to get comfortable, but it was a futile effort in the overfull vehicle. I felt lonelier now, crammed into a van among a group of strangers, than I had since leaving Sugarberry. Since Brian had shown up at my house with "Angel." Since Mom died.

I gave up trying to find a position that didn't cramp some part of my body and fixed my gaze numbly out the window while the group chattered incessantly on, trying to concentrate on the scenery we were passing in the dark night, and not on the way all of it seemed to suddenly be blurring around the edges.

# Eleven

I woke up in darkness in an unfamiliar bed in an unfamiliar room from a dream about Brian.

I couldn't remember the details—something about the ocean and sharks and a life raft that I knew wasn't going to hold us both, yet still I waved off the helicopter hovering above to rescue us.

I sat up, trying to look around and get my bearings, but the room was so dark I wondered whether I'd slept for only a few hours or an entire day and into the next night. Based on how I felt—exhausted down to my cells—I favored the former theory.

Millie and I did not get to have our promised chat when we got to her house. By the time we finally made all the "drop-offs" of the elderly passengers and crunched into an unpaved driveway to pull into a parking area underneath a stilt-built house, I was nearly asleep across the back seat of the psychedelic van. She ushered me up a set of stairs and through a dim house I barely took in as I stumbled after her, futilely trying to catch up to relieve her of the suitcase she'd grabbed before I could, and showed me into a room that could have been bare of everything except the cozy-looking bed in its center, for all I noticed. She murmured a few things about an attached bathroom and leaving a night-light plugged in, in case I woke up disoriented, and I was on the bed and out nearly before she shut the door behind her.

Now I looked around the room, mostly shapes in the dim illumination the tiny light cast. What time was it? I made out a nightstand beside me, a small analog clock on it giving off a faint glow. I picked it up and peered to make it out. Nine o'clock.

A.m. or p.m.?

Only one way to find out. I wiggled out the side of the large bed farthest from the door and stepped toward the curtains, yanking the cord.

Sunlight burst in like an atom bomb, and I closed my eyes against the sting of it. After a moment I slitted one open.

I was looking out over an expanse of water that seemed to have no end, light dancing off the top like a million shifting diamonds. A weathered gray-brown pier meandered from the sandy water's edge, ending in a platform where deck furniture was arranged as if in a living room. Grass carpeted the yard with Dr. Seuss trees improbably haloed in orange and yellow and purple blooms, and palm fronds dipped into either side of the large picture window I stood in front of, as if carefully staged by a photographer.

All I could think of was finding a cup of coffee.

Before collapsing into bed I'd taken time only to pull off my jeans and sweater, which lay in a crumpled heap on the floor— too wrinkled to put back on even if the sunlight streaming in from outside didn't make the idea ludicrous. I looked around for my suitcase—which I saw Millie had thoughtfully set on a luggage stand the night before—and took in the rest of the room: a tastefully decorated arrangement of furniture with subtle accents of coral and green that could have come out of a resort hotel brochure.

I pulled from my bag the first suitable outfit I could find—a pair of little-used walking shorts and a T-shirt—then pushed my feet into sandals.

The hallway off the guest room I was in led me out to the main living area, a vast open space that seemed centered in the house like a nucleus. The main area I stood in had light flooring running throughout—bamboo?—and mismatched pieces forming a sitting area: a chunky love seat in butterscotch-colored leather; a deep, pale sofa bursting with colorful pillows and several casually draped throws; and a bright orange armchair with wide curving arms and a high back that seemed to beckon me into it, all of it perched around a thick-pile white rug. The room spoke of comfort as much as decorator panache, the effect eclectic and a little over-the-top, but not unappealing—a little like Millie herself, actually.

Of whom there was no sign. The adjacent open kitchen area was empty, the house silent but for the distant shushing of waves I heard through the open French doors interspersed with the wall of windows at the back of the house.

"Millie?" I called uncertainly.

No reply.

I hovered in the middle of the space for a moment, unsure whether it was rude to wander any farther, but the rich scent of coffee pulled me toward the open kitchen at the far end of the room, where I found a full fresh-brewed pot and a note:

> *People tell me my coffee reminds them of me: full-bodied and stronger than they expect.* ☺ *Hope it's not too much for you. Help yourself—sweetener on counter and soy milk in the*

*fridge. Make yourself at home—I'm meeting with a client*
*but will be out shortly.*
*—M*

I didn't know what she meant by a client, or where she would be "out" from, but I followed instructions, pouring a cup into the clean mug I found beside the coffeemaker and adding a dollop of soy milk after a tentative sniff. I stood awkwardly at the counter, sipping it, as thick and dark as promised, which did happen to be the way I liked it—one of the few things I enjoyed about being divorced was finally not having to brew it pale and thin, the way Brian preferred his.

*Make yourself at home.*

It was a ludicrous instruction. I couldn't have felt more awkward if I'd broken in like Goldilocks and helped myself to a comfortable bed. And how could Millie Jenkins be so unconcerned about leaving a stranger to roam through her house? For all she knew I could clean her out of everything while she was away doing . . . whatever she was doing.

The fact that I'd clearly interrupted her routine—first last night, now today—didn't make me feel any more at ease, and I thought about just booking a return flight home.

But the sliding glass doors lining the back of the large living area were open, and a fresh sea-scented gust of air drew me toward the expansive screened porch that ran along the entire back of the house.

I walked to the edge of the porch, where the screening met the wooden railing, to take in the one hundred and eighty degrees of glittering water that danced in the bright sunlight. Spinning fans on the cedar ceiling shepherded along the breeze off the water, and the thick air filled my nostrils with the scent of brine and cut grass and something floral, like old-fashioned perfume—magnolia or gardenia. The sound of water lapping at the shore, mixed with the whispers of palm fronds jittering in the breeze, created a relaxing white noise. Millie's paradise post-card come to life.

I'd planned a trip like this for our ten-year anniversary.

I wanted to surprise Brian. It was six months after the doctor had told us his verdict about my damaged uterus and inadequate eggs, and I'd begun to hope we might be recovering. That Brian was accepting that children might not be a factor in the life we had together—but we could be happy anyway.

Until one evening two Januaries ago, after what turned out to be our last Christmas as a couple. As Brian and I sat in the living room reviewing our own estate plan, the way we did each New Year, he showed me where he'd earmarked ten percent more of our savings for long-term health insurance and medical costs. "We have to plan for assisted living now," he said, not meeting my eyes, and the cold truth sank into me that no matter what he'd said about our being childless, he wasn't okay with it. Not at all.

We'd both needed a break, a chance to reconnect, and with a big anniversary on the horizon I'd tried to imagine the most relaxing, romantic place I could think of: wide stretches of beach, turquoise sea, frozen drinks and hula music and every other cliché I'd dreamed of from Corona commercials and Elvis films: Kauai.

I'd sneaked my research in when Brian left the office for lunch, or in the evenings when he'd increasingly started shutting himself in his study at home and tapping on his computer all night, burying himself in work the same way I was—to avoid having to think.

I made lists of things we'd do: rent an ATV and drive through Waimea Canyon, hike the Kalalau Trail and the Hanakapiai Falls, kayak the Wailua River to the secret waterfall, ride an inner tube down the old irrigation canals on the Lihue sugar plantation—places that looked as luscious as they sounded in the liquid consonants and copious vowels of the Hawaiian language.

I pictured the frangipani-scented breezes softening the brittle edges we'd each developed by that point, the fiery sunsets melting away the tension and sorrow that had chilled our once-warm home, the waves ushering out the heaviness that had weighed us both down.

It would be a splurge—especially with the slew of my mom's medical bills that stacked up on the corner of my desk. But we needed it—needed to reconnect, relax, remember who we'd been before we'd found out that our family of two would be the only family we'd ever have.

But I never got to sit Brian down and tell him my surprise, to present my file full of printouts on Kauai. A month before our anniversary he sat me down instead and presented a plan of his own . . . one that no longer included me.

I ran my fingertips over the fine mesh of the screen that separated me from the view I'd imagined so often taking in with Brian standing beside me, my head on his shoulder, our hands linked.

Would things have been different if I'd booked the trip sooner? Would the vacation have done everything I hoped it would—erased the new distance that had grown between us as the disappointments heaped one on top of another and the strain started pulling at our seams?

Would they have been different if my disfigured uterus hadn't been incapable of giving Brian what I'd come to realize he wanted most?

An ache filled my throat and the picturesque scene before me blurred. My hand dragged along the screen as I set my half-empty mug on the railing and sank to the wood planks under my feet, my fingertips burning from the friction as I pressed them to my stinging eyes.

"Are you all right?"

I spun around at the deep male voice from my tenuous squat and ended up tipping back flat onto my rear. Pain from my fall in Brian's foyer shot up my tailbone, and an undignified cry rose up my throat.

"Holy crap! Are you okay?" A man in the shadowed corner of the porch shifted the computer in his lap to the tropical-print sofa he'd been slouching on and yanked earbuds from around his neck before shooting to his feet and taking quick steps toward me.

I scrambled backward like a crab, and he stopped where he was, a few feet away. "Who are you?" I barked.

"It's cool," he said, holding up his hands as if to show he was unarmed. "I'm waiting for my father."

"What are . . ." I swiped quickly at my eyes with a sleeve. "Your father's here?"

He nodded, his hands still in their silly stick-'em-up pose. "With Millie. They should be finished in another twenty minutes or so."

I just stared at him for a moment, trying to make sense of his words. Finished doing *what*?

Still holding his palms out toward me, the man—older than

I'd first thought, maybe early forties—took two slow, cautious steps in my direction, extending one hand toward me. "You want an assist?"

"No. I'm fine."

He stopped again. "Oh. Okay."

"Thanks," I tacked on ungraciously.

Keeping his eyes steady on me, he reached behind him to where an ottoman sat a few inches from a nearby wicker chair and hooked it with his fingers, the wrought-iron legs making groaning Chewbacca noises as he slowly dragged it closer across the wood deck. While I watched, bewildered, he lowered himself to it, finally moving his unbroken gaze out to the sight I'd been blindly staring at a few moments before.

"What . . . what are you doing?" I asked after a long awkward moment.

He didn't look at me. "I was watching you take in this view a minute ago, and I realized I'd been sitting out here for thirty minutes and hadn't even glanced up."

"You were *watching* me?"

He turned back to me and lifted both hands again. "I wasn't hiding or *skulking* or anything." The defensive way he emphasized "skulking" would have struck me as funny in other circumstances. "I thought you saw me at first, but then you went and stared at the water, and then it looked like you were kind of upset, and I wasn't sure what to do. I mean, I could have just kept quiet, but I figured sooner or later you were going to turn around, and then it would be weird if I was just sitting there watching you like a creeper. And I was going to say something, but you obviously thought you were alone, and when you started crying I didn't want to, like, intrude or embarrass you. Not that you should be embarrassed," he hastened to add.

He'd sunk into the same slouchy posture he'd had on the sofa when I first saw him, his cargo-shorts-covered legs wide-spraddled, his hands gesturing as he spoke. He wasn't a big man—Brian was six-three, with the broad shoulders of the football player he'd once been; this guy was built more like a wrestler, narrower and more compact, dark hair sprinkling his bare legs and forearms. He wore a yellow shirt that hadn't seen an iron since its last laundering, and had a flop of messy dark brown hair.

He looked altogether unthreatening, and my tensed muscles eased ever so slightly.

"I wasn't crying," I said.

"Oh. Okay," he said again. "Sometimes all that sunshine off the water can be pretty harsh. Especially if you aren't used to it. Make sure you wear sunglasses. Protects your eyes. Plus, you know." He flashed white teeth as he flipped his own sunglasses from the top of his head down over his eyes. "They make you look cool."

I should give him the laugh he was so clearly working hard for, but my eyes were prickling again and I looked away, trying to surreptitiously wipe the wetness on my face with my fingers. He was being nice by staying, by trying to cheer me up, but I wanted him to leave.

"Here."

He'd pushed the glasses back up to the top of his head and was holding something out—a handkerchief. Such an oddly genteel affectation for a guy who looked like an overgrown frat boy. Out of necessity I took it from his fingers, wiping at my tears and dabbing, then giving up and blowing my nose into the soft square.

"Thank you," I managed, a little more sincerely this time, the cloth crumpled in my fist. "I'll wash your hankie and make sure it's returned to you."

"You can keep it. It's my screen wipe."

"Oh, my God! Why didn't you say so?"

"It was all I had. And you seemed to need it," he said.

Fresh tears spilled over my eyes, and I went back to my sleeve. "Look, I don't mean to be rude—"

"Hey, I get it if you don't want to talk about it, and I don't even know who you are . . ." He let the trailing words imply a question.

"I'm . . ." I was Patricia Adams's daughter . . . Brian McHale's wife.

But I was none of those things anymore.

"I'm . . . Millie's niece. Great-niece," I finished finally. *Maybe.* "Grace."

His forehead wrinkled like a shar-pei's. "Great-niece Grace . . . are you okay?"

The greenish gold of his eyes was like early autumn leaves, the edges drooping down at the corners in a way that made him look comically worried.

"No," I admitted with another sniff, giving up and going back to the screen wipe to blow my nose again. It was a goner anyway. "I'm not."

"I had a feeling."

"No kidding?" The words rode out on the gust of a laugh, as if they'd been held behind a dam that had burst, at the combination of his understatement with his mournful, basset hound gaze. But rather than taking offense, his face relaxed into that little-boy smile again as if that were his default expression, easier on him than the concern.

"I originally thought about going into detective work."

This startled another laugh out of me. "Are you serious?"

"Not at all. As you can see, I'd be terrible at it. I'm a master of the obvious." He grinned again.

"I don't mean to be rude," I repeated—that thing people said only when they were being rude—"but who are you?"

He tapped his forehead with the tips of his fingers. "Oh, right—sorry. I drop my dad off a couple times a week and I wait for him, and no one else is ever here at the house. I'm Jason Davis." He put out a hand as if I were here to take a meeting, rather than squatting on the floor in a T-shirt and shorts, and it occurred to me that I could simply have answered his similar inquiry the way he answered mine—with my name.

"Grace Mc—Adams." I rubbed my palms along the cotton of my shorts and then shook his hand.

"Nice to meet you, Grace McAdams."

"No, it's . . . it's just Adams."

"You said McAdams."

"'Mc' was a mistake," I bit out, sharper than I'd intended. I took a deep breath, trying to get hold of myself. I was being very short to someone who'd been nothing but good-natured. "You drop your dad off here . . . for what?" I asked, remembering her note mentioning a meeting with a "client."

"You know . . . Millie's"—he waved his hands as if trying to find the word floating in the air around him—"services."

I just gaped at him for a moment, every concern I'd had about the woman blossoming up like a mushroom cloud. "Her"—I made air quotes—"'services'?"

He shrugged. "Yeah, I'm not sure what I think about it either, but my dad's lonely. If this is what he wants—if she can help him get there—then who am I to be a skeptic?"

Dear God. The woman was a geriatric hooker.

I pushed up to my feet. "They do that *here*? Like, right now, in there?" I said, pointing toward the house.

Jason didn't seem to feel any of the horror that was sweeping through me. "Well, yeah. I mean, I don't think my dad would be comfortable doing it in a public place."

"I would seriously hope not!"

I could call a ride-share right now and head straight to the airport. Surely I could at least find something on standby.

Jason had risen to his feet and he put one hand out as if to reach for me, calm me down, but I took a step back. "I'm pretty sure most of her clients come here, Grace. It's no big deal. People get lonely—especially if they've been all alone for a while. I don't guess you're ever too old to want love, are you?"

That stopped me. I pictured my grandmother in the weeks and months after Gramps died, her clearly broken heart, the way that something seemed to have filtered out of her with the loss of him. Remembered my mother and the way she changed after Dad left. I'd encouraged her for years to date, but it was as if when my father walked out on her he took her spirit with him. Would I have begrudged either of them a little pleasure in their loneliness—in whatever form it took?

And who knew—maybe one day when I was old and totally alone, I'd be willing to pay someone to show me a little tenderness too.

The outrage drained out of me and I felt my stiff shoulders relax a little. I didn't plan to stick around while this woman operated her geriatric call-girl service here in the house, but I'd at least refrain from storming out without any notice. "No," I said finally. "I don't suppose you are."

The shar-pei wrinkles on his forehead eased and his eyes got squinty with his smile. "I don't think they'll be more than another ten or fifteen minutes—they usually finish up around nine thirty." I suppressed a shudder at the idea of the routinely scheduled commerce of it and tried not to judge. "You want to have some more coffee with me while we wait? Millie lets me help myself."

I might be able to get my mind around what she was doing, but there was no way I could sit out here sipping coffee and making chitchat with this man while his father and my great-aunt were engaging in their little . . . "business transaction" in a back room.

"Um . . . no. I actually have some . . . work I need to do." I waved vaguely in the direction of where my room was. "You go ahead, though. Pleasure meeting you."

The platitude rose automatically to my lips despite the fact that no part of the last fifteen minutes had been at all pleasurable.

# Twelve

O f course I had no work to do.

I closed the door in the guest room where I'd stayed and leaned against it for a moment, trying to regain my bearings.

If this had always been Millie's "career," I guessed I had my answer now as to why my family had excommunicated her. I couldn't imagine my proper mother or grandmother or grandfather countenancing prostitution, whatever gloss you wanted to put on it.

I'd wait the fifteen minutes till Millie was finished—I suppressed another shudder at the idea—and talk to her. But then I was going home. Coming to meet her completely blind had been a ridiculous, impulsive idea, and I didn't belong here.

While I waited I folded my crumpled outfit from the previous night and laid it carefully back in the suitcase—it was just about all I'd unpacked—and changed into something more suitable for heading back into freezing temps: jeans and a long-sleeved T-shirt that wouldn't make me melt while I played out the rest of my truncated time in Florida, but that I could throw a heavy cardigan over as soon as I landed back in Missouri winter. I laid my sheepskin-lined boots on the top of the suitcase before closing it—I could change out of the sandals just before I checked the bag.

By the time I finished checking the flights for the day—there was a good chance there would be room on the 5:05—I could hear voices out in the rest of the house, and after a little while the sound of the front door closing told me Millie was likely alone again. I closed the airline app and braced myself for the uncomfortable conversation.

I found Millie bustling around in the kitchen, and guilt plucked at me when her face brightened with that same delighted smile from the night before, as if she couldn't quite believe her luck in having me here.

"There she is! Jason told me you were up and about, so I started breakfast. Fair warning—I'm a magnificent cook."

"Oh, I . . ." What was the harm? I still had seven hours till the flight I hoped to catch, and I had to eat, after all. "That would be nice, thanks. Can I help?"

She pointed with a spatula to the tall chairs on the other side of the prep island where the sinks were. "You sit right down and let me take care of things. I'd tell you that I don't like guests to have to work, but the truth is I can't handle anyone else in my kitchen while I'm doing my mad-scientist thing, as Ira used to call it. How about some coffee?"

I nodded, remembering my abandoned cup out on the porch, and eased myself onto one of the stools, watching her move as efficiently as if she'd been choreographed. She wore a pair of loose palazzo pants in a wild Aztec print, and a gauzy white tunic top with fluttering sleeves that stopped just past her elbows. Her long hair was loosely swooped up in some kind of complicated knot, and her makeup was as carefully applied as it had been the previous night, right down to the bright-lipsticked mouth. She looked more put-together at ten a.m. than I did on my fanciest night out—and if she'd been engaging in some kind of . . . well, exertion, there was no evidence of it now. She was humming as she fetched a clean mug from the cabinet and poured, a slight smile hovering on her mouth when she turned to set it in front of me. "Sugar's in the bowl," she said, pointing. "I've only got soy milk, but it's delicious, and we aren't baby cows anyway."

"You don't eat dairy?" I said nonsensically.

Her face furrowed. "No, but I'll pick you up some creamer today—what do you like?"

"This is fine," I said, not meeting her eye. It was hard to reconcile this thoughtful grandmotherly woman—however fantastically kitted out—with what her most recent "john's" son had told me on the porch.

"I have so many ideas for while you're here," she went on, "but I thought today we might just let you get your bearings— relax on the beach if you like, or I can show you around my little island. Maybe we could even go pick you up something a bit more seasonal to wear, if that's all you brought?" She pointed the spatula toward my cool-weather outfit. "In any case, plenty of time later this week to get more adventurous. How long are you planning to stay, Gracie?"

I shifted on my chair. "Actually . . ." Now that the moment was here it was harder than I thought to say it to her face.

She waved one heavily ringed hand, cutting me off. "Not important. You're welcome here absolutely as long as you like. I hope you're hungry."

Talking with Millie was like trying to keep up with the fastest mouse in the maze. It took a beat for her abrupt transition to sink in, and by that time she had placed a plate in front of me that was heaped with more food than a breakfast buffet and sat down beside me with one of her own.

Millie wasn't kidding about her cooking. She'd whipped up tender crepes filled with a berry compote and topped with fresh whipped cream, fluffy scrambled eggs, and perfectly cooked thick bacon, all accompanied by another pot of her good strong coffee. I'd thought there was no way I could even make a dent in the mountain of food, but as soon as I took the first bite I realized I was ravenous.

"Well!" Millie was beaming as if I were a prize horse. "I like a girl with an appetite."

"It's delicious," I said honestly. "Thank you."

The gourmet breakfast made it even harder to say what I needed to. I swallowed another bite, took a bracing sip of my coffee, and looked at her.

"Actually, Millie . . . I'm afraid I can't stay after all."

"What? Oh, no! Is everything okay?" Her face fell so completely it reminded me of the game my father used to play with me as a kid: swipe his hand up to reveal a smile, down to an instant frown, like a live-action tragicomedy mask. It was one of the few times I remembered him paying direct attention to me, and it always made me laugh, but Millie's crestfallen expression just made me feel bad—and so did her immediate concern.

"It's fine." I searched for the right words; telling my elderly maybe-relative I'd never heard of till twenty-four hours ago that I wasn't fully comfortable with her career as a sex worker wasn't one of the polite phrases in my arsenal. Blowing out a long breath, I set my fork down on the plate and decided to be honest. "Jason Davis told me why his dad was here . . . what you do, and it's not that I don't support your right to . . . to make a living however you want to, or really anyone's freedom to, well, to do their thing, whatever that is, as long as it isn't hurting anyone else. And clearly you aren't. I mean, I assume," I said, my face heating at a sudden unwelcome image of Millie as a rubber-clad, whip-wielding dominatrix. "But I don't . . . I mean, we don't know each other, and I shouldn't have just foisted myself into the middle of your . . . your . . . whatever this business of yours is. But I'm sorry, I'm just not feeling comfortable enough to stay, considering . . ." I finally trailed off miserably.

If I worried that my frank words offended her, her puzzled smile put that to rest. "Gracie," she said with a hint of amusement. "What is it you think I do?"

My face had to be bright red with the heat I felt pulsing into my cheeks. Had I gotten it wrong? Or was I thinking the worst of her? Maybe she was just some sort of sex therapist, like Esther Perel?

I squirmed—Millie was watching me with an expectant expression, her silence telling me she wasn't going to offer any clues. I hazarded a guess on the safer side of the spectrum: "Um . . . I think you do some kind of . . . maybe . . . relationship therapy?"

"That doesn't seem likely to upset you to this degree, does it, sweetheart?" She was full-out smiling now, as if we were sharing a marvelous joke. "Gracie, did you think that I was a hooker?"

I covered my burning face in mortification. "That's not it, is it?" I said, my words muffled behind my hands.

The sound of her laughter made me peek out from between my fingers. She was bent over the counter, gripping the edge as if she needed the support as she dissolved into helpless giggles. "No," she finally managed when she caught a breath, "but I don't think I've ever felt so flattered in my life."

While I tried to cool my burning cheeks, Millie mopped tears of mirth from her eyes.

"Finish your breakfast, honey, and then let me show you what it is I do."

I FOLLOWED HER down the hallway on the other side of the expansive open living area, opposite the wing where the guest room was located, and into the first door on the right—an office. The neat surface of the dark wood desk bore only a laptop, and the room—like nearly every one I'd seen so far in this unusually designed house—featured a wall of windows looking out onto that million-dollar view. Opposite the desk were two mismatched upholstered armchairs, and I sank into one, Millie reaching over to the laptop and pulling it toward us before joining me in the other. She opened it up and clicked a few keys, then turned the screen to face me.

It was a YouTube video headed, "Been There Done That."

I glanced up. "You want to show me a video?"

Millie tapped one perfectly manicured dark pink nail on the top of the computer. "Watch."

She clicked on one of the thumbnails, and suddenly I saw her face appear on the screen. In the video the woman sitting next to me now was in a gold velvet chair with a back so tall it towered over her head. She wore a gray-striped maxiskirt that draped to the floor, and a loose peasant blouse in a teal and yellow print.

"Today I'm taking viewer questions," Millie's image said without preamble. She lifted a stack of papers from her lap, the colorful bangles dripping from her arms making clanking sounds.

"This was an early one—I've learned to dress with the mic in mind," the real-life Millie said to me, but my eyes stayed glued to the screen, where the tiny bohemian Millie was reading from the top of the pile.

"'I want to meet a nice guy, but all I get are come-ons and dick pics. How am I supposed to respond to that?'"

I flinched at "dick pics," but Millie had read the phrase without a hitch. I wondered whether she had any idea what that meant, but on-screen she made a *tsk-tsk* sound, shaking her head, so I had to assume she did.

She looked up directly into the camera, an expression of gravest disappointment on her face. "I wish I understood young people's obsession with their own genitalia and capturing it for posterity." She sighed. "Honey, there's not one thing you can do about a man who lacks any class and the sense God gave him and insists on foisting his frank and beans onto your phone screen."

That startled a laugh out of my throat.

"But the way you respond to that sort of thing is *not* to respond," she went on to the camera, one imperious finger lifted. "You delete that rude picture and you block that boy. You don't engage with that kind of disrespectful shenanigans. But let's examine this a bit further"—she glanced down—"'Fed Up in Frisco.' It's time to take a good honest look at where you're digging up these uncouth young men. Are you swiping right and left and wondering why the men you wind up with are leading with their willies and not their wit?"

I sneaked a look at Millie to see whether this was some kind of joke, but she was staring intently at the screen as if she were fully absorbed in the question.

"You don't meet a long-termer on a short-term platform. If you want more than a crotch shot and a hookup, then you need to raise your standards and change your stomping grounds. Put down the phone and step away from your computer screen and get out there into the actual world. Find someone at a bar who has a nice look to him, and you go up to him in person and you say, 'Hello, there, my name is Frisco'—but use your real name, dear—'and I'd be very happy to buy you a strongly poured adult beverage or a lemonade and get to know you a little bit.'" She wagged her finger at the camera. "You get out what you put into something—if you want someone to treat you like a human being who's more than just a nice face and a set of genitals, then let's get you doing the same. Now, you write back to me and you tell me how that goes if you decide to try it my way, okay? I'm rooting for you, Frisco." She licked her thumb and sent the top paper flying off camera. "This next question is from a viewer all the way out in Portland."

Millie leaned over to click pause and froze the video, taking the laptop back. "Hmpf," she said, frowning. "I should have talked about other options. It's not that online dating is bad, per se—just that those swipe-right hookup sites remove all humanity from the equation. Finding love is about so much more than knee-jerk judgments. Well, as I said, this was an early video. I try not to Monday-morning-quarterback myself too much."

I was still trying to sort out the avalanche of input that had just crashed down on me. Between this sweet-looking grandmother type in front of me spouting phrases like "dick pic" and "crotch shot" and "frank and beans," all I could come up with was, "You realize that letter may have been from a man? I mean . . . a gay man?" I said cautiously, afraid of shocking her.

"Well, of course it was from a gay man, dear. Most of my viewers who write in about that sort of thing are. He wrote back a few days later and thanked me. Said he'd met a sweet boy at a place downtown and they had an actual date set up. I was very proud of him."

I shook my head as if that might clear it, like an Etch A Sketch. "So you . . . you give dating advice?"

Millie closed the laptop gently, leaning back in the chair. "Well, yes. That's part of what I offer. But it's really just one of the services on the menu. You can't be truly happy with someone else till you're happy with yourself. I help with all of it—everything from makeovers to dating coaching to getting at the root of what's keeping someone from letting themselves find the love they're looking for—anything that contributes to helping them find a good match. I'm sort of a one-stop shop."

"For who?"

"For anyone who needs it. It started with a few of my older friends—the Merry Widows, you met some of them. Dating is a tough proposition when you've been off the market for decades, not to mention how much things have changed since my cohorts were younger. I helped a few of them swim back out into the current, if you will, and then . . ." Millie lifted a shoulder. "Word spread."

My eyebrows high, I pointed to the laptop. "Word spread to *San Francisco*?"

"Ah. Well. That was something different." She opened the computer again, tapped the keyboard, and once more flipped it so I could see it. "This happened," she said dryly.

It was another video, this one not as carefully staged as the last one. Millie was standing in front of an easel in a large, sparsely furnished room. The lighting was spotty and harsh, and the camera shook a little.

"That's my studio—where we record the videos, among other

things," Millie said, never taking her eyes off the screen. "It's out back—I'll show you later."

In this one her hair was loose in a spectacular silver nimbus around her head, a leopard-print headband holding it off her face. She wore an artist's smock with ropes of wooden beads draped around her neck, dark blue–painted nails clasped around a paintbrush.

"No one values anything they get too easily," Millie was saying to a point just over the camera, as if to the person holding it. Large crystal earrings bobbed as she talked, gesturing with the paint-daubed brush she held. "You need to stop giving away the pooty, hon. Just cut that nonsense right out."

Close to the mic I heard a muffled snort. I knew I was goggling, but I couldn't help it—I couldn't get my mind around things like this coming out of the delicate pink mouth of the genteel older woman beside me.

"But we've been dating for almost a month." The female voice was louder than Millie's, the question coming, I assumed, from the camerawoman.

On-screen Millie had turned back to her painting, and the camera moved around to reveal what she was working on: a vividly colorful mélange of shapes I judged to be an abstract until I saw a real-life mise-en-scène of fruit spilling from a basket on a table next to the canvas. If I squinted, the colors and shapes were similar. "That's not dating," she said, her profile to the camera now. "That's just getting busy."

"What do you mean, busy?" The tone was disingenuous, teasing.

Millie arched a knowing look toward the camera. "You know exactly what I mean. Has that boy taken you out to eat one time? Or to a show?"

"We eat," the voice said defensively. "We see shows—we watch movies on Netflix all the time."

Millie turned to face the unseen camera operator, her eyebrows bunched in a line of displeasure. "Oh, I know all about that Netflix-and-chill nonsense. Him calling you over late at night for oral relations on the sofa is hardly what I'm talking about."

The camera shook as I heard giggles from the woman holding it. "Well, so what do you think I should do? Just stop seeing him?"

"You aren't 'seeing him' now. You're hooking up. Getting it on. Booty-calling. Whatever you kids call it these days." She was gesturing emphatically with the paintbrush on each phrase, and I could see orange paint splattering as the unseen woman continued laughing. "Is that really all you want, sweetheart?"

Millie's voice had gentled on the last question, along with her expression, and she was looking at a point above the camera with a warm, understanding gaze that pinched my heart. Clearly whoever had shot this video was someone Millie genuinely cared about.

There was a moment of silence, and then a quiet, "No. It isn't."

Millie nodded slowly. "I didn't think so. You deserve so much more than what you're asking for, my dear. You deserve someone who really *sees* you—just as you are—and thinks that person is simply marvelous. Who wants to spend time with you and talk to you and listen to you, and laugh and dance and explore, and celebrate *life* and how lucky we are to live it"—on the word "life" she raised both arms, palms up with the brush clasped between two fingers, as if to encompass all the wonder of the world—"luckiest of all if we get to share it with someone we truly love, and who truly loves us."

A throat was cleared, and then, softly, "Have you had that, Millie?"

Her face went faraway and beatific, a knowing, secret smile spreading across it. "Oh, yes, my darling, you know I have. And it was glorious."

Heat filled my eyes as Millie focused once again on whoever held the camera. "You must hold out for that, my love—for more than what you're accepting so little of now. If you don't know to your soul that you are worthy of such a thing, how can anyone else?"

She was smiling so kindly at the person behind the camera, her gaze searching but sympathetic, that I felt a lump in my own throat.

I wanted that too. I wanted it *back*. As Millie painted a picture with her words far lovelier and clearer than the one on her canvas, the pain of losing everything Brian and I had had together sliced into my chest like a fresh wound.

The camera was still trained on her inescapable, insightful gaze when the image went black.

Startled out of my thoughts, I blinked away the sting in my eyes and looked underneath the video, which was captioned, *Wise elder gives hysterical, utterly perfect modern dating advice.* "Oh, my God—this thing has almost a million hits!"

Millie nodded. "Yes. Bridget said it 'went viral.' Which wasn't something you wanted in my day, but apparently these days it's gold."

"Bridget?"

She gestured to the computer. "My friend who shot the video. She was just monkeying around as we talked about the boy she was seeing and said she had to record it so she could play

it back for herself when her resolve faltered. She wound up post-
ing it on Facebook, and then . . . well, things snowballed."

"Were you okay with that? I mean, did she ask your permission?"

Millie smiled. "Well, no, but it's hard to get upset when it
seemed to strike such a chord in people." She scrolled down so
I could see the comments—there were thousands, and thousands more ticks next to the thumbs-up icon.

"So it turned out to be a good thing, since ultimately it allowed me to reach so many people, who seem to really welcome
an old lady's advice for some reason."

"It's good advice," I admitted.

"After this we started making more videos and she created
the channel here on the YouTube. And that spread into my blog,
and—"

"You have a blog?"

"Mmm. On my website." She pulled the screen toward her,
clicked a few keys, and then turned it back to me.

On the home page, a hot-pink banner read, *Silver Linings—
Tips from an Old Dog with a Few New Tricks.* Beneath it was a
photo—a gorgeous stretch of beach, with Millie in what I was
coming to realize was her usual sartorial splendor: a white linen
blouse unbuttoned and tied over what looked like a red maillot
bathing suit, a Hawaiian-print sarong wrapped around her
waist. The modest effect was ruined by the sea breeze that must
have been blowing—the skirt fanned out over her bare feet with
their pink-painted toenails, revealing astonishingly good legs
for anyone, let alone a woman her age, and her long, loose hair
was blown back like silver ribbons behind her.

And speaking of ribbons . . . she held one: one of those ribbons on a stick that Olympic gymnasts used in their floor work. Its trailing red silk had formed a near-perfect heart in the air.

"We tried to get that shot for hours, but we finally had to Photoshop the heart," she said, frowning into the screen. "Which is too bad, because it took me weeks to learn to actually do that, but the trade winds had other ideas."

"This is . . ." I shook my head. "It's incredible. So you just offer love advice on here—to, what, subscribers?"

She nodded. "All eighty thousand or so of them, last I checked. Not counting the hits we get on the site and on my Facebook page—which is into six figures most months." She couldn't mask her pride—and rightly so. I knew enough about the Web to know that those kinds of numbers were lightning in a bottle.

"And that spread into, well, I guess consultations, we'd call them," she went on. "And then I started noticing that some of the people I was corresponding and talking with seemed like they might be looking for similar things as some other people I talked to . . . and I started making some introductions, the way I've been doing among my friends here locally for years. And that's wound up with a few marriages. I suppose in the end what I've become is a yenta of sorts—that's what I'm doing with Michael Davis, Jason's father: helping him find someone special."

My eyes started watering and I realized I hadn't blinked in quite some time.

Millie Jenkins was an internet dating sensation. An elderly online love guru.

"How old are you?" I blurted before I realized how rude the question was, but Millie merely lifted the corners of her mouth in a Mona Lisa smile.

"I'm eighty-one. At least for a few more months."

"What? You look amazing!"

"Good clean living." She winked. "At least, now that I'm old enough to know better. Really I suppose we have to credit fortunate genes and a very proficient team of aestheticians." She leaned to place the laptop back on her desk. "And now it's nearly eleven o'clock and your first day of vacation is getting away from us. That is, unless you're still wanting to flee my little den of iniquity here?" She lifted one eyebrow in a reproachful look, but the smile playing along her lips told me she was teasing.

"No," I said sheepishly. "I think I can probably handle it."

She clapped her hands and stood. "Wonderful! Then let's get you into something a bit more tropics appropriate, if you have it, and I'll show you a bit of my little piece of paradise."

It sounded infinitely more appealing than waiting all day at the airport for a flight to take me back to cold, gray winter to face Brian and "Angel" again. And it meant I'd have the chance after all to find out more about this long-lost relative.

It wasn't until after she instructed me to meet her in the main room in ten minutes and I went back to my bedroom to change that another thought occurred to me.

If she truly was part of my family and her job hadn't been the reason for her estrangement . . . then what was?

# Thirteen

I came back out of the bedroom in a pair of long walking shorts and a promo T-shirt from a local radio station that eager interns had pressed on me outside Lowe's one morning when Brian and I were picking up paint samples for our bedroom.

I hated that even the tiniest things in my life were attached to a Brian memory. I hoped Angelica hated Dream Weaver Blue—and that Millie's ready chatter would keep me from stewing too much over things I couldn't change anymore, like Brian . . . Angelica . . . their baby.

Their *baby*.

I also hoped it would give me a chance to do a little digging, see if I could find out more about her—and our family.

Millie was coming out of her side of the house when she caught sight of me and stopped dead. "No," she said.

"No?" I actually glanced around to see if maybe a disobedient dog had padded out silently behind me.

"Is this your favorite radio station?" she asked, wagging a finger toward my outfit.

I glanced down at the neon logo on my chest, not even sure what station it was. "No . . ."

"Do you work there?"

I laughed. "No, but—"

"Is that thing even in your size?"

I plucked the ample extra fabric away from my chest. "I don't know—don't T-shirts all fit the same?"

"Oh, my." She clutched her chest and staggered back a step as though a shock wave had hit her. "You're better than this, Gracie. You're better than a giveaway T-shirt. Come on."

"Where are we going?"

"No, no." She held up a finger. "No questions. We're in my wheelhouse now. You just let me handle this."

RATHER THAN TAKING the garish Merry Widows van she'd picked me up from the airport in, Millie backed out of the garage under the house in a sleek champagne-colored sports car. As I neared it, the chrome door handle that had been flush with the metal gracefully extended toward my hand.

"Nice," I said, settling into the leather seat.

"I like sports cars—this one is my baby. She's electric."

I turned away to reach for my seat belt and to hide a smile at the idea of octogenarian Millie imagining herself as Mario Andretti in her glorified golf cart.

But as soon as we cleared her street and got out on the main road, she mashed the accelerator and the car took off so fast it left my stomach behind us on the asphalt.

My hands shot up to grip the suede dashboard, and I wondered whether the wheels still touched the ground. "*What* was *that*?" I gasped out as soon as I caught my breath.

Millie wasn't even trying to hide her broad grin. "That's a Tesla, dear. The Electric CruiseBeast. Finest piece of engineering on the road today. What you just felt is called Ludicrous Mode. For obvious reasons."

By the time we pulled into a parking spot at a tucked-away cluster of low buildings just a few miles away, I'd made her do it a half dozen more times, whenever we had pole position at a stop sign and a long swath of traffic-free road in front of us, and I laughed giddily every time my head got plastered to the headrest and my stomach dropped out like we were on a roller coaster.

"That was *amazing*," I said, letting myself out on shaky legs. "Why doesn't everyone drive one of these?"

"With great power comes great responsibility," Millie said seriously. "And a great price tag. My Tessie was a bit of an indulgence. Not really the most practical car."

Maybe not. But I was beginning to see the appeal of impracticality. I glanced around the palm-studded crushed-shell parking lot. "Where are we?"

"My favorite clothing boutique," she said, coming around to my side. "If this is an example of the beach clothes you brought, we need to get you some proper vacation wear."

My feet glued themselves to the asphalt automatically—I hated shopping.

But she had a point about my fashion choices—now that I was here in balmy weather and blue skies I couldn't have imagined in the frigid temps back home, I realized that the khakis and polos I'd brought weren't exactly seasonal.

"Okay," I acquiesced. "Let's run in and grab a few things."

MY USUAL APPROACH when necessity dictated buying new clothes was goal oriented and efficient: find the section I needed, pick out a few things in my size, pay, and go.

But it turned out that for Millie, shopping was an endurance event.

She wasn't kidding about her favorite boutique; as soon as she wafted through the doorway of the shop, Bord de Mer, which seemed far too small to have any kind of significant inventory, a pretty woman with short, tousled blond hair who looked to be in her midfifties lit up and threw open her arms. "Millie!" she cried. "I didn't know you were coming today."

"Hello, sweetheart," Millie said, patting the woman's cheek as she went in for the hug. "I didn't either—this was a fashion emergency."

I tried hard not to roll my eyes.

"How's that handsome man of yours?" Millie asked the woman.

"Better all the time—thanks to you."

"Stop that. It was everyone. Now let me introduce you to my niece." Millie stepped away from the woman and extended one arm toward me. "Helene, this is Grace." She beamed like an overzealous mother presenting her daughter at a debutante ball.

Helene took in a dramatic breath and raised a hand to her mouth in what seemed to me to be unwarranted enthrallment. "Millie," she breathed excitedly. "I didn't know you had a niece. Welcome, Grace." I got the same treatment with the flung-open arms and the hug, which I had to admit was actually rather nice—Helene smelled like lilacs and candy. "We adore Millie—well, everyone does. I'm sure I don't need to tell you how lucky you are to have this wonderful woman for an aunt."

I wished she *would* tell me, actually. I had a lot of blanks to fill in. Like what was it Millie had done for Helene's husband? And who was "everyone" who had helped?

But there was apparently no time for chitchat in a "fashion

emergency." While Millie explained my sad sartorial situation to her—in terms that made me sound like a Charles Dickens character—Helene ushered us back into a private dressing area and pressed flutes of champagne into our hands as we sank into velvet-upholstered sofas.

"Let me assemble some of our *derniers vêtements* and I'll be right back," the bubbly woman said, breezing back through the velvet curtain.

"Assemble what?" I said, still dazedly holding out my glass where I'd accepted it.

Millie chuckled. "The latest fashions. It's French."

"I didn't know there was going to be French," I said weakly as she tipped back a long sip of the bubbling golden champagne, and despite the fact that it wasn't even noon yet I followed suit, fairly certain I'd need the fortitude.

Helene was back in an astonishingly short amount of time, rolling in a rack laden with what had to be half the small store's inventory. "Here we are," she said with a flutter of one hand. "This will give us a starting place—now let me go get a few accessories."

As she breezed back out I looked with a mild sense of alarm at the clothing spilling from the rack—dresses and skirts and silky tops and a wide array of items far beyond the few shorts and tank tops I'd been envisioning picking up.

"Oh, I don't need all this," I protested, but Millie put out one imperious hand.

"Gracie, you're a beautiful young woman," she began. "But you're a peacock dressing like a pigeon. Please let me treat you to a few pretties—it's my first time getting to do a little something for my niece, and it would mean the absolute world to me."

While I was still reeling between her compliments and kind

words and the slightly insulting assessment sandwiched between, she plowed on.

"Besides, we have a special event tonight and I know you may not have brought anything for a wedding."

"A wedding?" I yelped.

She was flipping through the clothes with the concentration of a museum curator and didn't look up.

"Yes, I'm so sorry to spring that on you, dear, but everything happened so fast and it plumb slipped my mind to tell you when you said you were coming right away, and obviously I couldn't reschedule."

"But it's Monday night," I said dumbly.

"They got a deal on the venue from the owner if they did it off-peak."

"But . . ." I said again, "I wasn't invited."

She glanced up with a bright smile. "You're my plus-one. I already called the bride. They told me I could bring a whole army if I wanted to."

I was pretty sure that was Millie hyperbole, but it wasn't my chief objection at the moment. "But I don't need to buy something fancy just for that. I brought a nice vintage blouse, with a work skirt that—"

Millie stopped and faced me. "No work skirts. Why would you even *bring* a work skirt on a beach vacation? And, honey, vintage is just a nice way of saying passé. This is my treat, since I sprang this on you."

Part of me, for just one second, wondered whether the wedding was an elaborate ruse so Millie could do a full clichéd *Queer Eye* makeover on me. But no. Eccentric the woman might be, but as far as I could tell she'd been nothing but forthright.

Even when it might have been more politic not to (the "passé" comment still smarted a little).

Not that she was wrong. It wasn't the first time I'd heard gentle (or not that gentle, in Millie's case) comments about sprucing up my wardrobe beyond the array of hand-me-downs and practical work clothes my closet had contained for more years than I could remember. There was no need to throw out a perfectly good skirt or pair of shoes, Mom always said, when I was plenty able to wield a needle and thread or a glue gun. You didn't get rid of something just because you might have gotten a little tired of it.

*Right, Brian?*

More than once girlfriends had tried to drag me to the mall with them for shopping sprees, or Susie would leave Macy's sale flyers tucked not so subtly amid the mail she set on my desk. But it never seemed to make sense to me to spend money on an item that simply needed to be functional, when I had plenty of things to wear already.

But Millie had been nothing but gracious since I'd foisted myself on her with zero notice—and even now she was regarding me with a warm, beaming smile. Wouldn't it be even ruder to disappoint her?

"Okay," I finally agreed. "But I'll pay," I added before she could jump in. "I haven't gone clothes shopping in years. I'm probably overdue for a refresh."

"Oh, Gracie!"

Maybe it was the way her face lit up like Christmas morning, as though I'd just given her a pony. Maybe it was the way she'd begun using the endearment of my name—no one had called me Gracie since my mom. Or maybe it was just the image of the suitcase full of boring, unseasonable clothes sitting in her guest room when the bold sunshine and riot of colors outdoors made me want to be a peacock, not a pigeon, for a change.

Whatever it was, I doubled down, thinking of Dorothy Fielding's instructions to do something just for myself: "Why not? In fact, let's really blow this out and get me a whole new wardrobe."

Millie's eyes practically rolled back in her head with delirious joy, and I worried I might have overstimulated her.

"In that case, let's get started," she said, clapping her hands. "We've only got five hours until the wedding."


WE CONSUMED NEARLY two hours (and a full bottle of champagne) in the dressing room, as I tried on outfit after outfit, Helene bustling around me pulling a tuck here, a pleat there, making already beautiful clothing look as if it had been made for me, Millie sitting on the sofa with her champagne, calling out her approval or suggestions or vetoes like a rowdy heckler at a comedy show.

"Good Lord, Gracie, you're stunning!" she crowed.

"You really are," Helene piped up. "Striking looks obviously run in the family."

*The family.*

Millie nodded as if in total agreement.

By the time we rounded up my outfits, which apparently didn't qualify as such without a full complement of somewhat useless accessories as well as several new pairs of shoes, I nearly choked at the final total—we'd managed to tip well into four figures. I doubted I'd spent that much money on my wardrobe in the past decade. So much for the bulk of Mrs. Fielding's mad money.

But I handed over my credit card without complaint. There was no denying the way I looked in the carefully fitted, well-made garments—or the way they made me feel: confident . . . bold.

Beautiful.

Not adjectives I was accustomed to claiming. But I hoped they followed me back to Missouri when I left and gave me a bit more courage to face Brian and the shiny Angelica outside my front door day after day after day.

But apparently a new wardrobe was only step one in Millie's multipart system for making me her personal Eliza Doolittle. From Helene's boutique we walked through the cluster of buildings. The Island Market was Cypress Key's only real shopping center, Millie explained as we passed a few specialty shops, like the Dragonfly, a gallery featuring local crafts as well as hand-made jewelry and pottery and walls lined with original artwork, but also a small food market and deli; Beach Beans, an eclectic coffee shop I peeked into as we passed its open door, lined with paintings and overflowing bookshelves that also functioned as a lending library, Millie explained—as far a cry from a soulless Starbucks as I could imagine; and a package store with an open-air bar and restaurant in the back serving fresh-caught shrimp and soups and simple sandwiches (amusingly named Something Fishy).

That was much of the commerce on the island, Millie said as we got back in the car. Residents who needed anything else had to head over the bridge and into Fort Myers—until new investors had bought the island's only hotel that previous investors had broken ground on and then abandoned in the housing crash of 2007, when Florida became the epicenter of the mortgage crisis. The finished building had sat eerily empty, built but not finished out, never open for business a single day, until it finally opened—with new owners—as the Turquoise in 2013, bringing a full-service restaurant and bar, shops and watercraft rental businesses, and new life to the island.

"You'll see it tonight—that's where the wedding is," Millie said as we stepped into the Tips and Tails Salon, a narrow space with two massage chairs, two low counters covered with nail polish bottles, and a few chairs lining the curtained front window. Inside it was soothingly dim after the bright sunlight, with some kind of calming steel-drum music playing softly and the scent of jasmine overlaying a faint chemical smell.

A dark-haired woman reading a magazine with her feet up in one of the massage chairs, whom I'd taken to be a lone customer, looked up when we entered and, just as Helene had, beamed at the sight of Millie. "You're two days early this week!" she said, coming over with arms wide.

"I had a surprise visitor—this beautiful girl is my niece. Grace, meet Pilar, the finest aesthetician on this or any island."

The woman scoffed and made a dismissive gesture but couldn't hide her pleased reaction as she gave me the same embrace and cheek kisses she and Millie had just exchanged.

"I thought you might be full of bridal party today," Millie said.

"You're in luck—Ysidra and her mom and sisters came yesterday. I'm closing early to get to the wedding, but of course I'll take care of you. What are we doing for you ladies?"

"Just Gracie today—we need to go get ready too."

"Oh, I'm fine," I protested. "I don't really do my nails."

Millie looked pointedly at my ragged fingernails and scaly winter feet as if she were assessing a used car. "That's evident, dear," she said sweetly. "Mani-pedi for sure, Pilar, and, Gracie, are you swimsuit ready?"

I frowned. "I brought mine, if that's what you mean. It's a few years old, but I've only worn it a few times, so I don't need a new one."

But apparently that wasn't the path Millie was traveling. She raised an eyebrow at Pilar, who was wearing a matching expression. "Sounds like we need a wax too, hmm?"

"Definitely." Pilar nodded.

"Oh, I'm sorry, no—no waxing." I'd seen enough of that in movies and TV shows to know I wanted no part of it.

Millie turned to me with a patient expression and laid a hand on my shoulder. "Gracie, honey, you don't want spiders creeping out at the bikini line, if you catch my drift."

I caught it, my face flaming at the picture she'd created. No, I most certainly did not want that, and since the warm sunshine and tropical setting were already beckoning me to a beach, chances were better than good that I'd be wearing my one-piece at some point. I reluctantly acquiesced, and Pilar led me to a back room whose soothing décor and gentle music gave no indication of the horrors that ensued several minutes later, in areas that only Brian and my ob-gyn had gotten quite that up close and personal with.

"How is this necessary?" I yelped in pain as the first strip of cooled wax was hostilely ripped away, along with what felt like a strip of flesh.

Pilar patted my hand with a deceptively innocent smile. "Trust your aunt—beauty comes from the inside out."

"Not this far inside," I gritted out as another strip was yanked away.

Afterward I followed Pilar out—walking in a wide-legged John Wayne gait—to the massage chairs, where Millie was already settled in, her head and body rocking gently side to side with the vibrations of the massage mechanism.

"How'd it go?" she asked brightly, as though she hadn't heard my outbursts.

"I think you know," I muttered as I climbed into the chair beside her.

But all was forgiven as Pilar soaked my feet and gently massaged all the way up my calves. It felt delicious, as did her expert ministrations to my calloused feet and my toes, which looked delicate and pretty, I had to admit, once she finished off with the polish—a bright, sunny coral that Millie talked me into instead of the clear I'd requested. I got the same wonderful treatment for my hands, though this time I prevailed with the polish.

I was feeling pampered and utterly relaxed—until Pilar capped the bottle of topcoat she'd just finished layering on my fingernails and suggested we visit someone named Anders for something called a "Brazilian blowout."

"Whoa, no. I am done with Brazilian anythings," I said, stiff-arming the woman.

Millie laughed. "It's just a hair-smoothing system, sugar—a straightening treatment. But I wouldn't want to pull out those gorgeous waves," she said to Pilar. "Anyway, we need to get home and get ready for tonight."

"Let her dry first," Pilar said, reaching behind me and restarting the massage feature I realized had timed out, and Millie nodded.

"Just add it to my tab, Pilar."

I leaned up. "No, that's okay, I—"

Millie reached over and squeezed my arm, her skin age-softened but her grip surprisingly firm. "Please let me treat you to a little something, Gracie. You can't imagine what a pleasure it is for me to have you here." Her blue eyes—the same shade as mine, I realized with a jolt—were as warm as her hand, and I nodded with an unexpected tightening of my throat.

As Pilar bustled off, I leaned back in the massage chair and turned to look at Millie. Her eyes were closed, and I couldn't tell whether the light lavender of her lids was a result of her eye shadow having worn away to reveal the tender skin beneath or the makeup itself. A small smile hovered over her lips.

She looked fragile and small in the huge chair despite her imposing size, and a strange tenderness crept up in me like a slow incoming tide.

Millie's eyes flew open, her gaze directly meeting mine as if she'd known I was watching her. "What's going on in that pretty head of yours?"

She'd startled me. "I was just thinking . . . that I'm glad to finally know you."

"That's lovely." She smiled, then cocked her head as if she could see through the partial truth. "What were you really thinking?"

I could feel color surge into my cheeks. I didn't want to hurt her feelings—but I'd learned long ago that a lie always showed on my face.

"I was thinking . . . well, you seem so nice, and . . . kind." I swallowed. "I was wondering what happened that cut you out of our family."

The smile disappeared from Millie's face as if I'd waved a wand, and for a moment I regretted being the cause of the melancholy expression that replaced it.

But I wanted to know. I *needed* to know what could have been so awful that Mom wouldn't have called her only remaining relative when she grew ill, when she realized she was going to leave me completely, utterly alone.

What could Millie Jenkins possibly have done?

Millie let out a long, streaming sigh as though I'd pulled a stopper out of her, and looked down toward her jiggling legs.

*It's complicated*, I expected her to say. *It's a long story.*

"Your great-grandfather—my father—didn't approve of . . . the way I lived my life."

I stared, waiting for more, but her eyes closed again and that appeared to be all she had to say.

What did that mean?

I thought about what I knew of Millie so far from the less than twenty-four hours since I'd met her—her terrible but enthusiastic painting, her teenage-boy enthusiasm for fast cars . . . her group of what might have been lonely widows that she organized and got out into the world, and the genuine delight in seeing her of everyone I'd met so far . . . her funny, kindhearted videos, and her easy acceptance of the people who sought her advice, regardless of their lifestyle.

The way she'd dropped everything to welcome *me*—a total stranger but for an accident of shared blood—into her home, her life.

What about any of that could my great-grandparents and my grandmother possibly have found objectionable? And why would my mother have gone along with it once she became an adult and could make her own decisions?

But Pilar was somewhere within earshot in the back room, and this wasn't the time to pry into what might be dark family secrets, even if Millie hadn't effectively put a stop to my questions.

I reached down to touch the loose, mottled skin of her arm and her eyes flashed open again. "I'm supposed to stick my feet under that cancery-looking purple light over there," I said, covering my unsettled thoughts with a smile. "See you in a few minutes?"

"I'm right here whenever you're ready." Millie closed her eyes and patted my hand where it still rested on her arm, and that odd tenderness swept through me again.

How could this kind woman I'd been getting to know be the same person who'd done something awful enough to make my close-knit family not only disown her, but erase her existence entirely?

# Fourteen

Parties weren't really my thing under the best of circumstances, let alone when I knew no one there—barely even the person I was going with—on top of being slightly jet-lagged. All I really wanted was to curl up in Millie's comfortable guest bed—or perhaps under it—and lose myself to sleep.

But Millie had been so excited about bringing me to meet all her friends that I couldn't back out. I made myself unwrap my new clothes to change.

Helene had kept a few items I bought so she could take in a seam or a hem here and there; she'd promised to deliver them to me in a few days. But on the way back to Millie's car we'd stopped in at Bord de Mer to pick up the rest of my purchases she'd held while we shopped, including the dress I'd picked out (or, more accurately, that she and Millie had picked out for me) for the wedding.

It was easily the most beautiful thing I'd ever owned. The floral pattern suggested the tropics, but the light colors—watercolor brushstrokes of peaches and yellows and a touch of teal—kept it from being too overtly *Miami Vice*. The deep vee at my chest and the cap sleeves framed a bodice that, with a few quick subtle tucks Helene had taken while Millie and I were at Pilar's salon, perfectly hugged what curves I had, then draped softly to my knees, where the light silky fabric alternately out-lined and fluttered around my legs. I did an experimental twirl to watch the liquidy silk flare and sway and then settle, and immediately felt foolish. I took my hair down and brushed it, then put it in a fresh ponytail and went out to wait for Millie.

The living room was empty, and the sound of some kind of disco music coming from the other hallway suggested she was still in her room. I wandered around, debating whether to just sit and wait or go let her know I was ready, when the framed pictures dotting the bookshelves along one wall caught my at-tention. Family photos? I walked over to look more closely.

Some of them seemed to date back decades, black-and-white and grainy, and I recognized Millie as the tall, smiling young woman in culottes and a safari hat standing with a group in front of a towering waterfall in a lush green jungle; amid a rowdy-looking group drinking wine at a patio table in some European café, Millie easily identifiable despite her enormous sunglasses and large-brimmed hat; or arms linked with two other women on a whitecapped mountaintop, bundled up like a snow bunny with only her eyes and wide grin revealing her identity. I could have identified her by her definitive fashion choices, if nothing else.

As the photos began to be in color, more modern, the woman more closely resembled the Millie I knew, now with the addi-tion of a slight, angular man beside her in many of the pictures. The two were almost comically mismatched, but it was easy to see how happy they were from their broad smiles and the way they leaned into each other in nearly every picture: bending over the mouth of a volcano, pretending they were about to jump;

arms wound around each other's waists in the surf on a black sand beach; standing before the Taj Mahal with their hands over their heads, mimicking its shape. This must have been her husband.

Something stirred and uncoiled inside me. I'd fantasized about traveling like this, once—seeing the world before I came back home to take over "the family legacy," as Mom always referred to the firm. But something in her had changed after my father left, gotten small and tired and easily overwhelmed, and I was afraid that if I didn't come back immediately after college my mother would simply collapse in on herself completely.

I used to think that was a hidden blessing—the silver lining of a dark cloud. If I'd done what I'd once dreamed of I wouldn't have been home when Brian came back to work in the practice . . . his family legacy too. After we started dating, being anywhere else lost a lot of its appeal—I was too ecstatic to have finally gotten our perfect fairy-tale ending.

*Ha.* It *was* a fairy-tale ending of love reclaimed . . . I just hadn't been the princess in that story.

The next photo I picked up showed Millie and her husband not all that long ago from the looks of it, on some kind of boat. The sun was setting behind them and it was hard to make out their faces in the dim light, but the two of them were pressed close together, their heads turned toward each other as if they'd each just heard something marvelous from the other. I set that frame back down, but I couldn't so easily get rid of the feeling of melancholy the photo had given me—and then a black-and-white picture on the next shelf caught my eye and froze me in place.

Because it was my mother.

There were no other family or childhood pictures displayed.

Not a single one. Except here was my mom as a young girl—I'd seen enough photos of her amid family albums to know her at once—somewhere around nine or ten. She was striking a sassy pose I'd never seen from her in life, one hand on a cocked hip, a brash, pursed-lip vogue into the camera. Beside her was a young man—my grandfather? I couldn't tell. There was something familiar about him, but he was slightly bent over, laughing at my mom, his head tipped down so that his features weren't fully clear. How old was Gramps when he met Grammy? They'd grown up in the same town and married young—this must have been him. I picked up the frame and looked for a date in the white margins of the photo that were visible but saw nothing. I'd have to take it out of the frame to look harder, but I didn't want Millie to come out and find me literally tearing apart her things.

I looked more closely at my mom. She looked so . . . lively. Even before my dad left I didn't remember her like this—bubbling over with vivacity, clearly cracking my grandfather up with her antics.

That creeping feeling of tenderness clutched at me again—for my mom, and for the fact that Millie clearly cared enough about her, even now, that this was the sole family picture she chose to display.

The thread of doubt I'd still been harboring about Millie's identity fell away. My great-aunt. I had an *aunt*.

"There you are," Millie sang out, coming into the room, and I startled, nearly dropping the frame. "I was just coming to see if you needed—" She saw what I was holding and stopped dead, her sunny smile fading. "Oh," she said softly.

"You have a picture of Mom," I said, holding it out.

Millie was looking at me, not the picture—peering at me,

actually, as if leery that I might resent her possession of the photo.

"Yes . . ." she said hesitantly.

"You really are my relative."

Millie tried—but failed—to hold back an oddly sad smile. "Were you hoping to find out otherwise?"

I shook my head. "No, I just . . . I didn't . . ."

My feet were moving when my tongue seemed to freeze, and before I realized what I was doing I'd stepped over to Millie and flung my arms around her like a little girl.

If she'd been a daintier woman I might have knocked her over. But she was tall and solid, and instead her arms came immediately around me, one clutching me tight, the other hand softly stroking my hair as I clung to her.

What was the matter with me? I breathed in the gardenia scent at her neck as a thick lump caught in my throat. I was hardly what anyone would call volatile, but first there was my crazy explosion on Brian and now this maudlin display. I seemed to have lost all ability to regulate my actions, let alone my emotions, and as the absurd sob I'd been trying to hold back finally ebbed, my mind raced, trying to find the least embarrassing way to extricate myself from this childish embrace.

Millie took care of it for me, ending the hug as naturally as breathing and briskly changing the subject. "I was coming out to see whether you needed a wrap for tonight. It can get a bit chilly after dark—down to the sixties."

I was amused at the Florida idea of "chilly," and the bubble of emotion in me dissipated—not as though it had never existed, just as if it had found its way free.

"Yes, thanks. I'd appreciate that."

She frowned at me. "I've mussed your ponytail."

I reached up to straighten it, but Millie put a hand on my arm. "Actually, dear, I happen to be rather amazing at hair." Millie seemed to feel she was rather amazing at everything. "I wonder if you'd do me the honor of letting me get my hands on those gorgeous waves. I've been itching to since I first saw you."

It felt like every cliché from every rom-com movie ever made, but Millie had an infectious enthusiasm about her, and a way of making it seem as if the answers to all problems were just so simple. I was starting to see why she'd become an advice guru.

So a few moments later I found myself in a dainty Queen Anne chair in front of the vanity in her spectacular bedroom—which was decorated in a riot of hot pink and yellow—while she bustled around me with an arsenal of brushes, irons, and sprays.

If I closed my eyes I could imagine her gentle touch was my mom again, running a brush impossibly patiently, gently, through the snarls in the waist-length hair I was so proud of—like Rapunzel—and threatening every night to cut it all off if I didn't start taking better care of it. But I secretly loved the bedtime ritual. Along with the stories Mom read me in bed, it was almost the only time I had her to myself, had her full, focused attention on me, so leaving the knots for her to detangle was worth the risk of her making good on her threat.

She never did, though.

What I wanted to ask the woman brushing my hair now was *why*. Why Millie obviously cared enough about my mom even now to display a photo of her decades after she'd last seen her—my entire lifetime, and probably longer—in a home where Patricia Bean Adams had never set foot, yet she had absented herself from my mother's life, from my life. But that wasn't what came out.

"What was she like?"

"Your mother?" Millie smiled, running the broad-bristled brush back along my temples, and appeared to be thinking about her answer. "Well . . . do you know that old nursery rhyme about the little girl with the little curl in the middle of her forehead?"

"'When she was good / She was very, very good, / But when she was bad she was horrid'?" I laughed. "You can't be talking about my mom."

Her eyebrows went up and she met my eyes in the mirror. "In her defense, mostly she was very, very good."

"How was she bad? You have to tell me. All I ever heard my grandparents say was what a well-behaved girl she was."

"Yes, I suppose they would." The look that momentarily tightened her features disappeared like a passing cloud, but there was a story there. I wasn't comfortable enough yet to ask for it, though, and her next words knocked the thought right out of me: "Well . . . when she was twelve she stole my car."

"What?"

"Hold still, dear. My convertible—an Austin-Healey Bug-Eye Sprite I'd scrimped for since it rolled off the line in 1958. I finally found a used model I could afford four years later—Speedwell blue, like a powder puff, with a cute little froggy face of a grille. But that baby had a 948 engine and roared like a beast." She was smiling again, doing something to the back of my hair with a curling iron, but I didn't think she was really seeing it.

"You do like cars," I said.

"Always have—there's nothing like having something gorgeous and finely engineered underneath you." She winked and I couldn't help laughing. "I loved that car—and so did your mother. As soon as I brought it home Tricia begged for rides anytime I saw her. I'd drive her up and down your grandparents' street, and every time we hit the cul-de-sac she'd make me go around and around and around. 'Faster! Go faster!' she'd scream out, till I worried I'd spin us right out of the car, and the whole time she'd just giggle."

I pictured it—my mom goading Millie up and down her parents' street in her sleek little sports car—the same street I lived on now. "That doesn't sound like my mom. Dad used to always tell her she drove 'like an old lady.'"

"Lovely," Millie said dryly.

"Yeah, well . . . Dad wasn't what you'd call PC."

"I'm familiar with the type. Did he pass away too?"

The question was innocent enough, natural . . . but it threw me. I wasn't used to having to explain him. "No," I said tightly. "He left her. Left us. For someone else."

Millie stopped, straightening from the back of my head and meeting my reflection's eyes. "I'm very sorry. For both of you," she said.

I shrugged. "Thanks, but it's no big deal. It happened a long time ago." I lowered my eyes to my lap, tipping my head to encourage her to finish whatever she was doing back there, but I knew from her stillness that she was still watching me in the mirror.

"Do you see him very often? Talk to him?"

I lifted one shoulder again. "I suppose I could. If I wanted to. But no. He has his life, and I have mine."

One of my biggest worries at my mother's funeral had been that my father would show up—with Nan—and I'd have to face him for the first time since they'd moved to L.A. And what would I say to him? It was hard enough interring my mother; I couldn't face unearthing things between me and my father that had been buried long before. He'd made his choices when he'd left us and never looked back. I didn't need him pretending my mother had mattered to him now, and though Brian thought I should at least let him know she'd passed away, I did nothing. I didn't know whether or not Brian had told him anyway, but the result was exactly what I expected in either case: My father never showed.

"What about Mom?" I redirected when I still felt no touch on my hair. "How did she steal the car?"

In the long silence that followed I was afraid she'd just stand there, waiting me out. I pulled my hands into fists, digging my nails into my palms, but finally felt the tug of the brush at my crown and let my fingers relax.

"Well, she used to beg me to teach her to drive it," Millie said slowly as she began pinning up my hair in the back. "So I'd sit her on my lap and show her—she'd steer and I made her tell me when to press the clutch so she could shift gears." I couldn't see her expression, but I heard the smile in her voice.

"You're the one who taught Mom to drive?" Mom had never told me this story. Of course, she'd never mentioned her colorful aunt Millie at all.

"Oh, yes—your mother took to a manual transmission like a worn-out debutante takes to the bottle." A startled laugh escaped my lips. "I wouldn't let her drive on her own, of course, no matter how many times she begged. So one night when I was staying with her while your grandparents were in St. Louis, she sneaked out of the house while I was sleeping and just up and took it."

I was riveted now, watching her intently in the mirror. "What happened—did she wreck it?"

"Oh, goodness, no. Frankly she drove it like a grandma down Shirl's street—your grandmother—and was back a few minutes later. She couldn't have gone farther than out to the main road and back."

"You were watching?"

One eyebrow rose. "Sweetheart, that engine could wake Keith Richards from a three-day binge. Of course I was watching—I wanted to make sure she knew what she was doing."

"Why didn't you stop her?"

Millie had finished arranging the back of my hair into some complicated updo and came around in front of me now, looking pensive as she wielded the hot iron at the strands around my face. "Everyone needs the freedom to stretch their wings and find out what they're made of."

I couldn't believe that what my responsible, hardworking mom was made of was grand theft auto.

When I was seven years old, while Mom checked us out at the grocery store, I'd wandered over to the front counter and helped myself to two cheap plastic sleeves for photo albums that were stacked to one side. I didn't realize I was stealing them—I thought they were simply there for the taking, like flyers or coupons. Together they couldn't have cost more than a dime, but when I proudly showed them to Mom when we got home, pictures already displayed inside and the pages tucked into gaps in a glue-bound family album, she turned off the stove where she'd been making dinner, took my hand, loaded me and the sleeves in the car, and made me return them to the customer service desk and apologize, my cheeks so hot I thought they'd catch fire.

She'd hugged me in the parking lot afterward as I sobbed out my shame. "I know you didn't mean to do it. But stealing is wrong, even if your intentions are good," she told me gently, rubbing my heaving back.

It made an impression—Brian used to tease me for returning change to servers in a restaurant if they gave me back too much, or correcting checkout people if something rang up for less than its posted price.

"Did Mom get in trouble?" I asked Millie.

"Well, I was staked out on the sofa when she crept back inside—nearly scared the britches clean off her when I greeted her in the dark—and I gave her a stern talking-to. But I never told her parents."

"Why not?"

Millie looked out the bay window. The sunlight bouncing off the water outside revealed the loose crepe of her skin but lit her light blue eyes like marbles, making her look at the same time both old and oddly young. "She told me she only wanted to see what it felt like to get outside the neighborhood. I didn't want Walt and Shirley to bring the hammer down. Your mother was a good girl. I just told her that stealing was wrong, even if her intentions were good. That was enough."

I started at her words. "My mom told me that once. *Exactly* that, when I accidentally committed petty theft as a little kid."

I thought she'd laugh, but instead to my shock I saw Millie's eyes grow shiny. "She did? Well." She swallowed and then turned away to set the curling iron back on the vanity. When she turned back to me she'd gathered her composure. "It's nice to hear that a few memories stuck. We made a lot of them together."

She finished whatever it was she was doing and sat on the vanity facing me, blocking my view as she assessed me. The focused attention might have made me uncomfortably self-aware, except that her intent stare was impersonal, like an artist regarding her canvas.

I remembered the caliber of her messy still-life from the video she'd shown me.

But what was the harm? Worst-case scenario, I could put it back in its usual style. Or nonstyle, if I were being honest.

"Sweetheart," she began with a winning smile I was beginning to recognize as her charm offensive when she wanted something, "you're simply beautiful just as you are . . . but would you indulge an old lady and let me dab just a few cosmetics on that perfect face of yours? I happen to be rather an artiste with makeup, but this poor old skin of mine makes a disappointing canvas. I rarely have the pleasure of working with a gorgeous smooth complexion like yours."

I laughed at her utter transparency. "You want to do the full-on *Pretty Woman*, don't you?"

She clasped her hands at her chin. "More than life."

Millie was the one who had a timetable for the evening—if she thought there was time and it made her this happy, who was I to stifle that? I was relishing the chance to find out more about my mom, my family. I raised my hands in surrender. "Sure. Why not?"

She was wielding a puffy brush at me almost before the words left my lips.

"Did you ever do this with my mom?" I asked after a few minutes.

Millie's breath washed over my face as she let out a light laugh, carrying the pleasant scent of coffee. "Oh, my, no. That would never have been allowed."

An odd way to put it. Grammy and Gramps had been fairly strict, deeply conservative in their child-rearing values, but I couldn't imagine them objecting to a harmless game of dress-up. But the soft bristles and gentle strokes on my face felt as soothing and good as what Millie had done to my hair, and I closed my eyes and just enjoyed it. Not as much as Millie was, I surmised, when her happy little humming started again as she worked.

"Nearly finished!" She brandished a tube of gloss that smelled delicious when she opened it and brushed the wand over my lips, then set it back to the glass-topped vanity with a click before stepping away from where she blocked my view of the mirror and gesturing to it with an excited flourish of her hand.

I took myself in.

"Oh. Wow," I managed.

What snagged my eye first was hair. *Big* hair. Millie had piled it high on my head in a pouf that gave me at least two inches in height, leaving a few strands to stream down like waterfalls across my shoulders and back. As I stared unrecognizingly at myself, she pulled a few more little wisps out with what looked like my mother's silver cake rake, leaving them to straggle beside my cheeks—which seemed sharp as razor blades with the deep shading and highlighting she'd done. Above their artificially angled planes she'd painstakingly created what I had to admit was a magazine-ready smoky eye, but all that gray and black made me look like an anime character—and my lips were so shiny and sparkly with gloss I swore they bounced sunlight back into the room.

Millie was standing beside me, beaming like a trainer with a prize show dog. "What do you think?"

"Well," I said carefully, and swallowed. "This is . . . something else."

Her cheeks collapsed. "You don't like it."

I turned away from my reflection and faced her. "No, no—

it's not that . . . exactly. I just maybe look"—*tacky, garish, a little like a drag queen*—"well, not really like *me*."

"What do you mean? This is all you. I didn't even *touch* the fake lashes or lip plumpers or face tape."

"Face tape?"

She put a hand on either side of her head and pulled backward, the skin of her face growing taut. "Poor woman's face-lift. An old model's trick." My expression must have conveyed my horror. "Not that *you* need that, of course," she assured me. "Every bit of this is you. Just . . . enhanced."

"I don't know. There's just"—I gestured vaguely around my head—"a lot going on here. It's not that it's not, um, pretty," I hastened to assure her at her crestfallen expression. "I think maybe it's just not quite right for me."

Millie tipped her head, examining my face. "Well, I don't know you very well yet, sugar, but all I saw from the second you stepped off the escalator was a beautiful girl." She touched one papery hand to my cheek and turned me again toward the mirror. "Try taking a look through my eyes for just a moment, the way I first saw you. If you were seeing this woman for the first time . . . what would you think of her?"

I looked up again, at the image of the fastidiously put-together woman in the mirror, and tried to do what Millie had asked: see her as a stranger.

The first thing I noticed were her eyes. Against the contrast of shading on her lids and her dark lashes, the blue of this woman's irises was luminous as sea glass—like Millie's eyes, I realized, remembering how the older woman's had lit up just like this in the sunlight. Wisps of hair framed high, elegant cheekbones above her soft, sensuous mouth. Her smooth skin glowed like the perfect magazine ads I'd always envied.

I caught myself up on that last thought with a short laugh. Millie was right—if I forgot that I was looking at my own reflection, what I saw in front of me was a woman who simply looked sleek and polished. Confident.

Like Angelica.

"Yes," I said, nodding slowly as I turned from side to side, and then again, "*Yes.*" Millie was right—I wasn't changing who I was on the inside. But what was the harm in dressing that up a bit in pretty wrapping to make the package more exciting?

I pulled my gaze away from the striking figure in the mirror and stood, leaning up to press a kiss to the soft give of Millie's cheek. "Thank you. I can't believe you made me look like this."

Millie gave me a cautious side-eye. "Is that a euphemism?"

I laughed. "No. I love it—really."

An incandescent smile took over her face like springtime. "Well, the hell with that, then—we're going full-body hug." She grabbed me into one, and I let her.

For a moment I closed my eyes and imagined that it was my mom, once again holding me to her in the warm, comforting embrace I'd missed so badly.

But Millie was tall—much taller than Mom, even a few inches taller than I was, and I could smell the light scent of gardenia lingering at her neck where my mother always smelled of Chanel No. 5.

I opened my eyes, my throat thick with loss.

Yet with Millie's strong embrace still holding me close, her body unexpectedly solid despite her advanced years, I thought that despite whatever had been lost in my mother's family years ago, maybe something else had finally been found.

# Fifteen

The wedding was more than the modest affair I'd pictured.

And Millie was more than simply a guest. No wonder the couple—who were also not the elderly pair I pictured on a second or third marriage, but a young bride and groom in their twenties or so—had told her she could bring an army: Millie had set the two of them up nearly two years ago.

And she was their officiant.

We'd arrived early at the paved parking lot of the Turquoise, the town's sole resort hotel Millie had told me about where the wedding was being held, so she could handle last-minute arrangements with the couple and their wedding planner. She directed me to the back of the waterfront hotel—a string of pastel single-story cottages with beckoningly wide beachfront decks fronting a charming two-story driftwood-colored building that seemed to have grown out of the environment. As she left for the bride's room, I walked through the foliage-filled lobby looking out on where the ceremony would be held, white chairs set in neat rows on a swath of grass overlooking a strip of sandy beach and the sparkling gulf beyond it. I meandered toward the outdoor tiki bar, trying to stay out of the way as the staff bustled around in tightly directed formation, readying everything for the reception.

A dark-haired man in a shirt embroidered with pale thread in a subtle Hawaiian pattern glanced up to where I loitered awkwardly, sending me a smile as brilliantly white as his uniform.

"Would you like a drink while you're waiting for things to get started?"

I waved a hand. "I don't want to disrupt your preparations."

"No disruption. What's your pleasure?"

"Oh, um . . ." I wanted something to settle my flutter of nerves and the feeling of being completely out of place. "I guess a glass of wine? White if you have it."

"Chardonnay, viognier, sauvignon, or pinot grigio?"

I sighed. "Again with the French. It seems to be a theme for me today. I don't know much about wine."

"Ah." He stopped what he was doing behind the bar bordering the poolside deck, where tables were set with white cloths and bold-colored tropical centerpieces for the reception, and put his elbows on the teak surface, leaning toward me. "That's my favorite kind of customer. You get to tell me what you like and I can find the perfect fit for you."

I laughed. "You sound like my aunt. Great-aunt, actually. She's a matchmaker—she's the one who introduced the couple getting married today."

"You're Millie's niece?" That wide smile took over his face again, and he pushed up straight and extended a hand. "Pleasure. I'm Bud—Millie set me up with my wife, Sharon."

I shook his hand, bemused. "Boy, everywhere we go around here she seems like some kind of celebrity."

"Millie knows everyone."

I smiled. "Six degrees of Millie Jenkins?"

He laughed, his Adam's apple bobbing in his tanned throat. "Something like that. She's always been really involved in the community, but yeah, once she started matchmaking I think she made it her mission to get to know every last resident of Cypress Key."

"That's . . . extraordinary."

"It is, right?"

The female voice came from behind me, and I turned to see a tall brunette woman wearing purple. A lot of purple. Her floor-length dress hugged every inch of her body like a giant encompassing grape—at least, where it actually touched skin: The top plunged low enough to reveal a broad and deep expanse of cleavage that left nothing else to the imagination either, filled only with a chunky silver-and-purple necklace that dipped into the shadows of the valley between her impressive . . . well, décolletage, I supposed, keeping with the French theme. Her hair glinted purple too, I could see as she stepped closer, and long amethyst earrings dangled from her ears.

"Don't let her get her mitts on you if you aren't into that kind of thing, though," she went on. "She keeps trying to matchmake me, but I like to pick out my own cut of beef at the meat market, if you get my drift."

I shook my head. "Sorry . . . what?"

The woman lifted a hand and thunked herself in the forehead with it so aggressively I winced. "Good Lord. Sorry. I'm Bridget. You're Grace. Millie told me. Nice to meet you."

Her hand shot out toward me, and I took it as her words continued pelting me like machine-gun fire: "And you want the chardonnay if you prefer full-bodied and oaky; the viognier if you like light, floral, and fruity but dry; sauvignon for citrus; and there's just no point messing with pinot at all."

Bud laughed. "Come on, Bridge, you're making me obsolete."

Bridget grinned and came to stand next to me at the bar as I ordered the chardonnay. "Bridget McGuire. Best friend of the bride. Relieved from my maidenly duties while Ysidra goes over the vows one last time with Millie." She glanced up at Bud. "And I'll have a—"

"Cab, I know," he said, pressing a red wine into her hand that he'd already poured as we—and by "we" I meant almost exclusively Bridget—talked.

"You're a bridesmaid?" I finally managed.

"Maid of honor. Heavy on the 'maid,' as Ysidra keeps telling me. Which reminds me . . ." She looked at Bud. "I need something to bring her back down from eleven. How about a shot of vodka?"

He lifted an eyebrow. "You sure?"

"Yeah. Nobody wants gin breath for their first marital kiss. Put it in a water glass, would you, so her judgy new mother-in-law won't think she's a lush?" She shifted the full force of her presence back to me as Bud poured. "Millie said you were out here. She's so excited you're visiting. I can't believe you never knew about her before. Don't you love her? She's the total tits."

"Well, I . . ." I took a gulp of my wine to give myself a chance to recover my bearings. "I don't really know her very well yet. But she seems . . . well, great, yes."

Bridget put a warm hand on my arm and squeezed. "You'll only like her more the more you know her. And me too—you'll be seeing more of me if you stick around, since Millie and I are pretty close."

Suddenly I caught hold of why her voice sounded so familiar. "You made the video with Millie—the one that went viral?"

Bridget spread her arms expansively and gave a wide, infectious smile. "That's me, baby. Woman of many talents. She owes all her success to me."

"Oh . . . that's nice."

"I'm just kidding—please, it's all her. Hey, we'll talk more, okay? I gotta get Ysidra a drink or she's going to have a total come-apart."

Something sharp jabbed my chest as I remembered my own wedding, the nerves that had made me shake so hard I worried I was pollinating the entire church with my quaking bouquet as I walked down the aisle toward Brian, where he waited with casual ease and a smile that steadied my racing heart. "Bridal jitters are pretty common," I murmured, staring into my glass.

Bridget laughed. "Uh, no—Ysidra's so excited she's practically bouncing off the wallpaper. If I don't tether her back down to earth at least a little, girl's gonna levitate down the aisle instead of walk. I gotta go. See you out there, Grace. Thanks, Bud."

*Excited.* I'd been almost giddy with excitement, unable to believe this man had finally chosen me, when I'd loved no one but him all my life. I wondered now if my nerves as I trembled my way down the aisle toward him were partly because, until we heard "man and wife" and the ring was slipped onto my finger, I'd never quite believed he was actually mine.

I guess, looking back, maybe he never really was.

"Hey, Grace!" Bridget's shout pulled me out of the funk I was spiraling into. Glancing back, I saw she'd gone only a few feet before she'd turned around, a glass in each hand. "Listen, I didn't mean to talk you out of doing Millie's yenta thing if that's your bag. She can totally pair you up." She tried to wave, sloshing wine and shaking her head at herself as she steadied the glass, shrugged, and strode off back to the bride.

Bud was grinning when I turned back to him. "That's Hurricane Bridget. Category five at all times. But she's a good egg."

"She seems it," I said, but my voice sounded thin.

It wasn't Bridget that had depressed me. It was just being here, amid so much celebration and love and happiness—the first time I'd been to a wedding since our divorce. I didn't want Millie to "totally pair me up." I didn't ever want to feel again the way I had when Brian walked into my house with his new baby mama, as lit up and glowing on the inside as Angelica was on the outside.

I ALWAYS CRIED at weddings. Whether I knew the couple or not, something about the boundless hope and happiness and expectation that radiated from every face brought tears to my eyes every time.

Seated on white folding chairs on the broad expanse of grass overlooking the gulf phosphorescing in the moonlight, about seventy-five guests watched the bridal party come down the aisle between the chairs and take their places. Bridget caught my eye as she stepped solemnly along behind the last bridesmaid, pulling an exaggerated widemouthed *can you believe this?* grin that spoiled the effect of her slow, deliberate steps.

Millie followed, resplendent in her full-length muumuu in watercolor shades of blue and green, chunky Swarovski crystals glinting at her neck, a three-ring binder in one hand.

The music swelled louder into the familiar strong chords of the "Bridal Chorus," and something pinched hard in my sternum as I stood with the crowd. Wearing a soft-white strappy dress that fluttered around her knees in the salt breeze, the petite dark-haired bride, Ysidra, made her way steadily toward where Millie and the rest of the party stood watching her.

But Ysidra had eyes only for her groom—Josh, Bud told me. Just as Bridget said, the bouquet of fronded greenery and bird-of-paradise was steady as iron in Ysidra's grasp, her smile unwavering, her step just a little too quick for a proper bridal march—as if she couldn't wait to get to her soon-to-be husband.

Millie's eyes were warm and shining on the bride, the binder now held open between her hands; Bridget practically danced from foot to foot with excitement as she beamed at her best friend; and Josh . . . Josh was looking at his bride with an expression that made my cheeks flush, as if I were intruding on something deeply intimate.

Brian hadn't looked at me that way as I walked down the aisle to him. I didn't remember him ever looking at me that way. There was always tenderness in his gaze . . . and so much love sometimes it stole my breath. But not this naked, joyous *intensity*, as if the center of his world resided within me.

My stomach lurched with a sudden realization: Brian was too traditional to let his child—I caught my breath: *his* child—be born out of wedlock. One day not far in the future, he would be standing where the breathless groom stood now, watching his pregnant girlfriend (fiancée?) walk toward him, probably looking at her with the same naked joy I saw on Josh's face—that I'd already seen on Brian's even when he'd glanced at Angelica in my living room.

I barely heard as Millie instructed everyone to sit with a patting gesture in the air. I didn't really register her words as she welcomed the guests and spoke about love. The vows were unfamiliar—not the traditional ones Brian and I had spoken—

but I couldn't have said what they were even moments after the still-smiling bride and groom softly repeated them after Millie. They must have been poignant, because I heard a smattering of sniffles throughout the audience and was grateful for the excuse for my own wet eyes and cheeks.

Something was bubbling up in my solar plexus, into my chest, threatening to push up and out my throat. I held my breath, hoping to stifle it, but that only made it feel as if my ribs would explode from the pressure. As Millie presented the couple for the first time as husband and wife, my heart started pounding as if I were in a burning building, my breath suddenly stuck in my throat.

The crowd burst into applause and music crashed into the still evening again—something loud and fast and bass-heavy that thudded through my chest—and while everyone's attention was fixed on the joyful exit of the wedding party, literally dancing back down the aisle, I used the opportunity to rush past the few people between me and the other side of the row, desperately needing to get some air into lungs that felt as if they were screaming for oxygen.

I raced back toward the tiki bar, where Bud nodded when he caught sight of me streaking past, misunderstanding my desperation: "Almost there—ladies' is on the right."

I pushed my way into the door he'd indicated and locked myself in a stall, leaning against the metal wall, heart punching at my rib cage and lungs burning for air. Tears were running from my eyes—not from sorrow now, but from my frantic struggles to breathe.

*Calm down. Get hold of yourself. It's all in your head.*

The words did nothing to ease the vise clamped around my chest, and suddenly I wondered if I was actually going to die.

I braced my hands on the other wall, the brushed steel cool against the flat of my palms, and pushed hard, the pressure seeming to ever so slightly ease the one in my sternum. Leaning all the way forward I pressed my wet, hot cheek to the cold surface. *Breathe. Breathe!*

Something gave way around my rib cage and air shot sudden and cool into my lungs. The relief of it brought the air back out on a sob.

I heard flushing, a click from the stall beside me. Despite still screaming for oxygen I held my breath again, mortified. When the water turned on I let myself sip a few breaths, and as soon as the door closed behind whoever had been in here with me, I sucked in deep lungfuls until my racing heart steadied and my eyes finally stopped streaming.

I tore a handful of tissue from the dispenser to dab at the wetness on my face, remembering Millie's painstaking makeup job. Letting myself out of the stall, I walked cautiously to the sinks and mirror.

I looked . . . fine. Maybe a few streaks through the soft bloom of color Millie had swirled onto my cheeks, but my eyes weren't the swollen red balls I'd anticipated—if anything they looked bright and alert with the residual shine from my tears. My lids still bore the shadowing and liner, my lashes as long and artificially sooty as Millie had made them earlier.

Good Lord. What the hell was in this stuff?

Reaching into the beaded clutch bag Millie had loaned me, I patted powder over the slight streaks on my face, evening out the color with the little sponge as the bathroom door cracked open and a flurry of chatter filtered in with a handful of women, all talking about the beautiful ceremony.

I washed my hands quickly, avoiding eye contact, and slipped out before the door shut behind the last woman; I wasn't up for social chitchat. But instead of heading back to the reception, I hooked left out of the restroom, hoping for a few more moments of privacy.

The wedding party was clumped together in the secluded grassy area behind the tiki bar, framed by curving palm trees whose fronds rustled in the breeze overhead as the photographer directed everyone into various groupings. Bridget caught my eye and lifted both palms in a wave, like jazz hands. I waved back as she nudged Millie, beside her, who looked a question at me. I shot her a reassuring thumbs-up, feeling silly, but her relieved smile was enough reward. I didn't want to spoil her enjoyment or the couple's blissful reverie with worry about me.

As the petite photographer summoned Millie and Bridget into the picture with the bride and groom and their attendants, I slipped away from the well-lit hotel grounds and toward the wooden boardwalk, down to the darkness of the beach and the gulf beyond.

The gentle sound of lapping waves hit my ears and a thick marine smell filled my sinuses. I leaned left and then right to pluck off my new sandals so I could feel the cool sand against my soles and walked all the way to where it dampened.

Standing in the purple night, staring out at the indigo ocean under the moonlight, I let a long, slow breath leak out of me.

"So I guess this is kind of our 'thing' now?"

The male voice nearly startled a scream out of me, and I whirled to my left. "Holy—" I bit down on the unaccustomed curse word that had almost flown out of my mouth and heard a chuckle.

"Sorry." A man sat directly on the sand about ten feet away, knees angled up, so still I hadn't noticed him in the darkness. "I couldn't decide whether it was better to startle you or keep quiet and risk looking like a creeper again. Not sure I chose right."

At his words I realized who he was: Jason Davis. Of course. Of *course* he'd be the one person out here catching me hiding from the crowd and trying to rein in my self-pity—again.

"What are you doing here?" I heard the edge in my tone too late to sand it down.

His mouth curved up in that ready grin I remembered from this morning. "Same thing you are, I'm guessing. Playing hooky."

"I'm not—" I stopped the reflexive denial, knowing it wasn't true. "What are *you* avoiding?" The question—and my tone—was rude, but that was too bad. I wasn't the one lurking on the beach.

I mean, not really.

"Are we avoiding things?" He was playing with the sand—scooping up a handful and then letting it hourglass back to the beach, one eyebrow cocked up like a mischievous satyr. He *looked* like a truant kid.

"Well, I can only speak for myself," I said stiffly.

"You could join me. I've got a *bunch* of sand."

It was a stupid, childish comment, but playing in the sand sounded weirdly simple and innocent and nice. "I'm not exactly dressed for making sandcastles."

"That's an amazing dress on you." He blurted it as if it had been hovering just behind his lips, and then immediately followed it up with an uncomfortable chuckle. "Sorry. I wasn't sure if it was okay to say that, but since you brought it up . . ."

Warmth flushed my cheeks. This made twice now that I'd been sharp with this man, and he'd returned only good-natured kindness. "Thank you," I said. I scuffed the sand with one toe, avoiding his gaze. "Listen . . . I think I might owe you an apology."

"Oh, yeah? For what?"

"I . . ." I looked out over the water. "I've been a little rude."

"Eh. Kind of my bad—I stuck my nose into a private moment. Both times. And in your defense, this morning you had no idea who I was."

Heat flamed in my face. "Yeah, well, I had a . . . a theory about that that turned out to be pretty spectacularly wrong."

"This I'd like to hear."

I shook my head. "No. It's too embarrassing."

"Now I *really* want to hear it." He wore a half grin, an up-curving inverted triangle bracketing one side of his mouth as he looked up at me, his fingers still sifting through the sand.

Suddenly I wanted to feel its grit against my palms too. I gingerly lowered myself to the sand, cool on my rear and thighs under the thin silk, stretching my legs out together in front of me to maintain some kind of decorum, and dug both hands in, palms down. It wasn't gritty at all, smooth and cool, almost like cold silk. "I thought Millie was a . . . prostitute."

"Wow." In the beat of silence I could almost hear him fighting not to laugh. "She must have *loved* that."

"She did, actually," I admitted.

"And you thought my dad was her . . . john?"

"No offense."

He held up a hand, grinning. "None taken."

I dug my fingers deeper into the sand. Underneath the loose, dry surface it was moist, colder, and sand clumped together around the shape of my hands as I pushed them through, digging trenches.

The chatter and the beat of the music filtering from the reception didn't drown out the night noises of the beach: the slapping splashes of slack tide, the rustle of palm trees like tongues of gentle flame, the breeze in my ears. Away from the lights of the hotel the sky wasn't black but a deep aubergine, lighter at the horizon.

"Good memories."

I started when Jason's voice broke the silence. I'd almost forgotten he was there. "What?"

"You asked what I was avoiding, and I was thinking about that. I think it was good memories."

"Of what?"

He shrugged. "Another wedding . . . My wife."

"You're married?" It came out as an accusation more than a question.

"Was, yeah. We've been divorced awhile, but saying 'ex-wife' feels weird to me. Not like I'm in denial, or that I want things back the way they were. It's just . . . it's weird to me, defining someone by what they're not anymore, instead of who they are. Plus it's in this narcissistic self-referential frame—like I can't even define this person outside of how they related to me at one point in the past but don't anymore. And it kind of implies they did something wrong, right? 'This *was* my bank teller—until I shit-canned her.' Oh, shit—excuse the cursing." He stopped. "I'm talking too much, aren't I?"

"*Did* she do something wrong?"

He looked surprised by my question. "Well, I mean, yeah. We both did, right? Considering, you know . . . divorce."

"That doesn't necessarily mean someone did something *wrong*," I bit out.

I felt him looking at me, but I kept my eyes straight out on the horizon.

"I didn't mean wrong like she screwed up. Or like I did. I guess all I mean is . . . it seems funny to define people based on how they relate to us, instead of who they are. '*My* mom. *My* boss. *My* ex-wife.'"

"Well, it would be even weirder to try to not use those identifiers. 'This is the woman I lived with most of my preadult life who brought me food and tended to my needs.'" His laugh startled me away from the picture of my mother in her last days that had started to form in my head, when the roles were turned and I was the one bringing her food and tending to her needs. The sound unwound some of the tightness in my jaw.

"'This is a person I knew when I used to daily enter the same workplace with her, and who oversaw all my business dealings.'" Jason had picked up a stiff pod-looking thing and was drawing shapes in the sand with it, not looking at me. "'I know this person because at one point we made some vows and signed some legal documents and cohabited with common goals.'"

This wasn't the kind of conversation you had with a stranger. "Until we didn't," I said tersely.

Jason looked up at me for a long moment, then nodded. "Yeah. Until we didn't." He wiped the indentations away with his hand as I watched, smoothing it like a Zamboni, and only the shushing of the low gulf waves filled the silence. "So you have one of those shit-canned exes too, huh?"

"He shit-canned himself." The word felt strange in my mouth . . . but satisfyingly harsh.

"Mine too."

I brushed back the hair that had blown into my face and

tucked it behind an ear to anchor it, watching his hands—wider and thicker than I'd have expected from his compact frame—busy themselves in the sand. After a moment I reached over to the space between us and scooped up a handful of my own. I opened my palm and sifted it with my thumb, watching as the sand dropped back to where it came from. I hadn't talked about Brian and our divorce to anyone except Brian, really. I didn't want to burden Mom when she had so many struggles of her own, and talking about our relationship to anyone else felt like a betrayal of our vows to each other . . . even as we were ending them.

But this man didn't know Brian. He didn't know me—or anything about me. With the spill of light from the party behind him he was just a limned shape beside me. That made it easier to face his steady, straightforward gaze in the shadowed night.

"Was that hard for you?" I asked. "That she was the one to end it?"

He looked out at the dimly phosphorescing surf. "I don't mean this to sound as bad as it's going to . . . but it was actually a relief."

"You didn't love her anymore."

"God, no. I loved her like crazy. That was why it was a relief."

"That doesn't make sense."

I felt the sand creak under us as much as I heard it as he shifted to face me. "You ever have braces?"

The subject change threw me. "I did."

"You remember when you'd go see your ortho and he'd tighten them up to move the teeth some more? That awful ache for days after?"

As he said it, the sensation rose up viscerally: the constant dull throb at my gums that made me want to scream, no matter how many aspirin I took or how much ice my mom put on it. "Yes," I said, reflexively clenching my jaw.

"I used to grab a towel and just bite down as hard as I could."

"Ow! God!" No matter how delicately I tried to hold my jaw, anything I'd done—eating, talking, even *moving* my mouth sometimes—it seemed like the pain took up my whole consciousness. I couldn't imagine trying to make it worse.

"Right? Stupid to make it hurt even more. Except . . ." He held up a finger, a professor bringing home his point. "After a few minutes of mind-numbing, head-exploding agony?" I shuddered, imagining it, and he shrugged. "It abated. Not all the way, but faster than just waiting it out."

I gave a skeptical laugh. "You mean when your ex—"

"'*My* ex.' The ex of *me!*" His smile and the fist thumping his chest like Tarzan took the edge off his teasing. "Anne," he added.

I liked that he humanized her even as I doubted the easy acceptance he seemed to have of their divorce. "When Anne finally ended it, it hurt worse, but at least you could get the pain over with and feel better faster.

"Oh, don't get me wrong. It felt pretty agonizing for a long time. A *long* time." He shook his head. "But things were headed that way well before she finally called it. At least then I knew where we stood and we could both admit that it wasn't working. It wasn't so easy on Anne either. We both meant that 'better or worse' thing when we said it."

To my dismay I felt my eyes heat. I had the emotional control of a two-year-old lately. "Everyone means it when they say it." Didn't they?

He nodded slowly, and this time I wished I could see his eyes. "Yeah. I guess that's why I'm out here. It was a little hard to hear it again. To see . . . well, all that hope."

It was a perfect summation of the way I'd felt earlier. "What does it even mean, then?"

I wasn't really asking the question of him, but he answered anyway. "If it isn't actually 'till death do us part'?"

I nodded, afraid that speaking would trigger the absurd wetness I felt gathering in my eyes.

He looked back out over the waves, and I watched his features in silhouette against the dark backdrop of the sky. "I guess it means we did our best. All of us."

He didn't say anything else, and I didn't have an answer. I turned to face the water with him, and we sat like that for a long time, listening to the surf and the muffled noises of the party we were both avoiding. After a while I felt calmer, my tight throat loosening. I crossed my arms on my tented legs and rested my chin on them, watching the sea.

We sat for another moment before I reluctantly unfolded. "I guess we ought to get back."

"Yeah." He nodded and pushed to his feet, then turned to offer me a hand. "This feels familiar," he said, his eyes crinkling at the corners.

I breathed out a laugh as I let him help me up. "Maybe this *is* our thing."

He didn't let go when I found my feet. We stood almost eye to eye—he was only a few inches taller than I was—my hand warm inside his.

He turned it into a slow handshake, the inverted triangles lifting the corners of his mouth. "It's nice to finally meet you properly, Grace. You look really pretty, by the way."

The compliment threw me. "Well, a lot better than this morning, anyway."

He shrugged. "You looked pretty this morning too. Just a different kind of pretty. They're both good." He let out his quick grin. "I talk too much, don't I?"

I smiled back. "Not as far as I'm concerned. Thank you. That's a nice thing to say. A nice thing to hear. I'm glad you happened to be out here," I blurted, my cheeks growing warm.

"Yeah. Me too."

He held on to my hand for a long moment and I let him, relishing the simple feeling of connection, until finally he let go and we started side by side back up the beach and toward the music and voices and lights.

"Who are you here for—bride or groom?" I asked as we walked.

"Oh, I'm not a guest, actually. I'm part of . . . well, I guess the planning committee."

I raised an eyebrow. "You've been shirking your duties?"

"My duties are done for now. I'm shirking the overly fastidious event coordinator. She takes her job really, really seriously."

"That sounds like an ideal quality for an event coordinator."

He threw his head back and guffawed. "Touché. I'm probably making her job a little more challenging. I guess it's good we're going back."

"I guess so." But as the sounds of the party grew louder, the lights brighter as we got closer, I wished we could have stayed in the quiet peace of the deserted beach.

When we reached the boardwalk he put a hand on my arm, stopping me. "Hey, Grace . . . it's not that I've lost all faith."

"In what?"

He gestured in front of us, where laughter and music carried to our ears in the clear night air. "That. Hope."

I let the sounds of joy wash over me for a moment; then I let out a long breath. "Nothing ventured, nothing gained?"

"Something like that. So what do you think? Should we give it another chance?" He extended one arm toward the board-walk, like a maître d' showing me to my table.

I shrugged. "Sure. Why not?" I said as we fell into step together again.

# *Sixteen*

Jason veered off as we came back up the boardwalk and into the hotel grounds, no doubt to resume his duties, and I felt an unexpected vacuum as he vanished into the main building. It was easier to walk back into the party when I wasn't doing it all alone.

But I quickly found Millie standing in a group of people near the pool. She turned if she'd been expecting me.

"There she is! I wondered where you'd gotten to."

"Just catching a quick breath. You were a wonderful officiant, Aunt Millie."

Her head fluttered back as if a bug had flown in her face, and I realized it was the first time I'd called her that. She put one hand over mine and squeezed. "Thanks, sweetheart. Wish I could take the credit, but I cribbed the whole thing from *Love Actually*, *Four Weddings and a Funeral*, and *Mamma Mia*."

"Seriously?"

She winked. "No. Except yes, a little. Was that Jason Davis I saw you talking to again?"

The question was asked nonchalantly, but I had a feeling she'd been holding on to it since I'd stepped up beside her.

"I went out to the beach for a breath of fresh air, and he was there too."

She looked at me, considering, as if mentally piecing together a puzzle. "Well, how about that . . ."

Millie the matchmaker. I shifted the topic. "Did you get all the pictures done?"

She let out a great sigh. "Sadly, yes. I do enjoy a photo shoot."

"I'm sure you looked beautiful."

"You know, I think I really did. Not that it's about me, of course."

"Of course," I said, fighting a smile.

Millie beamed. "Let's get you something to drink, my dear."

As if she knew it would be difficult girding myself to be social all night, she led me to the bar and exhorted Bud to keep my glass filled, then shepherded me from group to group to introduce me with an affection and pride I didn't feel I'd earned. But the bride and groom's joy was apparently contagious, and everyone we talked to bubbled over with warmth and welcome, as if I were part of the island, not just a temporary visitor. To my surprise I even knew some of the guests—Pilar from the salon was there, and I tried not to think about the fact that a few hours ago she'd been the one to create the unfamiliar *aware* feeling I had between my legs. And Helene from Bord de Mer, with a shorter dark-skinned man whose arm seemed stapled to her waist who introduced himself as Ayodele, her husband. Amid the conversation with her and a few others, I finally got the answer to the question I'd had from the moment she'd said her husband was fine thanks to Millie: When Ayodele had battled prostate cancer the year before, Millie spearheaded a GoFundMe campaign to help him and Helene pay for his medical expenses.

"All good on the back end now," he said with a thumbs-up when someone inquired as to his health. I was as impressed by my aunt's big heart as I was by her internet savvy.

When dinner was announced Millie went to sit with the wedding party, and a few of the people I'd been chatting with chose a nearby table, inviting me to join them. The meal was an old-fashioned shrimp boil with locally caught fat pink shrimp curled amid perfectly cooked red potatoes and corn on the cob. Waiters passed out bibs and Wet-Naps before upending the pots in the center of each butcher-paper-covered table. Guests in pressed pants and linen shirts and gauzy tropical dresses tucked the bibs into their collars and dug in with their hands, laughing as they tore off shells and bit into the corn, and I followed suit, my hands sticky with brine and butter.

At our wedding Brian and I had served a choice of chicken cordon bleu or filet mignon, plated and served by white-gloved waiters. Our guests—mostly Brian's extended family and our twentysomething friends—had wrangled with the array of forks and spoons at their places as course after course came out, looking uncomfortable and bewildered amid the sedate formal service.

"It's a wedding," Brian had argued when I'd floated the idea of a more casual buffet dinner. "It's traditional."

By contrast, everyone at my table—and the others, I saw, glancing around—wore big buttery grins, their chatter lively and their laughter loud. By the time the empty shells and plates were cleared away and we'd all taken turns washing our hands at the rinsing station set up for that reason, the music shifted from something unobtrusive and sedate to bouncy eighties tunes, and I realized I was actually enjoying myself. I looked around to see whether Jason too had been drawn into the mood—despite ourselves—but I couldn't find him among the staff.

My dinner companions excused themselves one by one to head toward the improvised dance floor on a deck overlooking the pool, the last to go the couple to my right, Ernest and Julio. "Seriously, like the wine?" I'd blurted out when they introduced themselves, my internal filter thinned a bit. "'Hoo' like an owl, not 'jew' like . . . well, a Jew," the shorter of the two men explained with a wink, as his husband elbowed him. "It's okay; I'm Jewish by marriage," Julio had added in a stage whisper, and I'd had to laugh at their clearly well-rehearsed shtick.

"Aren't you dancing, honey?" Ernest asked, leaning over as they walked past.

"Oh, I don't really dance," I said. "Not like this." I gestured over to the dance floor, where Bridget was leading a contingent of wedding guests in a rendition of the Morris Day and the Time dance as "The Bird" blared over the speakers. Half a dozen people swung their legs side to side like pendulums, laughing so hard they couldn't maintain the rhythm for more than a few oscillations before leaning over and gripping one another's shoulders in hilarity.

Ernest rolled his eyes. "No one dances quite like Bridget."

He winked, then darted off to catch up to Julio. Alone now, I leaned back in my chair, sipping my wine and once again scanning the party for Jason. Maybe he was working behind the scenes, or had already been relieved of his duties and left. Disappointment curled into my belly like a dog settling into its familiar bed, and I shifted my gaze to watch the dancers.

At our wedding, for our first dance Brian had surprised me with a meticulously choreographed routine he performed with his frat friends to Usher's "Yeah." Some of the guys were pretty good—Brian among them, his easy athletic grace always making him seem as if any physical activity were effortless. And it was adorable, all those big burly men stepping and spinning to me like some kind of command performance for the queen.

Brian and I did the obligatory slow dance after that—Maroon 5's "She Will Be Loved," which we'd picked together. But I wondered how long he'd practiced the other routine with his buddies, thought about what it would have been like if we'd planned one together, rehearsed it for weeks, giddy with our surprise for our guests. I probably wouldn't have had the courage . . . but it looked like so much fun.

On the dance floor other dancers had picked up on what Bridget and her group were doing, and before long a little flash mob assembled behind them, including Julio and Ernest, who were surprisingly adept. When the song ended the entire crowd burst into applause and high fives, and despite the ebullience of the wedding guests, my chest ached.

"It's a crime to see a beautiful woman sitting alone at a party." I heard Millie's voice just before I felt her drop a kiss to the top of my head.

"Oh . . . I don't mind," I said, embarrassed.

She lowered herself into the chair Ernest had vacated a few moments before, setting two bottles of water on the table between us. "Oh, honey. I didn't mean you were some sad wallflower. I know sometimes a woman just wants a moment to herself."

"You don't seem like one of those women."

Millie beamed as if I'd aced a test question. "That's true. I must say I'm a girl who's happiest in a crowd. My Ira was the same way."

"Ira was your husband, right?" I said, remembering his name from the video Millie showed me.

"Ira was the center of my world." Millie's smile was soft, but her eyes dipped at the corners. "Talk about a zest for life. He loved being surrounded by all the people we loved."

"You mean your children, grandchildren?" It hadn't occurred to me till this moment that there might be other relatives too.

"We love children, both of us. But no. We always knew we couldn't have any of our own."

I could have swallowed my tongue. Of all people I should have been more sensitive to such a question.

Millie didn't seem fazed. "But we both felt we had our family in the people we were lucky enough to gather around us here." She was looking out over the party fondly, like a mother hen watching over her chicks.

I wanted to ask how they'd handled their infertility with such easy acceptance—both of them. I wanted to ask how she had dealt with the crushing loneliness of losing the person she'd loved so dearly.

Most of all, I wanted to ask about her actual family—*my* family. But it wasn't the time or the place, and even if it had been, the sight of maid-of-honor Bridget striding purposefully our way as if she wore combat boots instead of purple-dyed satin heels meant our private moment was over.

"What in Cupid's sweet name are you doing drinking water?" she said to me before looking over at the bar and snapping her fingers in the air. "Bud, for God's sake, you're falling down on the job—get the girl a drink. All of us girls."

I laughed. "This girl's had enough, I think."

"Not for me either, dear—I'm the DD," Millie said.

Bridget shook her head as she plopped down in the chair on the other side of me. "I don't understand you people. Less is not more—*more* is more. We've got a party to keep going. We've got to overcome that weird ineffable sadness that comes over people at weddings."

It sounded like "neffable" with her words mashing into one another, but I knew what she meant. Apparently Jason and I weren't the only ones who felt that odd sorrow. I glanced around the room, but if he'd been working the party I hadn't caught sight of him all night.

"I never really understood that word," Millie mused. "What is 'effable'?"

Bridget shrugged. "I don't know. Someone else found their happy-ever-after and not me, so I feel pretty effed."

"Honey, how many times have I told you, if you'd—"

Bridget put her hands over her ears like a tantruming child and cut Millie off. "La-la-la-la. Not hearing it."

Millie gave a long-suffering shake of her head and looked at me. "Bridget insists on going it utterly alone, despite my many qualifications and my lengthy list of success stories."

"What can I say? I'm just an old-fashioned girl," she said.

My laugh slipped out before I could stop it at the picture she made slumped back in the chair, legs sprawled carelessly at loose angles and her plunging neckline barely keeping everything in check.

Bridget grinned back sloppily at me. "It's funny because it's true, right?"

Apparently Bud had heard her summons over the music and the chatter, because he appeared at my side with a tray of filled wineglasses. "You bellowed?" he said to Bridget.

"Thank you, handsome, but I'm driving," Millie said, waving him away as he moved to set one of the glasses in front of her.

"But she's not, right?" Bud asked, pointing at Bridget, who had clearly enjoyed more than a couple of drinks already.

She waggled her eyebrows and wiggled her fingers at him in a goofy wave. "No, sir. One for me and one for the lovely lady from the winter hinterlands."

I held up a hand. "Not me, thanks."

"Oh, come on," Bridget said, sitting up. "At least just hold it so I don't feel like a total alkie."

I obeyed as Bud retreated to the bar, and Millie pushed to her feet. "All right, ladies, I need to get back to the bride and groom—we still haven't signed the license. You'll be okay for a little bit longer, Gracie?"

"I am keeping her very good company, Miss Meddly Millie Matchmaker, and I will see to it that she has fun whether she wants to or not." Bridget's words blurred around the edges, and Millie arched an eyebrow at me as if to verify that I didn't mind being left with her.

I smiled a reassurance. "Take your time. We'll be fine."

She patted my shoulder. "All right, dear. I'll be back shortly. And you . . ." Millie sent Bridget a mock frown and gestured toward the bottled waters she'd brought over. "Drink at least one of those in its entirety." Bridget stuck out her tongue and Millie sighed. "Gracie, I'm counting on you to be my enforcer."

I laughed. "I'm on it." As soon as she walked away I leaned forward to pull the bottles closer and handed one to Bridget, wincing when a sudden sting reminded me of the afternoon's overly intimate wax session.

"Take off the shoes," Bridget advised. "That's a key element of party stamina." She twisted the top off the water and took a long swig, making a face.

"It's not that." I shifted in the chair, trying to get comfortable. "Millie took me for a full makeover today. Including some, um, personal grooming I'm not quite used to."

Understanding swept over her features. "First time stripping the taco?"

"What?"

"The lady portal. The bizniz. Sweeping the stairway to heaven." I stared. "Come on, you know—waxing Madame Bovary. First time you got the full monty?" She made a diamond of her hands around her groin area.

"Uh, yes. I . . . That's what I did. *Really* sorry about it now."

"Eh. It's overrated. A remnant of a patr'archal society where our value was based on our attractiveness to men. Screw that noise." She pointed an imperious finger at me. "You leave that bush gloriously unpruned if that's your thing, girl. Be proud."

Brian used to tease me about being too serious—"I think you may have been born without a funny bone, Grace"—but Bridget had a way of dragging the giggles out of me. "I can't believe I'm sitting here in public with someone I just met, talking about my . . ." I waved a hand vaguely in the air.

"Vagina! Say it. Pubis. Mons veneris. Labia majora."

I set my untouched wine on the table and covered my ears as she'd done a moment earlier. "Stop it."

Bridget reached over and pulled one of my hands away. "It's science. Don't be scared. Own the pooty."

I shook my head.

"Own it!"

"Fine," I managed, my face aching from my smile. I spread my arms to the sides. "I own my vagina! I'm proud of my genitals! Are you happy?"

"Boy, if I had a nickel for every time someone told me that . . ."

Heat seared my face without my even turning around, knowing who I'd see. *Now* he finally showed up.

"Hey, Jason," Bridget said. Of course. Apparently everyone knew everyone on this tiny little island.

"Hey, Bridge." Jason Davis was still standing just behind my eyeline—if I'd been able to raise my head, that is. Bridget had to have seen him walking up and didn't warn me. The way she collapsed across the table in a fit of giggles confirmed it.

"Okay, very funny," I said. "Ha, ha."

She sat up as Jason stepped into view. "I'm sorry," she said, pulling her face into dramatically serious lines. "You have to know I would never have done that if I were sober." She dissolved into laughter again.

"There's a shuttle if anyone wants a lift home, and we're offering pickups to bring folks back tomorrow for their cars if they want it," Jason said.

"Aw, you know me too well, buddy. Sign me up. Hey, I want you to meet someone. This is—"

"We've met," I said to the tabletop.

"A few times now. I got caught up with work, but I was hoping you might still be here."

I finally glanced up. Jason wore that smile of his as if we shared a secret.

My embarrassment ebbed like a tide just beginning to turn. "Jason Davis," I said. "Beachside duty shirker."

"Hey. That's poolside duty shirker to you. As you can see, things have evolved."

"Well, I'm glad there was a little intermission in there of actual work."

"A beautiful woman reminded me that I shouldn't leave someone else picking up all my ample slack."

I didn't want to like his compliment as much as I did. "I'm

willing to give you the benefit of the doubt and say I caught you in a weak moment. Sounds like you made it up to your boss."

From the corner of my eye I saw Bridget's head oscillating back and forth like a fan as she followed our banter. "Well . . . I can see no one needs my conversational felicity . . . facilitaty . . . dammit. My help." She shook her head as if to clear it and stood. "Clearly it's time for me to sleep it off. I'm gonna go get in line for that shuttle."

"Can I walk you over?" Jason asked.

She cocked her face in his general direction. "Mr. Davis, sir, you are a prince among frogs. I'm good, but thanks for the ride, pal." She punched his arm—hard enough that it had to hurt, but he didn't let it show.

"Anytime, Bridge. See you tomorrow."

"Have fun, kids," she called breezily over her shoulder as she headed toward the hotel. "Don't do anything I'd do . . ."

I kept my eyes on her as she wove her way unsteadily across the patio in case she stumbled into the pool. "I think she meant *wouldn't*."

"You have to know Bridget. I'm betting she meant it just the way she said it." He gestured toward the chair she'd just vacated. "Mind if I sit?"

"Won't your boss be mad?"

"She's the one handling the shuttle. Judging by Bridget trying to get into the equipment room over there"—he gestured to where she was wrestling with a clearly locked ventilated door, till a woman with a sleek bun and a severe suit approached and led her toward the hotel door instead—"it may take a while to herd everyone aboard."

"That's the event planner? I haven't even seen her tonight."

"Viviana's like a ninja with event management," he said.

"She prides herself on operating as invisibly as she can. She says if the guests see her, it's like discovering Oz behind the curtain. Ruins all the mystery and glamour of their special occasion."

"Wow. She does take her job seriously."

He grinned. "You have no idea."

"Don't you even feel guilty?"

"I do. Totally." He was shaking his head despite his words, and I laughed.

"Jason! There you are. I'm going to send the first shuttle off."

The woman we'd been talking about had appeared at the side of our table so suddenly I nearly jumped. Up close I could see she was younger than I'd guessed from her austere style, with features I'd have called delicate if they weren't held in such stiff lines. Jason widened his eyes at me and mouthed, *Ninja,* as she came into his sight line, and I smothered a smile.

"Okay, Viv. You're in charge," he said smoothly, making no move to get up, and I marveled at his cheekiness.

She crossed her arms over her chest. "I didn't know if we should wait for a few more people in this batch, but there's a bit of a . . . high-spirited guest shouting about a party bus and getting the show on the road."

Jason loosed his grin directly at me. "One guess who." He seemed completely unconcerned about his boss's very clear annoyance with him.

"Hi, I'm Grace," I said to the woman awkwardly, adding my now-customary conversational lubricant, "Millie's niece."

But the woman merely nodded. "Viviana Hargrave. Pleasure." She didn't extend her hand, so I followed suit, wondering whether I should excuse myself so Jason didn't get in further trouble.

"Do what you think's best, Viv. It's your party. You know I trust you completely."

At Jason's words the rigid lines of the woman's face relaxed slightly, and she turned back to him. "I do know that, Jason," she said. "But it's your hotel."

For a moment I thought I'd misheard her.

"Let's go on and get Bridget home, and whoever else is on board," he said.

She nodded. "Right."

"Does she need a personal escort?" he asked, all business now.

"I think she's okay, but liability-wise maybe?"

"Okay. See if Javier can get away for twenty minutes to ride along and see her inside—tell him I'll count it as overtime—and have Ricardo pick him up on the way back after the other drop-offs."

"Brilliant, thanks. It's done." She stepped off without another word or even a glance to me, her heels clacking purposefully on the flagstone pool deck.

I was still staring at the man in front of me, who'd morphed from a good-natured beach bum into an incisive businessman in front of my eyes.

"You *own* this place?"

"Well, yeah. Part—my dad helped me put up collateral."

"You didn't actually mention that earlier."

Jason grinned—"*My* hotel!"—and I couldn't help laughing. "Okay, now the guilt is good and setting in, you'll be happy to know—I guess I need to go help Viv out with the end-of-night stuff."

"No guilt. Who knew you were the boss?"

"Hey . . . how long are you here?"

"I think Millie may be ready to head home in a few more minutes, actually."

"No, I mean here on Cypress Key. I'd like to see you again."

"Oh." It had been more than a decade since I'd been asked on a date. If that's what this was. "I don't, uh . . . It's not that you're not . . . I just, you know." I nodded, and then realized that was sending the wrong message and shook my head. "I don't think so. I'm sorry."

He held up his hands, palms out. "No apology needed. That was a completely open-ended question." He slapped his hands down onto his thighs and pushed himself to his feet. "It was really nice meeting you, Great-niece Grace. Honestly. And I hope you have a great visit with your aunt."

That smile curled up the corners of his lips like the ridiculous tips of jester slippers, and he gave a quick silly little wave before turning to follow Viviana while I watched him go, suddenly wishing I had given him a different answer.

# Seventeen

illie's hands were solid on the wheel of the CruiseBeast as we pulled out of the hotel grounds twenty minutes later, but I could see the toll all the evening's activity had taken on her. Pouches I hadn't noticed under her eyes made her look tired, her customary bright lipstick had worn off, and for the time since I'd met her she looked her age.

"Did you have fun, Gracie?" she asked, her voice slightly hoarse.

"I did, actually." I heard the surprise in my tone, and Millie must have too, because she smiled.

"I was so glad you met Bridget . . . she's one of my favorite people. And you and Jason seemed to be enjoying your chat," she added. "*Chats.*"

"He's . . . nice," I said carefully.

My phone was in the beaded clutch Millie had loaned me— I hadn't touched it all night, but now to avoid her searching gaze I found myself unsnapping the clasp, pressing the screen light, glancing surreptitiously down at it.

I stared dumbly at the screen.

"Brian called." I didn't know I'd said it out loud till I heard my own voice. "Just a few minutes ago."

Millie shot a glance at me as I wrangled the phone all the way out of the small bag, the rubber edges of my OtterBox catching on the silk lining. "Brian?"

"My—" I caught myself. "We used to be married," I said.

"Oh."

She sounded surprised, but I didn't bother to elaborate as I hit the voice-mail icon and pressed the phone to my ear.

"Grace." Silence followed the single syllable of my name, and I pulled the phone away to glance at the screen, thinking that was the end of the message. It was still playing back, I saw, just as I heard him speak again. "I guess it's late and you're probably . . . well, I don't know what. Or where, actually." He laughed, the manufactured one he used when courting new clients. "But anyway . . . just . . . let me know you're okay, okay? It's weird not to know where you are, and I wanted . . . Well. I hope you're having fun. Or whatever. Can you just let me know you're okay?"

My heart was racing, my hands shaking as I dropped the phone to my lap, staring out my window at nothing, all the pleasure of the evening blown away like dandelion fuzz. The silence in the fancy electric car was total.

"I should probably tell you I could hear that," Millie said gently.

I bit down hard, clenching and unclenching my jaw. Jason was wrong—it didn't make anything feel less bad.

"It's a weird situation," I managed finally, still staring at the blackness outside the passenger window.

I didn't want to talk about it. Didn't want the eternally upbeat Millie trying to cajole me over to the bright side. I didn't even know what bright side there was at the moment. Why did he call? Why the hell did he think he had the right to know where I was?

What was it that he'd started to tell me he wanted?

I chewed on all of it like gristle, my hands clenched and my stomach bunched into a knot, praying Millie stayed silent.

Miraculously, she did. I stared down at the phone in my lap. *Brian*, the screen still read.

I wanted to beat the phone against the window until one or the other broke. Wanted to drop it to the floorboard and stomp it till the glass shattered. Instead I lifted it almost in slow motion and hit the off button that sent the name fading to black.

We made the rest of the drive home in silence.


I WASN'T GOING to call him or even text him. He had no right to know where I was—no right to worry about me at all. What if I had answered his call? Would we have had some stilted, superficial conversation while Angelica listened in? The way we would have to now for the rest of our lives?

But I also knew I wasn't going to sleep. Not for a long time. So when I heard clanging sounds from the kitchen that told me Millie was still awake too, I let myself back out of my room and slid onto one of the barstools at the island facing her as she poured milk into a saucepan on the stove.

"I needed something to help me sleep," she said without turning around. "Would you like some?"

"Yes. Thank you."

I watched as she broke two squares of baking chocolate into the saucepan, stirring to help them melt in the warming milk, then added a healthy pour of sugar. She retrieved several small jars from a cabinet and I knew before she did it that she would add three shakes of cinnamon, a dash of cayenne, a scrape of fresh nutmeg from a grater over the pan. By the time she poured two glasses of the thick hot chocolate and turned to set one in front of me, my vision had blurred.

Her expression grew alarmed. "What is it, my love?"

I wrapped both hands around the mug. "This is my mother's hot chocolate," I pushed out past an aching throat.

"Your . . ." One hand fluttered up to her mouth. "Oh."

"You taught her."

She nodded. "I picked it up traveling in Mexico. Made it for her when I came back and she loved it." And then her eyes were watery too, and that made my tears crest and fall.

I took a sip, closing my eyes, and for just a moment my mom was here, the comfort of her presence wrapping its warmth around me.

I opened them and it was Millie, but looking at me with the same soft, loving expression my mother always had.

"It's perfect," I said, and attempted a smile. "It never makes me sleepy, though."

She tore a paper towel off and handed me one, using another to dab her eyes. "The chocolate's just for something warm and sweet to wind down the evening," she said, reaching into a drawer and plopping a prescription bottle onto the counter. "Ambien is to help you sleep."

I gave a shaky laugh, picking up the bottle and rolling it in my fingertips. "I think I'm going to need that tonight."

"I can tell you're unsettled."

"I'm pissed off is what I am." It came out sharp and hard and surprised us both.

"Brian," she said simply, and I nodded.

And I told her. All of it, including my mortifying outburst and what I'd done to his car that led to running away and coming here, to hide with her.

"He's been family my whole life, and I care about him, even if we . . . we won't be together anymore," I finished, thinking of the way Jason talked about Anne. "I keep reminding myself of that . . . but I'm *furious*. All I want to do even now, right this minute, is bash his face in—and *hers*."

As soon as the terrible, violent words left my mouth I was horrified, and I slapped my hands up to cover my burning face. "That's appalling," I moaned behind my fingers, wishing I could disappear into the ground. "I can't believe I have these hateful thoughts." My heart was racing, my temples throbbing, and my throat had closed so tightly that for a moment I worried I was on the verge of another panic attack.

I felt Millie's hand on the small of my back, rubbing gentle circles. "You're angry," she said softly.

A hard, incredulous laugh shot out of me at the understatement. "You *think*? I know that. That's what's upsetting me so much—I can't get past it. It keeps geysering up—not just on Brian, but on everybody—Jason Davis . . . you. I can't make it go away!"

She didn't recoil at my shouted words, just stayed beside me making those soothing circles on my back. "It seems to me you have every reason to be angry, sweetheart," she said in a calm, conversational tone. "Why do you need to make it go away?"

I was breathing in little gasps now, like a hysterical child unable to get hold of her emotions. "Because I . . ." I gulped for air. "I've never felt like this before. I can't keep feeling like this. All I want to do is lash out. I want to . . . *hurt* something." I was repelled by my own words, and tears stung my eyes, but the poison kept fountaining out of me. "Everything changed and no one is who they pretend they are, and you can't count on anyone and I want to *destroy* things . . . destroy people. I can't dam it all up anymore."

Millie sat down slowly on the stool beside me, never taking her eyes off mine. "Anymore?" she said, so, so softly.

With that single word, the dam broke. Angry sobs tore out of my throat so harshly it hurt, my chest and my stomach and my shoulders heaving with the force of them. I clutched the edge of the counter as if it were the only thing holding me up, feeling as if it might snap beneath the white-knuckled force of my grip, fury and outrage and pain ripping their way through me, and I feared the devastation they might leave in their wake.

Years before my husband decided he didn't love me anymore and walked away from our family of two—because it wasn't enough for him when I couldn't offer him more—moving on and not looking back, my father did the exact same thing.

My mother did it—however inadvertently—when she shriveled with his betrayal into a husk of the woman she'd been . . . and then died and left me alone in the world.

Brian wasn't the thing that had started this bonfire burning me up from the inside—he was just the accelerant that turned long-banked angrily glowing embers into full-out flames.

Millie still sat beside me, her hands resting in her lap, silently watching me—not like the train wreck I was, but with a neutral, nonjudgmental expression. Acknowledging my pain without trying to alleviate it.

Something about that—about her bearing witness to my anguish, just letting it be—slowly eased the vise around my sternum, and as air rushed back into my lungs my sobs tapered off and finally stopped. I took a shaky deep breath, everything in me letting loose—before mortification tightened me back up again.

"I'm s—"

"Don't you dare apologize," Millie said, cutting me off. "You're angry. You let it out. So what? We feel things. We don't ever have to be sorry for that—screw it." I startled at the harsh words from that kindly face, but Millie didn't seem perturbed. "In fact, anytime you start to apologize for yourself for feeling anything true, that's what I want you to say instead: 'Screw it!'"

I couldn't help a weak laugh.

"Anger's not the enemy unless we chain it up—then it turns back on us."

I shook my head. "I'm just not an angry person."

Millie burst into laughter, shaking her head. "Oh, sweetheart, what nonsense. We're all angry people sometimes. Sometimes we're sad. Sometimes we're lit up with joy from the inside out. We don't get to pick and choose which emotions we want to feel—we just feel them. All we can do is decide what to do with them."

I looked at the woman in front of me—the picture of a sweet little old lady (well, not so little), with her twinkling eyes and sunny, untroubled expression. "You're angry?" I said, skepticism thick in my tone.

Millie's face abruptly tightened and her eyes grew as hard as her voice when she bit out, "I've been angry every day of my life for the last seventy-five years."

The transformation was so sudden, so total, I instinctively leaned away.

But the storm clouds cleared as fast as they'd gathered, and her expression relaxed. "I just learned how to channel it. I'm not saying you shouldn't blow it all up, Gracie—sometimes that's what you have to do. I'm just saying that if you light the grenade, make sure you let go of it."

"That's what you did, then? Blew it all up with our family? That's why I never knew about you?" I said with a flare of bitterness from a well that clearly wasn't yet empty.

Millie didn't answer. She looked down at her half-drunk chocolate—undoubtedly lukewarm now—and sighed, a long exhale of resignation.

"I know you want to know the truth, Grace. You deserve it. And I promise to tell it to you. All of it. But it's a long story and it's been a long night. Are you willing to wait until the morning?"

The muscles in her face seemed to have collapsed, making her look suddenly tired and every second of her age, and remorse bit at me even as I agreed.

I wanted to know what had happened to estrange her from our family, yes. Desperately.

And yet . . . part of me now feared hearing it. In the brief amount of time since I'd known her, I realized I'd started to care about Millie. A lot. She was the only family I had now. What if whatever she had to say was terrible enough that it took that away from me too?

But I was the one who'd pushed for the full story. If she was ready to tell it to me, I couldn't backpedal now into blissful ignorance.

For better or worse—and I was starting to fear the worst—tomorrow I was going to hear secrets about my family that had been kept longer than I'd been alive and might tear away whatever illusions I still had left.

# Eighteen

My troubled dreams were stronger even than the Ambien, which I'd finally broken and swallowed half of at two a.m. when sleep still wouldn't come, and I woke up when the sun knifed through the crack at the edge of the curtains, unable to remember the images that had played through my head like an action movie all night. My eyes felt puffy and crusted and my dry mouth tasted like I'd licked a dirty sock.

Millie looked not much better when I found her waiting for me ten minutes later, a cup of coffee in front of her on the dining table along the wall of windows. Absent the usual impeccable makeup on her face, her long silver hair drawn severely back in the kind of workmanlike ponytail that was my default style, shadows of exhaustion darkened her eyes, and the lines alongside her normally smiling mouth were carved deep. She wore a plain track suit, colorless white, the jacket zipped up like a suit of armor. I might not have immediately recognized this subdued, solemn version of her if I'd run across her anywhere but her own home.

I'd never understood the phrase "heart in my mouth" before

that moment, but as I walked toward the kitchen it felt as though that organ had ceased its beating in my chest and I held it behind my tense jaw, along with my breath.

"Good morning," she said, pushing out a tired smile I tried to return as I poured a cup of coffee of my own.

"Good morning. Warm-up?" I offered, holding up the pot.

She shook her head. "No, thank you. I didn't bother with breakfast, but I put out cereal if you're hungry."

I saw the array of boxes plunked haphazardly on the counter—minus bowls, sugar, spoons, napkins, the full setup I'd have expected from Martha Stewart Millie—and the omission sent a fresh shaft of unease through me.

"Not right now, thank you," I said. We were both being so carefully polite.

I moved toward the chair at her right, where she sat at the head of the table, and noticed that beside her untouched coffee cup lay the framed picture I'd found the previous day—the sole photo I'd seen here of my mom, of anyone in our family—alongside an old-fashioned metal lockbox.

"I never said goodbye to your mother," Millie began as I started to sit, and I dropped the rest of the way to the chair, coffee sloshing onto the table.

A tight flick of her lips. "Sorry, dear. I'm a rip-off-the-bandage kind of person." I nodded wordlessly as she slid over the napkin under her own cup and I wiped the spill.

"I wanted to," she went on as though the interruption hadn't happened. "But I wasn't permitted. By your grandfather. Which was Walter's right," she added when she saw my reaction. "Tricia . . ." She glanced down at her mug and gave a sad smile. "Patricia was his daughter. To raise as he and my sister—Shirley, your grandmother—saw fit. Your mom was thirteen years old. Still a child, but I could already see the woman she would grow into—willful and strong-minded and audacious."

My mother had many wonderful traits—she was loving and soft, reliable and kind and warm—but I couldn't reconcile Millie's description with the woman who'd raised me. In the years before my father left had she been the firebrand Millie described? I didn't think so. Whatever had changed in her, if Millie was right about her as a child, had happened long before I'd come along. I slid the photo toward me, peering into the sassy little girl's face as if I could see what had happened to alter her so fundamentally.

"I was twenty-four years old, and I'd just tried to kill myself."

Her bald words shot past my distraction, and I sucked in a breath, looking up sharply.

"I didn't succeed," she said, in a weak attempt at humor. "In case you were worried. Actually, looking back I'm not sure how much I wanted to. I swallowed a fistful of aspirin. Made my ears ring like sleigh bells for a couple of days, and I felt nauseated and woozy longer than that—my family never even realized. I think I knew, even then, that I didn't really want to die at all. I most savagely wanted to live."

I swallowed so loudly I heard it in my own ears and suspected Millie could too, but I couldn't speak—wouldn't have known what to say if I could.

"I'd been traveling off and on for a few years at that point, earning money to get by wherever I landed by doing all sorts of odd jobs. My family . . . *our* family," she corrected herself, "had long since withdrawn from me in any way that mattered—holidays, family gatherings, even the rare conversations we might have had were short and superficial and painfully one-sided—and it was easier to be away. I'd always had the travel bug anyway."

*Me too*, I wanted to say.

"But when my mother grew ill and went into the hospital, I came home. I needed to see my mom." Millie tried to give a quick small smile, but her lips trembled and her eyes had turned glassy. She put a fist to her mouth and let out a sharp exhale behind it, as if trying to gather her composure, blinking to clear the shine from her eyes. "My father—your great-grandfather Martin—did not let me into her room," she said in a flat voice. "She died that night. The last time I saw her had been two years before that."

The horror of that washed over me, and my eyes heated and stung. "That's why you're so angry. That's why you have no pictures of our family anymore except for this one." I picked up the photo of my mom and my grandfather. "You wanted to shut them out of your life the way they'd done to you, to leave your past behind so thoroughly you didn't even keep any pictures of yourself." I could relate to that too—I'd come here with a suitcase and an attitude and left everything else behind, and right now I felt I could happily never again see any reminders of anything that had happened to me before this trip.

Why had our family treated Millie the way they had? She hadn't offered any explanation for that yet, but frankly it didn't matter to me. Family was family—people weren't disposable. You couldn't just cut them out of your life like a tumor.

"One," Millie said, and it took me a moment to catch up with her answer to my statement. She was looking at me with an intense stare that felt unnerving, as if I were supposed to understand something that was completely opaque to me. "I kept one picture of myself from my past."

"Which one?" I asked, as if that somehow mattered.

"You're holding it."

It took a moment for me to make sense of it. To understand what she was saying. And then, as if dragged there by a magnet, my eyes fell to the tall young man in the photograph who was clearly so enchanted with the little girl who was my mother, and I knew.

"This is you," I said quietly.

"*This* is me," Millie said immediately, arms spread. "But yes. I am in that picture with your mother."

I looked down at the framed photo in my hands with new eyes. I could see it now—the downward slope at the outside edges of the eyes, the shape of the nose above the hand shielding what was clearly a widemouthed laugh, the angle at which the man held his head. But that was the extent of the resemblance. His expression spoke of someone else—not the confident stance with a tipped-up chin that I was used to from the woman I knew, as if she were daring the world to bring it on, but a drawn-in protective posture, as if shielding himself from anticipated blows. This person seemed to be missing something, a muted black-and-white version of Millie due to more than just film stock.

I looked back up at the live full-color version—who was all Millie even without her normal sartorial splendor. She faced me directly, shoulders back and expression neutral, but her eyes sharp and focused. Watching me.

"This is why they cut you off," I said bluntly.

"We cut each other off, if I'm honest. I didn't have to leave. I didn't have to stay away—especially after my father died. But that wasn't until quite some years later. In that time I'd been living my life this way—as who I am—and my father had long since made it clear that I was not welcome in his home . . . or with the family . . . as anything but what he needed me to be. Milton Bean. His only son."

Milton. Millie.

"But Grammy . . . your sister. She was an adult. She could make her own choices. And my mom . . . she was grown by then too," I protested.

Millie rolled her lips inward, biting down on them. "Yes. Shirley was in a . . . difficult position. She had known about me for a long time by then—long before my father found out. In fact, she let me wear her clothes and her makeup when we knew we had the house to ourselves; it was the only time in my child-hood that I got to be the person I knew I was, and those times kept me sane. The way I was never seemed to matter to her—and I loved her for that.

"But my sister made a choice. When I refused my father's demand that I come back only in that *costume*," she said with a tip of her head toward the frame in my hands, "my father told her—told us both—that as far as he was concerned I was not part of his family. That I never had been. I was worse than dead to him—I had never existed at all. Shirley . . . didn't find herself able to defy him." Her throat worked and she tipped her head down, resting it against propped fingers, behind which I could see her gathering herself. "Oh, my," she said after a moment in a strangled voice, looking back up. "That part never gets any easier. Even after all these years."

Anger—becoming familiar to me now—swept through me like a brushfire.

I'd never known my great-grandfather Martin—Millie's fa-ther. But his was the legacy that all his descendants had been carrying on in our family law firm ever since. A portrait of him hung in the lobby of our office still, beside Brian's great-grandfather. Martin Bean was a man who looked as if humor were beneath him, a waste of valuable time, and when I was a little girl I used to imagine his stern face on the villains of the terrifying Grimm's fairy tales my mother read me.

I could easily imagine that forbidding-looking man rejecting his own child—his only son, I realized, the reason that the Bean family name carried on now only in the middle name of Martin's otherwise female descendants. But Millie's sister, Shirley—my grandmother? My warmhearted grandfather who always made sure to carry treats for me in his pockets?

My *mom*?

I reached across the table and took her hand, entwining my fingers with hers and gripping tight, but I couldn't manage words. What could I say?

At my touch something seemed to give in Millie, her rigid posture collapsing, and she gripped back tightly as fat tears spilled over her lower lids.

"Oh! My stars. It's been a lot of years since I've told this story. Since I've . . . been worried about telling the truth."

"Screw it," I bit out. "Remember? You're the one who told me not to apologize for myself."

"Oh, I'm not apologizing," she said forcefully. "Not one bit. Those days are long gone." But her resolute gaze softened as she looked at me and went on. "But finding you means . . . rather a lot to me, Grace. It turns out that I'm still afraid of being rejected by my family after all."

As she spoke I wondered why I'd felt it was so important to find out why my family had erased her existence. Why it had mattered to me, as if I'd been reserving judgment on her contingent on whatever had happened more than fifty years ago—

rather than on the woman I had come to know now, since I'd been here.

How could people who claimed to love her just turn that off simply because of her being who she was—someone they decided wasn't acceptable? Grammy. The soft, sweet woman who offered me nothing but warmth and love and acceptance all my life . . . she had turned her back on this woman—her sister—because their father had said she must. How could Millie bear living with that?

How could I? Everything I ever thought I knew about the people I loved had been an elaborate illusion.

"That's not going to happen," I said.

She nodded but didn't seem able to reply. "Good," she finally said in a strangled voice. "I'm . . . very glad."

A laugh drained out of me on a single breath, catching in my throat, at the normally hyperbolic Millie's sedate reply. "Me too. You never saw anyone in the family again?" I said. "Your sister—Grammy . . . not even Mom?"

Millie took a long inhale, her shoulders lifting, and blew it out. "Shirley and I had stayed in touch for a while—a good while, actually, through letters where she kept me informed about her family; the firm, which her husband, Walter, your grandfather, had become the family heir apparent to; the happenings in our hometown—you know, riveting things like how the high school football team's season was going, or who was dating whom, or how Imogen Schmidt had stolen the bake sale win right out from under Rebecca Faraday with a recipe that rumor said she'd cribbed out of *Good Housekeeping*."

"Oh, Sugarberry," I said with a roll of my eyes, but I loved the idea of my aunt having once walked the same streets I'd grown up on, even if I'd never known it before now.

Millie smiled. "Yes . . . good old Sugarberry. We kept it superficial—I told her about my travels, what I was doing for work. As long as we avoided any sensitive topics our letters were newsy and fine. But I knew better than to talk about anything deeper than that. To talk about anything personal, what I was experiencing and learning about myself. How my world was opening up the more I embraced who I really was. By the time my father died I was . . . not that person anymore," she said, pointing to the young man in the photo. "Not in any sense. And . . ." She let out another long exhale, looking out the window as if whatever words she was looking for might roll in with the gulf waves. "I was afraid, I have to confess. By that point I hadn't seen my sister in so long. And never fully as me—as Millie. I couldn't face . . . well, how she might react if I were to go back for my father's funeral. What she might say. Or what she might *not* say. To see her again and have her look at me like a stranger or . . . worse. To have her struggle to figure out how to talk to me . . . I couldn't bear the idea."

My throat ached. Not to be known by the people you loved. To be afraid to show them who you were.

"How did she act?" I asked, afraid of the answer.

Millie looked down at the table, then past me, out at the water. Finally she returned her gaze to mine with a tired smile. "I didn't go," she said sadly. "Shirley thought . . . it would be best."

I heard all that she did not say in the succinct answer, and I reached to touch her arm.

"What about my mom?" I asked, not realizing until the words were out how desperately I needed to hear that she had not turned her back on this woman she'd once loved.

Millie sat up, stiffening her shoulders as if preparing to support a great weight. "Ah, your mom." She smiled—mouth closed, sad at the edges. "We wrote each other after I left . . . for a time. I want you to know she gave me hope for a long while when I had little. She was the brightest ray of light from my past. I never forgot that." She reached to the metal box that sat on the table to her right and slid it over toward me. "These are her letters."

My breath caught as I touched the cool, sharp edges of the box. Inside it was likely I'd find the rest of the answers I'd wanted—the *why* of my family's revisionist history. That I'd discover a side of my mom that I'd never known as her beloved only child. Did I want to know?

Millie misinterpreted my hesitation, my apprehension. "I'm sorry I didn't show them to you before." She sighed. "As I said . . . I was afraid. I'm sorry for that. I thought I'd left those fears behind."

I was too numb to remind her again of her own words— never to apologize for what she felt. "I'm not upset," I told her instead, forcing the words out past my tight throat. "I'm . . ." What was I? The roiling tangle of disillusionment and resentment and hurt and bewilderment inside me was such a whirlpool I couldn't separate out any distinct emotion.

And rage. At the vortex of it all, that rising tide of animosity and bitterness that threatened to swamp me.

Millie's expression was placid and calm, though—an eye in my hurricane. After the story she'd told me, how could she even look at me without seeing the generations of our family who had turned their backs on her? I gripped the edges of the box so tightly I felt them cut into the tender flesh of my palms.

"How do you do that?" My voice was thick with anger. "Not hate them? Hate all of us—me? How can you sit here with me and offer me your trust and your kindness and your honesty after all you've ever known from our family is complete rejection? How can you still be so open with anyone—with everyone?" My face was wet, but my voice was steady and hard. "How do you go on in spite of all that unfairness—of someone not loving you anymore when you didn't do anything to lose their love?" I spat out the words.

Millie's eyes on me were soft and almost pitying. No, not pity . . . compassion. "Part of it was my own fault. Yes, they made a choice—but I made one too. I could have kept trying. I could have loved them anyway—the same way I wanted them to do for me. But I didn't. I couldn't for a long time. But finally I realized that I was creating my own reality. I was choosing misery and self-destruction.

"By the time I realized I didn't want to live that way anymore, it was too late—my sister was gone and my niece . . . your mother . . . Well. You can see for yourself, if you'd like." She raised one mottled, veined hand toward the box I still held.

I looked down at it as if it were a bomb and took in a deep, hitching breath, then another.

"They're for you," Millie said as I hesitated. "I don't need them anymore."

I TOOK THE box into my room. Sitting on the bed, the metal cold in my lap, I faced out toward the window and looked blindly out of it, my mind furiously buzzing.

One morning not long before my father walked out he stayed home sick from work, so after my mother left for the office it was just the two of us together in the house, never a fully comfortable experience for either of us. Puberty had begun to ramp up its impact on my body in earnest that year, plumping my flat chest into tiny buds I was ridiculously proud of and insisted on encasing in far more bra than they warranted, bringing with it hair in startling places, my period, and a new awareness of my appearance and body.

My father walked past the bathroom as I got ready for school, stopping when he caught sight of me in the open doorway. Never a hands-on parent in the best of circumstances, Dad had seemed to grow even more awkward around me since I began to change from the little girl who more often than not served as a vaguely annoying distraction from his work or his ball game that he nonetheless felt a sort of distant affection for, to a new being he didn't understand and didn't want to. He began avoiding looking at me directly, or squeezing my shoulder if I hugged him as if semi-returning the embrace, but then using the grip to move me away from him. But now he leaned on the doorjamb, watching me glaze Hard Candy lip gloss over my mouth.

"What are you doing?" he asked—and I remembered the unexpected rush of warmth at his unusual interest, his focus on me.

"Getting ready," I said, and then, feeling glamorous and fascinating and wondrously adult, I looked in the mirror at my own reflection and said something I must have seen in some R-rated movie once, with an arch, worldly tone, a languid indication of the impressive total package that was me: "You don't think *this* just happens, do you?"

He laughed, the sound setting my nerves on end. "Why don't you just be honest about who you are?"

I turned to him, my face hot, instantly an awkward adolescent again. "What do you mean? I am honest."

"Look at yourself, Grace." He nodded to the mirror and I did as he said from long habit. "How long have you been standing here with all *that*?" He indicated the small array of cosmetics on the counter and shrugged indifferently, as if the conversation had already grown dull to him. "Ask yourself why it takes you almost an hour to look so 'honest.'"

As he turned and went back downstairs, I stared at myself for a long moment and then slowly reached for a washcloth. A few weeks later he was gone.

For a long time there was a childish, irrational part of me that connected the two—my stretching my wings into womanhood and my father's sudden meanness, his abandonment. I'd changed and he'd left.

If the pain of that had shattered me—the loss of even his limited affection over something I could no more have controlled than I could stop time—I couldn't begin to imagine how much worse it must have been for Millie.

I noticed my phone on the nightstand where I'd left it, still plugged into the charger. With Millie's revelations I'd actually forgotten about Brian's message the previous night.

I set the box on the plush comforter beside me and reached for the phone.

3 messages.

Brian.

Not sure if u got my msg. U ok?
Im not mad abt the car. Can u pls just check in?
Grace? Just let me know yr ok?

The messages were spaced less than thirty minutes apart, the last one stamped after five a.m. my time. That was four in Sugarberry. Brian was an early riser—he rigidly enforced a ten p.m. bedtime on himself so he could get his seven hours of sleep each night before getting up for his morning run—but not that early.

I pictured him lying awake, worrying. Was Angelica sleeping by his side? Or was Brian up, restless, unwilling—unable—to slide into bed with one woman while he was texting another?

I'd been torturing myself over my outburst to him the other night, my actions in his driveway, and yet I didn't feel the flood of relief I'd have expected at the fact that he clearly wasn't angry at me, or repelled. Nor did I feel the guilt for making him worry and lose sleep that normally would have made me quick to respond.

What I felt was fury, my unpleasant new friend.

I jabbed out a reply:

**Don't worry about me. I'm on vacation.**

I pressed send and put the phone down, snatching up the box again and plunking it back on my lap.

Then, after a moment, I moved it to the nightstand next to the phone, stood up, and went out to find Millie.

CYPRESS KEY HAD started life like the rest of Florida—as a shallowly submerged spit of land on the supercontinent on which coral, shells, and the cast-off bodies of marine creatures began to build and form a limestone shelf. Over the millennia storms had ripped through, perforating the building landmass and iso-

lating atolls too small and insubstantial to entice early popula-
tions to inhabit them, as they emerged and submerged with the
years.

*I'm on vacation*, I'd texted Brian, and it was past time I acted
like it. I told Millie I wanted to get out and see some of the area,
and she excitedly suggested taking out the kayak tethered on-
shore behind her house so I could take in the "gestalt," as she
put it.

So now we paddled her red plastic two-man kayak in crazy
zigzags and circles on the gentle gulf just off the coast of the
little island till I finally got the hang of rowing in tandem.

She'd insisted on kitting me out with a wide-brimmed floppy
hat, a pair of oversize hot-pink-framed sunglasses, and a tube of
sunscreen, and despite feeling like a little kid playing dress-up,
I obediently lotioned and hatted up and slid the silly-looking
glasses on. I was grateful for it now; the sun baked my back and
arms and thighs and glared into my eyes even under the hat as
it sparked off the water.

I pulled my oar in a steady rhythm with hers once I got the
hang of it, relishing the bunch and stretch of underused muscles, pliable from the warmth of the sun on my skin. In the
motorless little craft the only sounds were the regular splashes
of our paddling and the gentle waves against our hull; the breath
in my ears, heavy and deep with exertion; the peevish cries of
the seabirds that arced overhead and occasionally arrowed into
the water around us, on the hunt; the distant buzz of a speed-
boat far out at the horizon.

Most of the shoreline of the little key was made up of stands
of branchy bushes with thick interwoven roots—mangroves,
Millie said. The tangled mess was the reason for the creation of
the new and more permanent island: the roots trapped the sedi-

ment of the river and kept the gulf from eroding the slowly building land away.

Finally, after paddling for so long that my out-of-shape arms started to feel like overcooked noodles, we rounded a bend and came upon a short stretch of sandy white beach. Millie directed me to aim us straight for shore, and once we slid up onto the sand I eased my stiff legs over the side and held us steady while she climbed out. It wasn't yet noon, and the middle of February, but the sun and the exertion already had me sweating. The cool water felt good on my calves and ankles as we splashed to shore, pulling the kayak farther up behind us.

"We could use a break," she said, producing two towels from a compartment in the top of the kayak. "And refreshments." A collapsible cooler followed. "The main beach is on the north side of the island," she said as I helped her carry everything to a dry patch of sand up the shore. "This one's really just for the locals, since you can only get to it this way. I was hoping we'd have it to ourselves." She handed me one towel and spread the other on the sand, then retrieved two waters from the cooler, ice-cold and dripping. She handed one to me and took a long pull from hers, finishing nearly half the bottle. She re-capped it and sat, her loose-skinned but muscular legs crossed so tightly the tops of her feet rested on her thighs.

"Ahhhhhh." The sound escaped from her on a long exhale, her eyes closing.

I opened my water and took a few sips, watching her, but she didn't open her eyes or move, just sat upright with flawless posture, utterly still. Finally I sank uncertainly to the other towel, propped upright by my outstretched legs and my arms tentpoled behind me, looking out over the water. After a while I lay back, the sun like a blanket on the bare white skin of my legs and chest and arms in my one-piece bathing suit, but sat up again a few minutes later, restless.

"What are we doing?" I said finally.

"Being present," Millie said without opening her eyes.

I was glad she couldn't see my reaction.

"Breathe, Gracie," she said after a few more beats of silence.

"I am breathing."

"No, really *breathe*."

She was watching me now, so I had no choice. I pushed up onto my tailbone and frogged my legs up the way Millie had, but all I could manage was a loose crisscross-applesauce. Apparently I was less flexible than the bendy eighty-one-year-old woman beside me.

I looked over at her, feeling silly, but Millie looked so pleased that I was glad I was playing along. "Now what?"

"Breathe."

Millie shut her eyes again, hands held palms-up on her knees, and drank in a deep breath, then let it out. She did it again. And again.

I obediently sucked in a gulp of air and let it huff out, repeating the action a few times until I felt myself get light-headed and had to lean forward till the dizziness passed.

Millie watched through one slitted eye, a grin at the corner of her lips. "You're not blowing up a balloon, sugar. No need to work so hard—just let your body do its thing. But pay attention. What does the air feel like in your lungs? Smell like? Taste like in your mouth?" She took in another deep breath, let it out. "Just bring your attention to this thing you do every single second without even noticing."

I was all for appreciating a moment, but she looked positively rapturous about a basic autonomic response. "Woo-woo," my dad would have called her—at least, the practical dad I knew before he ran off with a woman who cleansed her chakras and believed in horoscopes.

I pulled off the Barbie sunglasses and set them on the towel, closed my eyes, and copied her actions, taking in a long breath, letting it out slowly. In. Out.

I really tried to concentrate, but my thoughts were scattered by the calls of seagulls soaring overhead, Dopplering left to right, right to left with their flight. The shushing sound of the waves rushing up onto the sand, the slight foamy crackle when they receded. The whisper of palm fronds dancing behind us, like the flames of a campfire.

I tried again to do what Millie had instructed and pay attention to my breath: its temperature in my mouth—as if I could feel the sun-heated molecules of it on my tongue, warming my lungs, spreading into my chest. The smell of it—or the taste?— a little bit sweet, like candied orange slices. It was moist and slightly salty, as if the air and the ocean and the pH of my body were all aligned.

But I lost focus again, distracted by the sun washing the backs of my eyes red, enjoying its cape of comforting warmth on my shoulders, my shins, my upturned wrists.

"How do you feel?" Soft as it was, Millie's voice seemed to thrum through my whole body, and I slowly opened eyes that felt cakey, the sparkle of the waves dazzling my vision.

I stretched my shoulders and aching back, tipped the stiffness from my neck. "I guess I'm not very good at this. I couldn't tune anything out for more than a second or two." I waved a hand around me to indicate our surroundings.

Millie was smiling at me. "We've been sitting for about twenty minutes."

I stared at her. "Are you kidding?" I'd have sworn it was less than five.

"You asked how I handle being angry," she said, uncoiling herself from her pretzel position and stretching her legs out long in front of her. "This is one way. Being near the sea. Meditating."

I scoffed, trying too late to mask it with a laugh. "I'm not really the type who meditates."

"You just did. Being present—that's all it is. Not tangled up in your thoughts. Were you worrying about anything while you were sitting there?"

No, I realized. I wasn't—not Brian, not my dysfunctional family dynamics, not Millie's astonishing story and all the questions I still had about her. I'd just been hearing and feeling and smelling what was around me.

"Well, it's easy here," I said, drinking in the beauty of the place—the pure deep blue of the sky, the darker teal of the water capped with white, the golden sand, and the saturated greens of spiky palmettos to either side. "But I'm pretty landlocked in Missouri." Just the thought of going back to that drab gray winter deflated me.

"It doesn't matter where you are. Just be there as fully as you can. If you have somewhere at home that brings you peace and joy, go there. But if not, close your eyes wherever you are and go there in your mind. Come *here* in your mind, if that's what works for you." Millie spread her arms out, palms up, as if serving me up this tropical paradise on a platter. "It's always here for you." She faced me. "And so am I, Gracie. I promise I won't let go of our family again."

At her words it felt as if my lungs could suddenly hold more air. I nodded, not trusting my voice. I'd needed the comfort and security of a promise like that more than I'd realized.

"But the anger's still there," I said. "It didn't do anything."

"It did—for that little moment. It's a new moment now. Let's see what the next little moment brings."

I sighed noisily. "That sucks."

Millie let out a full-throated laugh. "It certainly does. But it's the best we've got, I'm afraid."


"YOU HAVEN'T ASKED me about her," I said as we paddled back sometime later—I hadn't glanced at my phone to see how long we'd lounged on that isolated beach.

All I could see of Millie behind me was the occasional flash of her oar, and she didn't ask who I meant.

Only the rhythmic splashes of our paddling and the water against the hull broke the silence, and then: "Habit, I suppose. It got too difficult to think about her, and so . . . I didn't."

I pushed my oar through the low waves, the pain in my shoulders now a hot, dull throb. I'd feel this tomorrow, but I was glad we'd done it. And not just for the beauty of the trip.

"Would you like to know some things? About my mom?" I asked, loud enough for the words to carry back to her despite the breeze at our backs as we headed toward her house— thankfully boosting the flagging force of my burning arms.

"More than I can tell you." The response was immediate and fervent.

So while we glided past thickets of snarled mangrove roots interrupted by weathered Florida cracker houses, squat concrete-block homes, and even one knobby little house that seemed to be sided entirely with shells—with a matching birdfeeder in the yard—I re-created my mother for the aunt who'd last seen her more than fifty years ago.

I told her about the Halloween when I was six, devastated because my mom had a work trip planned with a client in St. Louis, leaving me to trick-or-treat with only my dad. I pulled on my Ariel costume dispiritedly, trudging from house to house a step behind my father, who didn't dress up, didn't walk to the front doors with me, just waited on the sidewalk with a drink in a plastic cup, talking sports with any other fathers who lagged behind. After thin-lipped Mrs. Farnsworth doled out a single cherry Jolly Rancher in my bag I fought tears, stomping back to my dad to ask to go home, only to find a breathtaking sight: an enormous butterfly with three-foot neon wings standing in the driveway beside him, its body a long, solid column of black.

As I stood there gaping, the giant butterfly turned to me, crouched down, and threw open its arms, and I realized it was my mother. She had fastened two pieces of cut-out hot-pink posterboard to a black bodysuit and leggings, black tights pulled over her head. The wings fluttered crazily in the sharp fall breeze, making alarming popping noises as if they might tear off or carry her away. She must have been freezing, but it was the only costume she could think of when she'd decided to rush home and surprise me.

I told Millie how she sat at the kitchen table with me for every holiday, just the two of us making salt-dough Christmas ornaments, and "stained-glass" Valentine's hearts from glue and glitter and string, and Fourth of July confetti poppers filled with tiny pieces of red, white, and blue tissue we painstakingly cut and tore. All while the sounds of football or baseball or hockey, depending on the holiday, came filtering in from where my father sat in his chair in the living room, occasionally roaring out his outrage or approval at the TV.

But even on nonholidays I had so many memories. How I

always woke up for school to hear Mom already in the kitchen, putting things into the Crock-Pot so we'd all have a home-cooked meal later that night. How by the time I got out of the shower I found a glass of juice on the bathroom counter, and later my breakfast ready under a warming lid on the kitchen table, a sack lunch packed beside it. How my mom would read to me every night, even when she must have been exhausted from working late, still with hours of paperwork ahead of her. How she never just raced through the book or droned through the words she'd read a dozen times before, but brought every character to life.

Millie was quiet while I talked, and if it hadn't been for the steady sound of her rowing I might have wondered whether she was awake. Her strokes hadn't faltered—she had more strength and stamina than I did. Of course, she'd been doing this a lot longer than I had.

I told her how Mom picked me up early from school the last Friday of ninth grade before spring break, saying that she had a surprise for me, and in the car she had our suitcases already packed. We headed straight out from the parking lot toward I-70, just the two of us, driving two days to get to Disney World—my only other time in Florida. I was so ecstatic at the unexpected dream trip, at having my mom all to myself for a whole week, the two of us riding every ride and huddling together in our confectionary-colored hotel room at night like girlfriends, that it never occurred to me to ask why my father didn't come until we got home to find his car, the TV, and all his clothing gone. It was another few years before I realized that my mother must have known he was leaving and that the reason for the trip was so that I didn't have to watch him go.

That trip was the last time I remembered the bright, smiling mother of my childhood. After that she morphed to a dull gray shadow—late nights in her office at home or behind her closed bedroom door alone while I buried myself in books. The house became quiet and still and oppressive, and when it came time to go away to college I felt guilty at how happy I was for the chance to escape.

Telling the stories now made my throat ache—not just with the familiar pain of losing my mom anymore. Now it was complicated by the cloud of fear of what idealistic memories of her might be shattered when I opened the box that waited threateningly at my bedside at Millie's house.

# Nineteen

After we dragged the kayak back up the sloped sand beside Millie's dock, instead of heading back toward the house she directed me to follow her to an outbuilding at the edge of her property, near the water. I'd noticed it before, assuming it was a guesthouse or workshop, but as we walked up the three shallow steps to the octagonal building and Millie unlocked the door to let us in, I saw that both guesses were wrong.

The wide-open space was lined with windows that brought the outside indoors, as if we were in a waterfront treehouse. Wood-laminate flooring and a barre along one wall suggested it was some kind of dance studio. The easel and table splattered with colorful paint in one corner—a setup I recognized from Millie's video—told a different story, as did the yoga mats and cushions in a large open bin in another corner, and the enormous gold velvet chair I recognized from her video at one end, near a cluster of what looked to be stage lights.

"What is this?" I asked, trying to take it all in.

"This is my creative space," Millie said with obvious pride. "Ira built it for me so I'd have room to express myself."

I smiled to myself, imagining that the room Millie needed

to express all of her boundless self couldn't be contained in this five-hundred-square-foot building. "He sounds like a wonderful husband."

Her features softened. "He was. The finest any woman could ever ask for. I miss him every day—still."

"How did you meet him?"

Millie glanced over at me, surprised. "Most people ask me how he died first, as if that's the most notable thing about him. Singing karaoke in Thailand."

"That's how he died?" I tried to imagine it—a heart attack from nerves? Electrocution from a poorly wired mic?

Finally the wide smile I was coming to count on. "No—he died three years ago of a heart attack. Karaoke is how we met. I sang 'Love Me or Leave Me.' He went up right afterward with 'Come Rain or Come Shine.' After that we decided to try a duet—'Unforgettable.' And after *that* . . ." Her eyebrows waggled suggestively. "Well . . . we did another sort of duet."

"Please let me believe you mean something like 'Come Fly with Me.'"

She winked. "Well, you could say that . . . if by 'fly' you mean 'make love all night on a bed of kapok pillows.' You know how it is in the early days of infatuation."

It hadn't been quite that way for me and Brian. The night we'd finally made love I thought my heart would burst from my chest, but it was more Hallmark Hall of Fame movie than *Fifty Shades of Grey*. Our situation was different from Millie and Ira's; they'd kindled sparks as expatriate strangers in a faraway exotic land—we'd known each other so long before we actually became a couple, our consummation was more like a homecoming, long-banked embers finally forming a flame.

"That was in 'eighty-five," Millie went on, saving me from

my troublesome thoughts. "*Nineteen* eighty-five, to clarify," she said with an arch look, and I laughed.

I quickly did the math. "You didn't meet Uncle Ira till you were forty-something?"

"Forty-six. Best year of my life to that point. And there'd been some damn good ones." She wore a faraway smile.

From the way Millie talked about Ira I'd pictured him as her lifelong love—the way Brian had been for me. Imagined two uninhibited young twentysomethings meeting up while adventuring through Asia.

Something was tickling my consciousness about Thailand. "You were both on vacation?" I asked.

She was facing me directly now. "No. Ira was there for a real estate deal. I was there to transition."

It hit me just as she said it, something I'd read not long before—Thailand had been known as a place to seek gender-confirmation surgery long before it had become more widely performed in the United States.

"You met Ira before you . . ." I wasn't sure how to ask what I was asking. Or whether it was rude for me to even ask it.

But Millie nodded as matter-of-factly as if I'd inquired whether she'd like to try a canapé from a party tray. "I'd been living as a woman for many years by that point. But it wasn't until a few weeks after we met that I had the surgery." Her gaze was steady. "Ira knew—he couldn't properly have missed it, under the circumstances," she said with a wry lift of her lips. "But I told him, in any case. I'd learned long since that that was something best laid on the table right up front. He told me he was drawn to a person, not a portrayal."

I was swamped with emotion: awed and moved and a little bit envious of the unconditional love and acceptance of the uncle I'd never known. I couldn't begin to imagine the soul-deep loneliness of losing that. "He must have been extraordinary," I murmured.

Millie's eyes turned shiny and fervent. "My dear, you have no idea." She let out a breath as if blowing the thought away and clapped her hands together. "Ira's partly the reason I brought you in here—I had a thought." She gestured for me to follow her to a door at the back of the room and opened it to reveal a narrow storage closet that lined the whole wall, shelves built to the ceiling on both sides.

I followed her inside toward the back, where a jumble of what looked like exercise equipment was heaped—an exercise ball, a few hand weights, and even what looked to be a Thigh-Master. Millie pointed to a large beanbag-looking item slumped in the corner. She grabbed a bunched towel from a nearby shelf and slapped at the bag, raising dust. "My old heavy bag," she said. "Ira bought it for my 'fists of fury,' he said—those moments when my anger got the better of me and I needed to whale the tar out of something. It's unbelievably satisfying and soothing to hit things, Gracie—I thought you might benefit from it too."

I couldn't imagine myself engaging in that kind of primordial violence, but even if I'd wanted to refuse her offer, I couldn't when her obviously beloved Ira was so closely linked to the intimidating-looking bag—when he was such a presence with us in the room.

"Okay," I said, gamely reaching to tip the bag toward me and drag it out.

It didn't budge.

Millie was watching with a half smile, as if amused by the futility of my efforts.

"Oh, don't pop a hernia, sweetheart—we're going to need some help."

IF I'M HONEST, I probably knew that her help would involve Jason Davis. I didn't object, and when Millie let him and Bud in the front door a couple of hours later—after I'd showered and dressed and no longer looked like a rescued oil-spill seabird—I wasn't entirely surprised that I was glad to see Jason's quick smile.

"We meet again," he said as he saw me.

"It's our thing," I reminded him.

Bud waved a casual greeting, but Millie was watching our exchange like the black-masked terns we'd seen on our paddling trip, ready to swoop down onto their prey. I didn't want to disappoint my matchmaking aunt by reminding her that this . . . whatever it was with Jason—teasing, banter, flirtation—was just a momentary diversion, strictly short-term. Even if I weren't on vacation, the idea of dating—of being with someone new, someone not-Brian—was unthinkable.

In the studio the two men made quick work of carrying the heavy bag out of the closet and hoisting it up onto a hook in the ceiling of the main room.

"What's this for?" Bud asked as they got it attached and let go, the bag swaying like a wistful wallflower at the prom. "You gals learning self-defense?"

Millie winked at me. "Something like that."

"You need me to teach you some stuff? Remember when you make a fist, don't do it like this." He demonstrated with his thumb tucked inside his bunched fingers. "A girl can break a thumb that way."

As he released the ridiculous fist Millie grabbed his arm on the way down, lightning quick, and took some kind of hold on his fingers that made Bud yelp. "A girl can break a thumb in a lot of ways," she said matter-of-factly, and it was all I could do to hold in my laughter. She let go with a smile and a pat of his shoulder. "But thank you, Bud, for the tip. Why don't you show me a few moves?"

I marveled at the way she gently scolded him for his condescending if well-meant advice while still allowing him to save face. Millie was a lady through and through.

Jason stepped over to me as Bud took a *Raging Bull* pose at the bag and started throwing jabs at it, Millie evaluating his performance.

"You're starting to look like a native," Jason said, standing close enough to brush shoulders as we watched them.

"What do you mean?"

"The tan. The new highlights at the ends." He tipped a chin to the hair I'd left out of its ponytail, and I reached up self-consciously to pull a piece into my eyeline to verify. He glanced down. "The bare feet. You're a real islander already."

I laughed, and Millie glanced over from where Bud was showing her a complicated sequence of blows with some flashy footwork. I kept my voice low. "It's infectious—the atmosphere here. I don't know how you locals manage to actually work. All I want to do is relax and be out there." I indicated the wall of windows looking out over the water.

"Me too. That's why I like running the hotel now. It lets me do both."

"What did you do before?"

"I sold reinsurance policies to insurance companies and corporations." He made a face like he'd smelled something rancid, and I laughed again. "The secondary insurance market isn't nearly as exciting and glamorous as everyone thinks it is."

"I don't think anyone . . . Oh." I stopped as his eyes told me he was teasing again. "Well, it's a gorgeous property. And you guys did a great job with the party."

"Do you like parties?"

"Sure, I guess." I lifted one shoulder. "I liked one I went to last night."

He grinned. "Me too—I was glad I ran into you."

"All three times," I teased.

"Do you like the beach?"

"I'm growing pretty fond of it, yes."

"Hmmm. Do you like music?"

"Who doesn't like music?"

"Communists. Also, weirdly, cats, science has discovered. I saw it on PBS."

I laughed out loud. "Okay. Well, now you know I'm not a cat."

"Or a Communist."

I was full-out smiling now. "Is there a purpose to all these questions, or is this just a survey?"

"I was wondering if you'd like to go to a party on the beach with me Friday night. My favorite local band is playing."

My smile vanished, the lightness I'd felt evaporating. "Jason . . . you know I'm only here for a week, right?"

"Well," he said seriously, "the party probably won't last that long. Two days at most, and that's only if Fat Charlie thinks it's funny again to slip Ecstasy into the punch."

"What have you two been chortling about over here?"

Millie and Bud had stopped circling the heavy bag and come over to us without my noticing the punching had stopped, saving me from answering Jason.

"Just chitchat," I said, grateful for the interruption. "Show me some moves."

"I gotta get back," Bud said. "I left Ku to set up the bar alone. You staying, Jase?"

Jason kept his eyes on me, the edges squinchy with his smile. "Nah, I'm right behind you." Millie led Bud back toward the house, but Jason hung behind for one quick moment—long enough to hold out a business card.

"Hey, let me know if you feel like the party this weekend. It'll be fun."

I took it, warm from his pocket, no clue how to answer. But he didn't wait for one—just turned and followed Millie and Bud out the door, leaving me looking after him and flicking the edge of the card over and over with my thumb.

MILLIE HAD MOVES.

When she came back from seeing Jason and Bud out, she retrieved a set of old-fashioned brown boxing gloves from the closet and passed them to me, then lowered into a fighter's stance—slight crouch, fists upraised, head tucked—and demonstrated a few basic jabs and punches.

"Let's see you try," she said, straightening and coming over to help me with the gloves.

"How come you're so good at that?" I asked. "And that thumb thing with Bud—that was awesome."

"Self-preservation," she said, a little out of breath as she tightened the laces at my wrists. "When you're different, you figure out in a hurry that you'd better know how to defend yourself."

Her words made my chest ache. To have to go out into the world vigilant and fearful, simply for being yourself.

"Where'd you learn?"

"My father taught me."

The answer surprised me. "You mean before . . ."

"No, he knew," she said, not looking up from the bow she was tying at the wrist of one glove. "That's why he taught me." She met my eyes so abruptly it startled me. "He wasn't a horrible person, Gracie. None of them were. They just . . . Well, sometimes people are afraid of what they don't understand. But they feared *for* me too. I know that, and I know it came from love."

She was a better person than I was. Better than anyone I knew. I wanted to throw my arms around her, gloves and all, but instead I pounded them together and nodded, ready to learn a little self-preservation of my own.

# Twenty

Mornings were the best and worst part of every day.

The best because, if my dreams had been quiescent, there was a millisecond of time when I woke up and everything was right in my world again. My mother wasn't dead. Brian was mine.

The worst because the moment full consciousness skidded back in, the truth hit me like a fresh blow every time.

I'd had a long, convoluted dream where I was a fighter in some kind of real-life video game, progressing from level to ever-harder level as I fended off attackers with my fists and feet and fury. (It was more agreeable than it sounds.) So I did enjoy my moment of peace before reality charged back in—but this time the breath-stealing fresh sense of loss was followed by a flash of gratitude: Just outside that bedroom door my aunt Millie waited for me. Probably with breakfast.

I threw back the covers to sit up and almost screamed.

My arms were stiff poles of pain attached by joints that felt swollen too big for their sockets. Three hours of rowing followed by an hour of whaling on a bag full of sand were about three and a half hours more upper-body exercise than I'd had in years. I gingerly stretched, wincing, my arms like sides of beef.

But it felt good—the ache, the stretch, the feeling of having exerted myself, pushed myself past what I'd thought were my limits. The boxing had felt good too—Millie was right: Sometimes you just needed to pound on something. I'd started uncertainly, then, as the rhythm and motion of punching began to make sense to my muscles, with more force, more ferocity. When it grew hard to lift my fists higher than my waist I finally quit, sweating, winded . . . and calm.

After dinner—a flaky, tender fillet of local-caught snapper Millie had retrieved from her freezer, and before that from the Gulf of Mexico on a fishing excursion with friends—I'd collapsed onto the sofa like someone had removed my bones. Millie joined me and I suggested we stream *Rocky*, a cinematic classic I couldn't believe she'd never seen.

But for all her technological savvy where the internet was concerned, apparently it didn't extend to television. The woman didn't have cable. She didn't have *Netflix*.

"How do you watch TV?" I asked incredulously.

"Like this." She held up a book on the side table next to the couch, and I remembered seeing books dotting flat surfaces throughout the entire house, her studio, even the back porch, as if everywhere she sat down she laid out literary rations for herself. The living room was really just a glorified library, I realized, looking at the wall of shelves where I'd first spotted my mom's picture. A monument to reading—and to Millie's life in pictures.

So instead of watching television we talked. I pointed to various photos lining the shelves and asked for the stories behind them.

Millie wanted to know more about my mom, so I told her whatever memories popped into my head. My mother came back to life as I talked about her, and it made a warmth grow behind my rib cage, as if the stories returned her to me in some way—not just by evoking her, sharing her with someone who'd known her and wanted to hear about her, but by rekindling the spirit of the woman I'd lost when my father had walked out on us. I hadn't realized how much I'd missed it.

Of course, Pandora's box still sitting where I'd left it on the nightstand was a silent reminder that there was another side to my mother too. One I didn't know—and was afraid to. On top of it the edges of Jason's business card curled up, making it look like a tiny, threatening bird hovering there, and I reached—carefully, slowly—to pick it up, smoothing it flat on my thigh.

The previous night, when I changed into pajamas, I'd taken the bent card from my pocket, where it had sat all night, and stared at it for a while, wondering whether to throw it into the small waste bin thoughtfully placed in the bathroom for guests. *The Turquoise . . . a tropical resort hotel*, it said in raised dark teal lettering on thick cardstock, with Jason's name and several contact numbers discreetly in the lower right corner . . . one of them his cell phone. The background was a simple shoreline—white sand and the titular turquoise water, palm fronds edging in along the left side as if the trade winds had just blown them there. The simple picture instantly made me want to vacation.

Which I was, I reminded myself. I slapped the card back to the top of the box—wincing with the too-fast movement—and stood. At least my legs were normal functioning appendages, which didn't help much with the exercise in masochism of making my bed.

MILLIE HAD BREAKFAST in the works for me, as anticipated, when I came out—the fluffiest omelette I'd ever eaten, stuffed full with mushrooms, spinach, and cheddar, along with a juicy halved grapefruit we split, which she'd picked from the tree outside her window minutes before we ate it. And two Tylenols on the breakfast bar, next to a glass of juice that reminded me of the one my mom always had waiting for me every school day. I downed all of it gratefully.

As insistent as Millie was about not letting me help cook—"only one lioness per den, sweetheart"—she had no such compunctions about my doing the dishes when I offered, and we traded positions: Millie sitting at the island keeping me company as I cleaned the mess from breakfast.

I'd hoped to spend the day with her again, but she had consultations all morning and afternoon. "I could reschedule, but lonely hearts can be a little more fragile than normal."

I knew that was true.

Instead she gave me the key to the CruiseBeast—which wasn't a key at all, but what looked like a mini version of the car itself that magically operated the vehicle without ever leaving your pocket—along with a brief hands-on lesson for driving it and directions to the various beaches on the island. After Millie left to get ready for work, I changed into a bathing suit and shorts, grabbed the loaded beach bag I found waiting for me by the front door, and headed out.

I pulled up a map app to keep myself from getting lost, but it was a little pointless—a single main street bisected the whole of Cypress Key. Smaller residential roads striped either side—

some flaring straight off in a perpendicular line, some curving seemingly at random into little tucked-away warrens, some not even paved, the CruiseBeast's tires crunching over the crushed shells that made those passages navigable. I drove every single one, taking in the wildly varying architecture of the homes: everything from tiny squat shacks to grandiose mansions barely visible behind thick tropical foliage and private tennis courts, and the odd little shell house we'd seen yesterday from the water, even more bizarre up close.

The sun sank into my bare shoulders with the car's roof drawn all the way back, the warmed air vortexing in and bringing with it the rich briny scent of the sea and the sweet citrus perfume of the blooming orange trees dotting the roadside. There were no traffic signals, no toll roads, no high-rise tourist hotels, just the Turquoise parking lot I recognized from the road as I drove past, foolishly sliding down a bit in the leather seat as if Jason might be standing at a window waiting to come running after me to reiterate his party invitation.

When I found one of the beaches Millie had suggested—this one public, but still a little off the beaten path—I parked and hauled the beach bag and a folding chair I found in the back of the car down the rough sandy path to the open shore and set up camp. It was almost like a movie—the picture-perfect setting of teal-green sea lapping at white sand, a few wispy clouds artfully painted in a pure blue sky, palm trees dotting the frame.

Except this was better, because I could feel the warm wind tickling the hairs on my arm and gently swaying my ponytail, smell the rich marine base note of the gulf with its sweet overlay of gardenia and orange blossom, walk over smooth shifting sand to the tide line and feel the initial shock of the cool water as it rushed over my bare feet.

I was early enough to still have the whole beach to myself. The sun was already heating my skin, and I walked back to my chair and fished around in the bag Millie had packed for me, finding SPF 90—apparently she was really worried about my lily-white Midwestern-winter skin—which I liberally slathered across my shoulders, my arms, my back. I massaged it into my calves and higher, splaying my fingers along the warmed, pliable skin of the tops of my thighs and the soft, shadowed flesh along the insides. The sensation made me shiver despite the building heat of the sun. I stretched my shoulders like a preening bird, my braless breasts pushing against the nylon of the suit, and felt a new awareness of my body.

I wondered what the sun would feel like on *all* of my skin.

The picture of some nice vacationing farm family from America's heartland happening upon the shocking sight of a naked, waxed, blindingly white body lying on the public beach made me laugh, the sound startling in the peace of the deserted shoreline.

Preparations complete, I sat in the chair—and realized immediately that I'd forgotten to bring a magazine or book or anything to do. Millie's bag of tricks yielded nothing to entertain me—although I was gratified to see a small soft-sided bag provisioned with several icy bottles of water and some Ziploc bags full of snacks. Millie thought of—almost—everything.

Bored, I reached for my phone, opening my email, and felt my sore shoulders hunch back up as I scrolled through client inquiries, revisions to draft wills and questions about beneficiary designations, and continuing-education marketing emails.

Seeing an email from Susie, I decided to start there.

Mistake.

*Hey, hon!* it started. (There was just no chance that someone who watched me go from diapers to business suits was ever going to maintain professional decorum.)

> I'm refusing to bother you on vacay, despite the fact that certain bosses have repeatedly asked me to check with you on what seems like every little detail. My guess is that said boss might just not quite know what to do with the fact that you're not here for the first time, well, ever, and your whereabouts are uncertain. Don't you worry about things here on the home front; all your clients are just fine and I've rescheduled your appointments, so you just ignore any fires that look like they need putting out. I'm pretty sure I've got the hose trained on all of them. ;)
>
> And I just wanted to tell you too, even though it may not be my place to say so, that I've been thinking about you nonstop, and if your spontaneous getaway has to do with the porcelain princess who sailed in here like a parade float, asking an awful lot of questions about the practice and acting like queen of the May, well, no one on earth could blame you. <3
>
> I miss you. I hope you're having a whale of a time, sugar.
>
> XO,
> Susie

Instantly, whatever equanimity the last couple of days had restored dissipated like smoke, and rage—the familiar throbbing fury—surged up my throat and behind my eyes.

Brian had brought Angelica into *our* office? Introduced her to Susie?

As what? I fumed. My shiny new replacement? The new-and-improved future Mrs. McHale? It wasn't bad enough that she took over my home, my husband—now he had his perfect little baby mama waltzing through *my* law practice, digging for info?

For the first time I understood the phrase "seeing red"—my vision seemed to cloud over in a bloodred haze of impotent anger.

My hands shaking, my heart pounding, I smashed "reply" so hard I nearly jammed my finger.

**DO NOT LET THAT WOMAN ANYWHERE NEAR MY OFFICE.**

I went to mash "send"—when my better angel spoke in my ear.

*If you light the grenade, make sure you let go of it.*

My better angel sounded a lot like Aunt Millie.

Typing the angry all-caps message had felt really, really satisfying. But if I sent this it was out there, and while part of me really wanted to fling that grenade, I knew that all it was really doing was blowing me up. And the last person I wanted to throw it at was Susie.

But I was *pissed*.

I dropped the phone into my lap and punched my right fist into my left palm—twice . . . three times, relishing the slap and the sting of it. Let out a guttural roar, liking the way it ripped through the peace of the quiet beach.

I stretched my fingers out wide, as if preparing to play an arpeggio, and then picked up the phone and backspaced out the message deliberately, one letter at a time.

Taking in long, deep breaths, I typed a brief thank-you to Susie for the update. I promised to put a bounce-back message on my email so she didn't have to keep putting out fires. I told her I missed her too and I would see her Monday morning. With doughnuts, to make up for missing this coming Friday.

I even signed it with a smiley-face emoticon. Susie really liked emoticons.

I sent it, and a little bit of something ugly siphoned out of me as the email sailed away.

I put the phone away in the beach bag, folded myself on the towel in a rough approximation of Millie's pretzel position, and closed my eyes. I took a long breath and let it out. And then another one.

Angelica. Perfect, beautiful Angelica in my office, in the hallways of my building, talking to my friend at the receptionist desk, asking questions about *my* legacy. *My* family practice.

*The family practice of* me! Jason Davis's words popped into my head.

I focused my attention on my hands clutching my knees, trying to consciously make their grip relax.

Shiny, luminous Angelica . . . in my old home . . . my old bed.

I pushed my awareness to my tight forehead, my clenched jaw, deliberately easing the tension in them.

Fertile, pregnant Angelica carrying Brian's baby . . .

My breathing was fast and loud in my ears, and that was what I listened to, concentrating on it, hearing the slight shudder of emotion in it, feeling the cool rush as I inhaled, the warmth as it came back out, smelling the thick scent of the ocean.

Slowly I tuned in to more than just the sound of my rapid breathing. To the shushing white noise of the waves and the dancing rustle of the palms and the light fluttering of wind in the shells of my ears. I breathed in and out, in and out, let the warm salty air fill my lungs and felt the slow uncoiling of muscles. Slowly I opened my eyes and looked out at the white sparks jumping on the surface of the water.

The anger wasn't gone. But it was . . . manageable. Like a sore toe—you knew it was there, but it didn't cripple you. You could get by despite it.

Right now I was going to call that a win.

I HAD ANOTHER two hours on the little beach before I had to share it, spending the time walking as far as I could in both directions before the foliage was too dense to navigate, swimming in the water—cool but refreshing after the building heat of the morning—and finally lying on my stomach on the towel, the sand conforming to my shape and the sun an invisible blanket on my skin so that I felt myself dozing off, a pleasant half-conscious state where the waves and palm fronds and birds chittering filtered in as soothing white noise.

The sound of guitar music brought me fully awake to see a skinny young barefoot guy, board shorts hanging low on his hips, sitting directly on the sand near the tree line. He grinned when I sat up and gave a small wave. I waved back and lay down again, this time on my back, closing my eyes and letting the gentle strumming of the meandering melody and the sweet, heavy scent of his marijuana roll over me.

When I sat up again the kid was gone, replaced by a leathery brown woman with straw-yellow hair who might have been forty or seventy; it was hard to tell beneath the weathered skin. She'd planted an old-fashioned plastic-weave lounge chair on the sand and, judging from the loud snores that rose up, fallen asleep. I wanted to shade her somehow, or at least offer her my sunscreen, but I suspected that would defeat her purpose.

A little while after that came the family I'd worried about earlier when I'd idly contemplated nude sunbathing: a tall man with close-cut blond hair and a slightly shorter woman with impressively muscled arms and legs I coveted for myself, accompanied by their three small children. As the kids started chasing each other up and down the sand and shrieking, I finished my last bottle of water and figured I'd had enough sun.

Packing my supplies into the CruiseBeast, I headed back the way I'd come, realizing I was hungry. I was half tempted to stop in at Jason's hotel—I'd seen a restaurant on the premises the night of the wedding—and right now the idea of seeing him again felt appealing. But that party invitation complicated matters. If I ate lunch at his hotel I'd have to give him an answer, and it would be much harder to say no sitting across from his amiable smile and good humor.

Instead I pulled into the central marketplace where Millie had taken me my first day, remembering the shrimp shack there. A heaping plate of fresh gulf shrimp sounded ideal.

"Grace!"

The sound of a voice calling my name was disconcerting for a moment, as if I were back in Sugarberry where it seemed like everyone knew me, instead of an unfamiliar tropical town where no one did. I turned around to see Helene standing at the door of her shop, waving.

"I finished all your alterations," the woman said as I veered toward her. "I was going to send Becca over to your aunt's later today, but as long as you're here . . ."

I'd almost forgotten about the trove of clothing she and Millie had helped me choose, and when she handed me a pair of handled paper shopping bags stuffed full it felt like Christmas. As I left the shop she hugged me.

At the little package store/restaurant I sat at one of the three tiny tables inside, enjoying the shade but also the fresh breeze sweeping in through the open doors and windows, and plowed through two dozen fat, sweet peel-and-eats as though I'd last eaten days before, instead of feasting on Millie's cooking that morning.

My server came up to take my second batch of shells away. "You gonna go for round three?" she asked, grinning.

I rested my hands on my stomach like an expectant mother, then moved them abruptly when the gesture brought Angelica jolting back to mind. "I have to stop, but those are amazing. What's on them?"

She shrugged. "Just a little dusting of Tony Chachere's. When they're fresh like this they don't need much—those just came in this morning."

"They are literally the best thing I've ever eaten." I cringed as the words came out of my mouth, reminding me of Brian, but for once I could understand his hyperbole. Right this minute those shrimp actually did seem like the most delicious food I'd ever had. Amazing how much appetite you could work up lying on the sand.

"Hey, didn't I see you at Josh and Ysidra's wedding?" she asked as she wiped up stray bits of shell and severed shrimp leg from the carnage on my table. "Millie's niece?"

"Yes, that's me. I'm sorry, I don't remember you . . . ?"

She wiped her hand on her apron before extending it toward me. "Chelsea. I was the one trying to keep up with Bridget on the dance floor." She grinned again, as I speculated that that description covered a good third of the wedding guests.

"Grace Adams," I said as we shook, and for once my old name came easily.

Chelsea slipped into the chair opposite me—the place didn't exactly have a formal fine-dining vibe. "You look a little more comfortable here than you did the other night." She indicated the sarong I'd tied around my waist and my flip-flopped feet, sand still clinging to the sides. "Vacation or relocation?"

"Oh . . . just a visit."

"Winter runaway, huh? You're a little young for a snowbird."

I laughed. "I'm just here visiting my aunt for the week. But you're right—it's pretty great here compared to back home right now." My description of a Missouri winter made her eyes pop. Chelsea was born in Miami and raised in Naples, not far down Highway 75 on the mainland, she said, and hadn't roamed farther north than the panhandle.

"I'm probably gonna travel one day," the girl said—she couldn't have been more than twenty. "I always wanted to do some kind of international social work, like in Haiti or Africa or something. But for now, this is okay, you know?" She laughed and pushed herself back to her feet. "Who the hell knows where I'll end up? I'm just figuring it all out as I go. Whatever happens, happens."

My smile vanished at her youthful idealism, remembering when I'd felt the same way. As if every path in the world were open to me.

I'd fallen into a life I hadn't actually chosen—I could blame it on the family business and feeling I needed to come back to Sugarberry and take over from my mom, but she'd never asked me for that. I'd done it because I wanted to. Stayed when Brian turned into more than my childhood friend—became what I had always dreamed of and never dared to hope for. All these were choices I had made, yes. Figuring it out as I went, as Chelsea said. Whatever happened had indeed happened, and here I was, nowhere I wanted to be in life.

Except for . . . right here at this table, at this moment, in this run-down little hole of a restaurant with magnificently simple food, my skin stiff and sticky with dried salt and sunscreen, and more relaxed than I'd been in . . .

Well, maybe ever.

*Maybe it's good to make a* little *bit of a plan,* I wanted to tell her. *Because "what happens" is life, and before you know it you're caught up in other people's wake instead of plotting a course for yourself.*

But Chelsea was already gone, ducking back into the minuscule kitchen, and I couldn't imagine she'd welcome any advice from a woman pushing middle age who'd fled to this tropical paradise to escape from the real life she'd let herself fall into.


MILLIE WAS TUCKED away in her office with a client consultation when I got home. Still unsettled from the conversation with Chelsea and my own sticky thoughts, instead of showering I changed into one of Brian's old undershirts and gym shorts I'd had since high school and headed to the studio, where I spent twenty minutes pounding on the heavy bag before my still-sore arms and shoulders gave out.

Afterward I turned the shower on as hot as I could take it to try to soothe some of the ache, realizing with a yelp as soon as I did that I'd gotten some sun today after all, despite Millie's nuclear-option SPF. I had to settle for lukewarm, but even that felt good sluicing away the sand and salt and sweat residue.

I put on one of the outfits from Helene's boutique—just a

pair of cotton shorts and a billowy gauzy top, but they fit perfectly and made me feel . . . tended to. As if I were worth taking more care of than I normally did.

I barely recognized myself in the mirror. Even without makeup, with some sun on my skin I looked more vivid, my cheeks blushed with pink, my eyes brighter against the glowing golden tinge of my face and the lighter ends of my hair that Jason had noticed.

The thought of Jason brought fresh color to my face. I felt rude not calling, but though I couldn't deny that part of me would like to see him again, actually calling him, going with him to his party, felt too much like a date.

I heard voices as I came out to the living room and found Millie in the kitchen talking with a dark-haired woman sitting in my usual spot at the breakfast bar, her back to me. I didn't recognize her until she turned around with a broad wave and an open-mouthed smile. "Hey, girl," the tipsy bridesmaid from the wedding called out cheerfully. "Told you you'd be seeing more of me."

"Bridget brought us fresh shrimp," Millie said, holding up a clear plastic bag full of curling gray bodies.

"Plus I'm staying for dinner." Bridget grinned. "Hope you don't mind."

"Of course not," I said, omitting news of my all-shrimp lunch. "Can I help?"

"No," Bridget and Millie said in unison, and I laughed.

I took my perch at the breakfast bar beside Bridget while Millie retrieved a sweet onion from a bowl on the counter. She sliced it thin and tossed it into a pan with some oil, following it up with slices of red and green peppers from the crisper drawer of the refrigerator, then expertly beheading, peeling, and deveining the shrimp while the vegetables sizzled. She tossed the heads into a pot of water on the stove, along with the produce scraps. "Fresh shrimp makes the best stock," she told us. "You girls remember that."

"Millie is so full of good advice about everything, she can't help that it spills over," Bridget said, winking at me.

"It's unfortunate you refuse to heed any of it," Millie shot back, unperturbed. "It's excellent advice."

"Hey, I listen. I haven't hooked up with anyone new since I saw you last."

Millie glanced over her shoulder, one eyebrow raised. "Anyone *new*?" she said pointedly.

"I keep waiting for a little dementia to set in so she's not so much sharper than me," Bridget said to me in a mock whisper before looking back at Millie. "Javi doesn't count. We go way back. And come on—you can't expect me to go home alone after a wedding."

Javier was the name of the person Jason Davis had had his assistant, Viviana, assign to seeing Bridget safely home that night, I remembered.

"Yet somehow Grace and I managed it," Millie said dryly. Bridget just grinned and shrugged.

While Bridget asked me what I thought of Cypress Key so far and I told her what I'd seen and done, Millie rinsed and added the peeled shrimp into the mix on the stove, then assembled ramekins of sour cream, sliced avocado, and salsa, occasionally giving the pan a stir. She set everything along the counter with a packet of soft corn tortillas before sliding onto the stool on the other side of Bridget. The whole production had taken less than twenty-five minutes.

"This looks amazing," I said, glancing over the spread. "I can't believe how fast you threw that together."

"Honey, the day I can't whip up a meal spur-of-the-moment you should check my vitals."

We took turns reaching for tortillas and loading them up, and I took a bite of mine. The pink shrimp and caramelized onions were warm and slightly sweet, offset by the crisp crunch of the peppers, the cool creaminess of the sour cream and avocado, and the bite of spicy salsa. Millie managed to make even the simplest meals taste fancy.

Bridget shoved half her first fajita in her mouth and let out a sensual moan. "God," she said through a mouthful of food. "Someday I'm going to move in here as your home-health aide just so you can cook like this for me every day."

"When the time comes that someone has to live here with me and wipe my helpless bottom, I assure you he will be far younger, better muscled, and more macho than you are."

I covered my full mouth with my hand to hide my laugh.

"Millie's so morbid," Bridget complained good-naturedly.

"That's not morbid," I said, swallowing. "It's smart to have a long-range care plan in place. Such as it is."

"Whoa." Bridget held up her hands. "Let me stop you right there. Apparently I look a lot older than I am—it's a little early for me to be thinking about that kind of thing."

"Listen to Grace—she knows what she's talking about," Millie advised Bridget. "And it's never too early," she corrected. "I've had a will since I was twenty years old. You should too. You never know what can happen—remember that."

Bridget looked at me. "See? Always advising . . ."

"Ira and I had contingency plans for our contingency plans—we even made separate wills that specifically bequeathed everything to each other . . . just in case."

Bridget's eyebrows pulled together. "Just in case what?"

I didn't know Florida law, but I was pretty sure Millie was talking about complications from transgender issues. There were cases in the LGBT community of people who had lost everything when a partner died without a will. In the past, several states had even nullified marriages involving a transgender spouse, invalidating executed wills and claims, and in some cases ending parental rights. But I didn't know whether Bridget knew about my aunt's history—and it certainly wasn't my place to reveal it.

"Just in case Florida decided I was legally a man when we married," Millie said crisply.

I glanced quickly at Bridget, but apparently Millie's curt response was no revelation to her. She looked outraged—but not by Millie. "Those assholes could just decide your marriage had never been real and wipe it out of existence? That's bullshit!"

Fresh anger clutched my throat at the reminder that that was exactly what her own family had done to Millie—wiped her out of existence. For the first time I really thought, viscerally, about what Millie's life had been like. Growing up in my rural small town *now* would make it hard for someone who didn't fit ordinary cultural norms to be accepted—I couldn't imagine what it must have been like sixty-odd years ago.

Would I feel differently about Millie if I'd known her when she was Milton? I scrutinized my aunt as she filled another tortilla, trying to picture who she might once have been. I couldn't make myself see it—but was that because to me she'd always be who she presented herself as when I met her?

Was that how my great-grandparents had felt, Grammy, my mom? That they could never look at her and see Millie when they had known her for so many years as Milton?

But if it were the other way around—if she turned to me this second and pulled off her glorious cloud of silver hair, wiped away her makeup, and told me that she was actually a man—would I be able to adapt? Or rather, not to have to adapt and decide to keep caring about her anyway, but to feel the exact same way about her that I did now, regardless? Would it even be a choice I had to make, a battle I had to fight?

The thought flared jagged in my chest—of course it wouldn't. She'd still be *her*—Millie. What I loved about her—and I had come to love her in such a short time—was on the inside, not whatever shell that was clad in. The person, as Ira had told her, not the portrayal. If the joyful, warm, free soul heaping sour cream onto her fajita was a man, a woman, or a unicorn, what difference did it make? How could my family ever have felt otherwise?

*It was a different time*, my mind insisted on pointing out.

But how could Millie have managed to forgive so much?

Bridget leaned closer and bumped Millie's shoulder. "Those assholes wouldn't dare invalidate you. Grace and I wouldn't let them. Right, Grace?"

"I'd sure as hell fight their asses in court as high as I could take it," I said, surprised at the ferocity of my words.

"My niece is a lawyer," Millie said proudly, her sunny mood restored.

"No way," Bridget said admiringly.

I laughed. "Way. Estate planning, actually—so this is sort of my field of expertise."

"You make people think about their deaths every day? Whoa. I couldn't do it. It freaks me out."

I shrugged. "That's one thing I like about it. It's a chance for people to map out exactly what they want—not just for the people they love, the things they love, but for their own life. On their own terms."

"That's exactly how I like things," Millie chimed in. "On my own terms."

"Actually, the first question I ask new clients is how they picture the end of their life," I said, warming to my topic.

Rather than tippy-toe sideways into talking about areas that made a lot of people squirm, I liked to lead with it, to break the barrier of discomfort right away so it hopefully took the looming dread out of the subject that some people felt—Bridget, for one, judging by her horrified expression.

"Nope," she said. "Not gonna think about that. I'm just going to live fast and leave a beautiful corpse—hopefully not too young, though. No disrespect to James Dean."

I waved a hand in the air like a white flag. "Hey, I don't force anyone. But I do agree with Millie."

"You see!" my aunt crowed. "My advice is splendid." She looked down at the overstuffed fajita in her hands but didn't seem to be seeing it. "Ira and I always planned to go together when the time came. Just zoom right off a cliff side by side, laughing our tail ends off the whole way down."

I imagined Millie loosing a victorious, ecstatic war cry, the man I'd seen in her pictures beside her as they enjoyed one last ride of their lives. "Like Thelma and Louise," I said, smiling.

"Who?"

"Never mind."

"Millie knows more about most things than anyone I know," Bridget said, "but when it comes to pop culture she's hopeless."

"I'm far too type A to sit passively and let someone just pour their story on me," Millie said. "Books let you be part of the equation—they demand it, actually. A good author leaves room for the reader to fill in some of the picture. Ira and I would read the exact same book and have totally different visions of the story. Then we'd talk about them for hours." She wore a faraway look.

"I wish I could have known him," I said.

"Oh, my dear. So do I." Her smile was edged with regret.

"You'd have loved him," Bridget said. "Imagine a male Millie."

There was a moment of shocked silence where the awkwardness of her comment washed over all of us. Then Millie started to giggle—after a second, Bridget joined in, and before long the three of us were laughing so hard we had to put down our fajitas and hold ourselves up on the edge of the counter.

LATER, AFTER MILLIE had gone off to bed, I found myself too keyed up to sleep, and I quietly let myself onto the back porch and out the screen door, padding down the wooden steps. The stiff St. Augustine grass was chilly under my bare feet, but the air felt perfectly comfortable, as if it were calibrated to my body temperature, and even in the short sleeves of Brian's old T-shirt I wasn't cold. The moon was nearly full, a pure bright white that lit the sky indigo and shot a glowing silver path across the gulf as I walked down the dock. It was built too high for me to dangle my feet in the water but I sat on the edge anyway, the occasional splash tickling my soles, looking out to the black horizon.

I'd studied family law because I had to, because I knew that as an only child, especially after my father decamped, the family mantle would one day fall on my shoulders. At least, that was the narrative I'd always told myself. But Millie's comments had made me think. She was right: I did love it, the idea of balancing out the scales of what would happen with all a person had created in their lifetime, what would go on after them. I loved the visible peace of mind I could see in clients' faces after everything was taken care of, set up just as they wanted—after I'd helped to give them the ultimate happy ending, at least as far as the legacy that would outlive them.

Death was not something I'd ever feared—maybe because, growing up in our family practice, it had been such a constant presence in my life. Because it was the natural order of things. Because, for the most part, our loved ones didn't choose to die and leave us behind, and part of the covenant of loving someone was the knowledge that eventually you might lose them.

But it felt different when it was a choice, didn't it?

Even after my father had left us, my mother never said an unkind word about him. When I did—railing against his wannabe-starlet girlfriend, against the way he'd hurt my mom, against his minimal paternal efforts—she'd just held me and comforted me, reminding me he was my father, trying to convince me that he loved me, urging me to accept his calls and see him when he wanted to visit or if he asked me to come out to California.

None of which he ever did.

How could she be so conciliatory about someone who so little deserved it, and yet turn her back completely on her aunt, who eminently did?

The answers, if I wanted them, were waiting on the nightstand yards away from where I sat.

# Twenty-one

Propped up with pillows on the sofa in the living room, the small lamp on the table beside me casting a small circle of illumination over where I sat, I started at the back of the box, with my mother's earliest letters. The first one was dated 1961; she would have been thirteen years old, not long after Millie left for good, and the cursive was looped and childish, but I could still recognize the graceful slope of her hand.

*Dear Uncle Milt,*

The salutation startled me before I remembered.

*I cannot BELIEVE you slipped away while I was at school without saying goodbye! I didn't even know you had another trip planned . . . but I don't blame you for going—Mother and Father said you had an opportunity you couldn't turn down. I would have taken it too. But it is über-dull around here without you. That's a little German for you in honor of your travels to Austria—home of Mozart and* The Sound of Music *and Sigmund Freud. (I looked it up in our Encyclopedia*

*Britannica—there are a GREAT DEAL of interesting things
that come out of Austria, it turns out, including the man who
invented Porsches! I hope you are driving one.)*

There were a handful of letters like that, their contents revealing the path of Millie's—Milton's—travels after she left our
family for good, my mom faithfully researching every new lo-
cale where Millie settled for a time, and each one signed, *Love,
Tricia.*

*Dear Uncle Milt,*

*Well, apparently everyone here is entirely neutral about
Switzerland (a little national joke for you!) or any of the places
you are seeing. When I tell them about all the things you're doing, they just look bored or annoyed, and they don't even want
to talk about it, as if everything on earth you could ever want
is right here in dull Sugarberry. I wish I could travel with
you. Please take pictures, if you have your camera, and keep a
travel journal, like Charles Darwin did in the Galápagos.
Holy moly—you should go to the Galápagos Islands! Or wait
for me when I'm older.*

My mother had dreamed of traveling too? Why had she never
told me that?

Why had I never told her that I did too?

Her letters weren't filled with news about Sugarberry bake
sales and football games, the way Millie said Grammy's had
been. They were rich with not only my mother's admittedly
bossy thoughts about what Milton should see and where he
should go next, but the preoccupations of a thirteen-year-old
girl, like the new Patsy Cline record she was "wild" about, that

she thought Alan Shepard must be the bravest man in America to let himself be shot up a hundred miles above the Earth, and the fact that her parents wouldn't let her go see *Breakfast at Tiffany's* or *West Side Story*, and she wished Milton were there to sneak her in.

> *Dear Uncle Milt,*
>
> *Sorry this letter took so long. Your last letter almost didn't make it and the only reason I even knew that you wrote it is because I happened to see an airmail envelope in the bin when I took out the kitchen bag for Mother—it got mangled in the mail and Father thought it was trash. So I'm sorry I have no idea what you said, because it was too soggy to try to rescue, and it smelled exceptionally bad.*

My heart sank, understanding what my mom clearly had not. The next letter was dated almost a year later.

> *Dear Uncle Milton,*
>
> *I hope my letters are getting to you. I haven't heard from you in a long time. I know you said that you would be moving around a lot in Czechoslovakia, but I sent them to the hostel you said you would be checking with. I took this one to the post office myself in case Mr. Charles the mailman is losing them— remember how we used to joke that he'd chosen a strange profession for someone with so little sense of direction?*

I felt nauseous imagining my mother's letters to Millie—or to Milton—intercepted by her parents, probably winding up in the same bin where she'd rescued the one her dad—Gramps—

had tried to throw away. Millie far from home, wondering why my mother had stopped writing to her. Maybe fearing the worst.

> *Uncle Milton,*
>
> *I don't know why you aren't writing me. Father told me I shouldn't worry about it—that you were gone now and weren't coming back. Is that true? Are you gone forever? Why? Please, please write me back and tell me. When I ask Mother she looks as if she might burst into tears, and now I'm getting a little frightened. Are you ill? If something is wrong you should come home—you know we will take care of you. Family is everything—no matter what. You taught me that.*

Tears blurred the words from more than just the confused heartbreak of the young woman my mother had been. Along with "You get what you get and you don't get upset" and "You did it; now deal with it," "Family is everything" was one of my mother's most repeated truisms, usually after I'd said something hateful or dismissive about my father. It was another way Millie had been a hidden presence in my entire life without my ever knowing the first thing about her.

There were only two letters left now, and I dreaded reading them, knowing what was coming. But I made myself open the next thin blue airmail envelope, pull out the onionskin-thin piece of paper inside.

> *Uncle Milton,*
>
> *I don't understand anything. My letters aren't being returned to me, so I can't imagine that you're . . . No, I can't even write it. But I have been asking my parents to find out where*

*you are, because I am worried about whether you are all right, and they said it is no concern of mine and that I should accept that you are gone for good.*

*I said I didn't accept it. They are angry at me for contradicting them, but I don't care.*

*Then I overheard my parents arguing with Grandfather about you, and the things they said are . . . I can't even write that either. It's unthinkable what they are saying about you. Father says you're . . . unnatural and no longer a part of this family. Mother won't discuss it at all. I know you, and of course I don't believe it, but I really, really need you to write me, please. I don't understand any of this.*
*Tricia*

My chest physically hurt reading the words. I couldn't imagine what it must have felt like to Millie. The last one contained only a single awful line:

*Uncle Milton,*
 *Perhaps it's best if you don't write back.*
*Patricia*

MY SLEEP WAS restless, troubled by vague, disturbing images and snippets of dreams. In the only one I clearly remembered I was trapped somewhere in the basement of my house—my mother's house in Sugarberry, her parents' house before her. Above me the house was on fire, and I huddled in a dark corner of the cellar in terror, knowing no one would find me as I listened to the ever-louder crackling sizzle of flames over my head and smelled . . .

Bacon.

I blinked my crusty eyes open and shifted, disoriented, the bright sunlight that stung my eyes revealing I was lying on a sofa. Millie's sofa, I remembered, catching sight of the back of her head in the kitchen as she worked over something evidently pork-based on the stove. Around me were scattered the letters from my mom I'd been reading last night, and the sight brought their contents slamming back into my consciousness. I sat up, ignoring the crick in my neck and the residual ache of my shoulders and arms as I hastily gathered the envelopes into a random stack, hoping Millie hadn't seen me, that she didn't realize yet that I'd fallen asleep here after reading the terrible truth about my mother.

"Do you like it limp or crispy?"

Apparently she did realize.

I cleared the rasp from my throat. "On the limp side, please."

"Coming right up."

I thrust the stack of letters back into the metal box and swung the lid closed, leaning over to stash it beneath the small table beside the couch.

"You're likely to forget them there."

I jumped as Millie's voice came from immediately behind me, almost upending one of the plates she held as I swung around.

She smiled reassuringly. "I've already read them, you know. Too many times."

Settling next to me on the sofa, she handed over one of the plates, and suddenly the smell of the bacon and hot toast glistening and golden with butter, the sight of another of Millie's perfect omelettes folded neatly beside it like praying hands, all made me realize I was ravenous. We ate side by side in a silence broken only by the clink of our forks against the plates.

"What happened next?" I asked once the clawing in my belly began to be appeased. Because what other question was there to ask? "Mom was fifteen when she wrote you that last letter. Still living at home, still under Grammy and Gramps's thumb. What happened when she became an adult—when they couldn't control what letters or contact went in and out . . . when she was old enough to make more sense of everything, make her own choices? Did she . . . did she respond to you then?" As the breath froze in my throat I realized how badly I needed the answer to be yes.

Millie stopped chewing midbite, the food seeming to stick in her throat as she swallowed. She set her plate on the cocktail table, delicately dabbed her fingers with her napkin, examining them closely as if for stray crumbs. "I didn't write her again. Not for many, many years. By the time I finally did . . . well, I think it was too late. I'd let her down. Whatever we'd been to each other in the past was so long ago. She had a family of her own by then. You."

How many years had gone by before Millie tried contacting my mother again? Millie saw me doing the mental computations, the unexpected betrayal undoubtedly showing on my face.

"After your mother stopped writing me back I continued to travel—I found work wherever I wound up, made enough to live on, to get by," she said. "It was more than seeing the world, though that was part of it. There was such freedom in leaving my family and my history and the tight box of my hometown, my home *country*, behind me. Freedom in being away—so *far* away, and the farther I went, the freer I felt, the more the pain of my family's rejection receded into the past. It was the happiest time I'd known till then—finally at liberty to find out . . . or rather to *be* who I was. By the time I got to Thailand I knew I would leave Milton behind forever—or at least the shell of him.

For the first time there were . . . others like me. Women like me. And there was nothing wrong with them—they were just another face of society, another way of being."

"Thailand is where you met Ira," I said. I'd stopped eating too, no longer interested in food.

She nodded. "That's right. And Thailand is where I became Millie—at least physiologically. But, darling, the truth is that I have been Millie since the day I was born." She said it so gently, so tenderly, one hand resting hesitantly over mine on the sofa cushion, as if breaking terrible news to me and concerned how I might take it.

But of course she had always been Millie. Who else could she ever have possibly been?

"So you didn't trust Mom to accept you. You were afraid," I said, but there was no accusation in my tone.

"Afraid—no. I was angry and wanted to punish her." She pressed her lips together and shook her head, as if disappointed in herself. "Wanted to punish a young girl who was very much a product of her upbringing, her surroundings, her society—as of course we all are. How could she have reacted any other way than she did? How could I have expected her to? But all those insights came to me much later—too late for your mother to forgive me for giving up on her. When I needed them, I was still letting myself be eaten up with the anger, the resentment—the *unfairness* of it all. The great wrongs done to me." She put the back of a hand theatrically to her forehead, Sarah Bernhardt–style.

But I didn't smile, any inkling of blame for my aunt having dissipated with her story. "Great wrongs *were* done to you."

"Of course they were," she said, sobering. "Great wrongs are done to us all at some point. The question is, do we use them as a justification—or an opportunity?"

# Twenty-two

We spent the rest of the morning lounging on the comfortable reclining chairs on Millie's dock, idly chatting, reading side by side, or just looking out over the water, watching for dolphin fins as they arced up now and again, a fresh thrill every time. Around noon we went inside for lunch—Millie threw together a salad too decadent to be healthy, and I reflected that it was a good thing I'd been so active on this trip or I'd never work off the calories.

But I wasn't active today—after lunch when she excused herself for a client consultation in her office via Skype, I moved to the covered porch and lay on the hammock under the slowly swirling fan, letting the soft breeze and gentle lapping of the water lull me into a light doze. That night Millie made a jambalaya from the rest of Bridget's shrimp and her homemade stock and we read companionably together before an early bedtime—it was bizarre how lazy days in the sunshine could take all the energy out of you, I told Millie.

She only smiled. "Sometimes we don't realize how exhausting it is carrying around the loads of our lives till we get a chance to set it all down for a few days."

The next morning she drove us to yet another beach—this one tucked off the end of a cul-de-sac that mostly locals used, thanks to the lack of public parking or marked signs. We traversed a narrow path through the mangroves till it opened out into a small sandy area about twenty yards long, with gentle lapping waves thanks to its placement on the lee side of Cypress Key. Later she taught me to fish off the end of her dock, and we took our fresh snapper inside so Millie could expertly clean it and throw it into a pan with a dusting of cornmeal for the freshest fish lunch I'd ever tasted.

Lulled into bonelessness by our relaxing day, I suggested another quiet evening at home, but Millie had other plans. "I'm a member of an athletic league, dear, with some of the other Merry Widows, and we've got a practice tonight. Any chance you're a fan of sporting events?"

Which turned out to be shuffleboard. At a senior center.

It was the first elderly cliché I'd seen from her, but I refrained from pointing it out. As always, of course, she seemed to read my mind anyway.

"I'll have you know that shuffleboard was once the back-alley craps game of the English aristocracy."

"I didn't say a word." I begged off tagging along. I didn't think Millie would miss me if I decided to stay home.

Or maybe called Jason Davis to take him up on his invitation.

I had been separated from my husband for more than a year, divorced for months. Brian had clearly moved on, but I was holding on so tightly—first to him, then to the grenade of my anger and resentment—that I was stuck in place. I'd watched my mother shut down and give up after my father stopped loving her—despite my exhortations, she never went on a single date with anyone.

I wasn't going to do the same thing. Sooner or later I had to take that first step—and where better than hundreds of miles from where I lived, with someone who, if things went badly, I never had to see again?

It felt ridiculously awkward dialing his number from the card I'd left beside my bed—how long had it been since I'd called a man? (Technically never, since the last time I'd been in the dating pool I was barely a woman myself, and before that my mom had inculcated strict injunctions against my calling a boy.) How long since I'd gone on a date? (If you didn't count the Saturday-night dinner-and-a-movie that was Brian's and my ritual.) And it wasn't until it actually started to ring that I realized it was Friday afternoon, I hadn't bothered to respond to him all week long, and I hadn't given a second's thought to what I was actually going to say when he answered.

"Jason Davis."

My heart thunked against my rib cage; I took a deep breath and dived all the way in: "Hi. I'm sorry I waited so long to call you back about the party you asked me to, and if you already asked someone else or made other plans I understand. But if not, I think I'd really like to go." Silence greeted my announcement. "This is Grace Adams, by the way. Millie's niece—from the wedding. I'm sorry." I cringed. "It's been a while since I got asked out, full disclosure. As you can probably tell."

There was a long beat, and when he finally spoke I heard his curlicue smile in his voice. "Well, you said yes, so as far as I'm concerned you knocked it out of the park."

I WAS HOPELESS at the kind of makeover Millie had achieved on me earlier in the week. When I finished, my eyes looked bruised and my hair looked like I'd styled it with a stick blender. I washed my face, settling on just some light gold shadow over my lids and a little mascara, which I could do without putting an eye out, and lip gloss. I brushed out my hair and then just left it that way. No ponytail was going to have to be enough glamour for me.

One of my new dresses seemed like too much for a beach party, but jeans seemed too hot for the tropical weather. I pulled on shorts and a tank top, then worried about the evening temperatures near the shore, and whether I was showing too much skin on a first date. I finally settled on a new pair of ankle-skimming tan skinnies and a teal-and-cream knit top with a light short-sleeved sweater. Shoes were a whole new quandary.

I didn't remember dating being this stressful.

I presented myself in Millie's bedroom for inspection, where she was getting ready for shuffleboard (which apparently required flowing turquoise gaucho pants and a white fitted top neatly tucked in, a bright coral sash tied rakishly around her waist). "I'm not sure all the makeup and everything is my thing."

Millie looked me up and down approvingly. "Honey, it's not about wearing the paint and the pretties. It's about feeling that way no matter *what* you're wearing." She winked broadly. "Or not wearing."

"I'll be wearing this. All night long," I said dryly.

She smiled. "You look perfect."

THE PARTY WASN'T a hotel event, but a coming-out party for one of Jason's friends—literally. Gary had just come out to his parents and wanted to celebrate finally being out of the closet at age thirty-two.

"Why did he wait?" I asked as Jason dug in one of the coolers circling the pile of wood stacked on the beach behind a modest stilt house down one of the winding side streets of the island. It was clearly waiting to be a bonfire as soon as someone lit a match.

He examined his catch: a Michelob Ultra and a wine margarita. "His family is really conservative. Pretty religious. He wasn't sure how they would react."

I thought about my family and how they had reacted to Millie's news. How difficult it must be if the person you were didn't conform to the strictures of the ones who had raised you.

He looked over at me, brandishing the offerings. "I think I'm going to throw these back and try again—what do you think?"

I nodded, still feeling awkward, and he moved to the next cooler, where another couple was already rummaging around. "This is the money cooler," the woman said, grinning over her shoulder at us. "Microbrews. We're gonna sit on this one so no one else knows about it."

She passed two dark bottles to Jason and he saluted her with one of them before turning back to me. Behind him, sure enough, the man closed the cooler after they got their drinks and sat on top of it while he twisted off the tops.

"How did his family react?" I asked as I followed Jason away from the dormant fire pit and the crowd and toward the edge of the water.

He worked the top off a Key West Sunset Ale and handed it to me before opening the other bottle, dipping his head back toward the party. "That's his mom over there by the ice luge. His dad needed a little more time."

I watched the woman—she looked to be in her fifties, petite

and with a sweet, bewildered smile—nod at the people coming up one by one to kneel at the end of the ice sculpture and open their mouths for the chilled liquid a guy in a Hawaiian shirt hanging open over his bare chest was pouring into the top of the slide. A younger man stood beside her with an arm tightly around her waist and a smile so big it split his face, introducing her to everyone who queued up for a shot, and I assumed that was Gary.

"That's nice. I hope his dad comes around."

Jason clinked his bottle against mine. "To Gary's dad."

"To Gary's dad."

It was different standing here with Jason from the night we'd both been dodging the wedding. Then we'd happened upon each other and I could wander off anytime I wanted. Now we were here together. I was conscious of the way his throat moved as he tipped back his beer and took a long sip, of the dark hair on his forearm, matching the little thatch of it at the open collar of the pale linen shirt he wore. I was aware of my own bare arms and ankles, the way the wind rippled the thin knit of my top against my stomach. I shivered.

"You want to go get one of the blankets?" he offered.

"Maybe after the sun sets."

We stood side by side while it sank closer to the water, watching and not talking. I wondered whether Jason was as nervous as I was. He hadn't cracked a single joke since he'd picked me up twenty minutes earlier—Millie having left to pick up the Merry Widows already, thankfully, so I was at least spared the discomfort of her seeing us off like we were gawky prom dates.

"Know how you can tell the tourists from the locals?" he asked, when the sun had become a fat half circle of orange sitting on the horizon and was sinking fast.

I shook my head. "Cameras around their necks? Sunburn?"

Finally he let loose that grin and I realized I'd missed seeing it. "Sunset. Most people, if we're near the shore, will come out and watch it." I looked to our left and right and realized he was right; the few dozen guests already here had lined up at various places on the beach and were watching too, their faces lit up ruddy in the reflection. "But the tourists leave as soon as the sun's gone."

"What do the locals do? Isn't that the end of the show?"

"Aha!" He held up a finger. "The locals know that you only get the best part if you hang on past the end."

I laughed, but as soon as the sun sank all the way out of sight I could see he was right. The streaky clouds lit up like embers, the sky a fire behind them. As we stood there—it couldn't have been more than twenty minutes—the orange faded to coral and the clouds to dark red, then violet against a pink and lavender backdrop, before the whole thing finally faded to a darker and darker blue.

As the sound of applause started around us I realized my vision was shimmering. "That was amazing," I said. "I'm glad I had the inside track on sticking around."

"You're welcome," he said, toasting me again. "Let's get in line for the fish tacos."

Someone had lit the bonfire and the flames were crackling up the kindling and popping tongues out through the larger sticks and logs tepeed up above them, and the music from the portable speakers was louder now that the sun was down. The band was setting up on a clearly recently built wooden platform near the line of palm trees bordering the scrub line, and Jason and I finished our beers and cajoled another set from the gatekeepers of the "money cooler" before joining the growing crowd over by the grills.

"So what do you do when you're not on vacation, Grace?"

"I'm in family law—estate planning," I said. It was louder over here near the speakers, and I leaned toward him, raising my voice. I liked that I didn't have to stand on tiptoe to reach his ear, and this close I caught that same scent from before—soap and a little bit of coconut.

"You mean like wills, living wills, that kind of thing?"

I nodded. "That, yes, but not just that," I said. "There's a lot more to think about—health directives, financial planning for possible assisted living or extended care, and then a bunch of arcane issues you might never have thought about. A lot of people think that stuff will all take care of itself, but if you ask them they've got pretty definitive ideas over which family members they want making the hard decisions for them—or worse, the state."

He was grinning at me, and I swiped a hand over my face, worrying lip gloss had leached down my chin. The unfamiliar weight and slickness made me conscious of my mouth. "What?"

"Nothing. I like the way you talk about it. It's not boring when you talk about it."

His breath tickled the loose hair around my temples and I smoothed it behind my ear, watching his eyes follow the movement. "Brian—my . . . I mean, the person I know because I lived with him for years," I said, correcting myself, and was rewarded with a full-throated laugh. "He always says this is the dullest field of law."

"I'm starting to think Brian is kind of an idiot. No offense." He said it so good-naturedly I couldn't take any—in fact, I laughed.

We were at the front of the line now, and someone had set up a table with plates and paper towels and tortillas, all of which we stocked up on, then let the cheerfully swearing Rasta guy tending the grill heap some unidentified white fish flecked with spices onto our plates with metal tongs. After that was another table with condiments: a huge Lexan full of coleslaw, squeeze bottles of tartar sauce and cocktail sauce, jalapeños and tomatoes and cilantro. I took some of everything and waited for Jason to do the same; then we headed back around the fire where other partygoers had taken our beer buddies' idea and claimed the coolers as seats.

We sat directly on the sand, our plates in our laps, and used our hands to fold the overstuffed tacos together as well as we could, tipping our heads sideways to eat them as liquid ran out the backs and down our wrists. We licked that off too, laughing. The fish was spicy and tender and hot, a perfect counter to the cooling crunch of slaw. Afterward Jason took our plates to a trash bin tucked behind a stand of seagrass, and we rinsed our hands under the stream from a hose snaking to the house behind the thicket of seagrass and palmettos, drying them on our shorts.

"I'll be right back," he said, and pounded off up the sandy path toward the road, where we'd left his Jeep.

The band was warming up, a clashing of instruments and mic checks, and I wandered over to the stage area to watch. By the time the outdoor lights came on, illuminating the stage, and the crowd started to catcall, Jason was back.

"Here you go," he said, holding out a bright blue sweatshirt in one hand. "It gets cold after the sun's down if you're standing still."

I pulled it over my head, noticing his hotel's name embroidered on the chest. "Thank you."

But we weren't standing still for long. The band kicked in with a driving melody punctuated by the incongruous mix of an accordion and a rubboard and a violin, and almost without even checking in with me my body started to bob in time. We were close to the stage, and suddenly a flood of people surged around us, everyone bouncing and jumping and flailing in what I imagined was the only kind of dancing the frenetic beat dictated. I couldn't hear my own laughter over the music.

"What is this?" I shouted to Jason.

He was watching me, eyes squinting with his wide grin. "Kind of a funky zydeco thing. I love these guys." He threw up his hands, jerking his body and his head back and forth like some kind of orchestrated seizure, and I giggled helplessly until I realized he wasn't goofing around . . . he was *dancing*.

He looked like a crazed Muppet, all-out, full-throttle, total-body gyrating . . . but I'd never seen anyone *commit* like that. He threw his hands in the air like he just didn't care, along with everyone else in the crush that now surrounded me, and I couldn't remember why I'd ever worried about how I looked on the dance floor. Up went my arms, and I let the infectious crazy-fast beat dictate how my body moved. I still couldn't hear my own laughter, but I could feel it like champagne bubbles, rising up and up and up and popping free into the air.

BY THE TIME the band took a break, I was breathless and covered in sweat, the fleecy shirt Jason had brought me long since shed on the sand. He retrieved it for me as we shuffled back toward the coolers to find some water, and I left my shoes near the fire beside his as we walked to the ocean to cool down. The polite gulf waves slid along our bare feet, taking enough sand back with them each time that slowly our toes sank in and disappeared.

"I have an idea," Jason said, shifting his weight back and forth with a faint sucking sound in the sand.

"An idea?"

"About the dullest law field."

I smiled. "Okay. What's your idea?"

"What would you think about presenting a seminar about it here? I mean at the hotel."

I turned to face him, nearly losing my balance when my feet stayed anchored. "A seminar? You mean like a class in estate planning?"

He nodded. "A class, a workshop—whatever you think suits the material. We have this ridiculously large meeting room for an island the size of a Brazil nut." He swung his hand holding the water bottle behind him, indicating Cypress Key. "I've been wanting us to host more local events—not just for the residents, but bring folks over from Fort Myers, Tampa, Naples."

"I don't know. I've never thought about presenting something like that—it's generally kind of a sit-down one-on-one."

"You could add some Tony Robbins coal walking. To keep it lively."

I smiled. "Funny . . . I've toyed with the idea of writing a little booklet or pamphlet or something," I admitted. "A guide for people to think about some of these things well before they need to—and to talk about them with their families." My cheeks grew warm at words I'd never spoken aloud to anyone. "Most people treat end-of-life planning like a shameful secret—

something you don't talk about, that you pretend isn't there. But just like a good parent will have the facts-of-life talk with their kids when they're old enough, I think it's so important to be able to talk about the *other* facts of life—the facts of . . . well, death. It doesn't have to be the monster under the bed."

Jason was watching me appreciatively as the words fountained out—exactly as though I weren't boring him at all. "Well, this is kind of your target audience for that. Don't you know our state mottoes? 'Florida: home of the newly wed and nearly dead.' 'Death's doorstep.' 'Where America goes to die.' There is a *lot* of fertile ground here for estate planning."

"'Death's waiting room,'" I said, remembering the man on the escalator when I'd first arrived.

His teeth flashed white in the darkness. "There you go. We'd need time to get some marketing behind it to make it worthwhile, but you could stay . . . or come back for it. Maybe even as a regular thing, like once a month or something?"

There was a question mark at the end of his sentence, a lift of his voice as he watched me so intently that something fluttered in a panic in my stomach.

"I can't have children."

The words fell out of me like gumballs from a broken machine, and in the silence that followed them my stomach tightened. I'd never said it out loud before, and blurting it to a man I'd just met felt absurd.

"Oh, okay . . ." In the pause the swell of voices behind us seemed loud. "I can't play golf."

I shot a sharp gaze to him, uncertain whether he was mocking me.

"I mean it," he reiterated. "I've tried a bunch—I always end up unable to use my right wrist for like a week afterward. I'm pretty sure I'm doing it wrong, but damned if I know how. Do you know how embarrassing it is to tell people you injured yourself playing *golf*?"

"I don't think that's on the same level, exactly."

"It is if someone really likes golf."

"Do you?" I asked. "Really like golf?"

He met my eyes for a long moment. "I can play it or not play it—depends on the situation. I'm golf-neutral, I guess."

I frowned, the effervescence of the evening dissipated. "Brian wasn't neutral. At all. But I didn't know that until the doctor told us we couldn't. That *I* couldn't," I said, moving my gaze out over the water, the soft-glowing tips of the waves, the occasional twinkle of light at the horizon that told of distant boats, my throat closing up too tight to talk.

"To be clear, we're still talking about golf here, right?"

The laugh he startled from me came out as a snort just as a strong wave surged in over our feet and fountained upward. I squealed at the surprise and the chill of it and we danced back a few feet to a new line of safety.

"Look, Grace," Jason said as I brushed damp sand from the hem of my pants, and I looked up at the solemnity of his tone. "I don't know why things like that happen, or what it might have meant. But I spent a lot of time after Anne trying to figure it out. And what I came up with was that sometimes things are gonna go down a certain way no matter what." He stood a few steps upshore, and the lights from the party and the stage limned his shape and left his face in darkness except for the glint of his eyes. "I just mean . . . maybe you and Brian were together for the part of your paths that ran the same direction . . . until they didn't anymore. And that was going to happen regardless of anything either of you did or didn't do. You just each moved on to a different part of your map."

I could hear my heartbeat in my ears even over the music someone had started up again from the speakers, feel it jarring my rib cage. I took a step toward Jason, and then another one, and when I reached him I stood there for a long moment, our eyes locked, and then I slowly, very deliberately leaned closer until I could catch the slight tang of dried sweat on him, feel his breath.

His mouth was soft, a hint of stubble, and he stood, hands by his sides, and let me take the lead. I was grateful, little by little exploring the small cleft above his top lip, the tender inside of his bottom one, the *new* taste of him. His arms lifted and then dropped, as if he'd willed them down, and I reached for his hands and moved them to my waist under the thin fabric of my shirt, wanting the feel of his fingers on that hidden skin, and he splayed his fingers wide and pulled me closer.

I shivered, not from the cold.

The sonic boom of the band starting to play again broke the moment, and when I pulled away he let me. We stood with only a few inches separating us, breathing each other's air.

Finally his face broke into the smile that looked like its natural resting position, those little upward-flicking triangles at either corner. "You want to go listen to the second set?"

I smiled, nodded, and let him take my hand and lead me back to the party.

AFTER EXHAUSTING OURSELVES with another frenetic dance session I pleaded exhaustion—I hadn't had as much exercise in the last year as I'd had in the past few days. Jason retrieved two more bottled waters icy and dripping from a tub and we walked away from the light and noise and music, down the beach and into the darkness, talking.

By the time we'd turned around and headed back to the car, the crowd had thinned and I was surprised to see that more than an hour had passed.

"This is usually the time of night when the kids drive to the mainland and go gorge themselves at the Waffle House," Jason said. He'd taken my hand when we'd turned around and held it for a while, and I liked the feeling of his fingers threaded with mine, but as we got closer to the party he let go, as if unsure whether I wanted to make an entrance looking like a couple amid a group of people I'd likely never see again. It was silly and sweet and thoughtful.

I smiled. "Is that what the kids these days do?"

His eyes drew to slits as he grinned. "Sometimes I open my mouth and my dad falls out."

"Yeah. I notice that too, with my mom. The other day I had to actually stop myself from warning a kid at the beach to wait thirty minutes after eating before she went swimming." The idea warmed me, though—that part of my mother lived on inside me. As angry and disappointed as I might feel about her right now, it was comforting to dip into the well of love that lay underneath it and realize it was still there.

"So what do you say—want to reclaim our youth and go grab some late-night waffles?"

I was tempted but shook my head. "I probably need to get back to Millie's. Tomorrow's our last day together before I go back."

"I get it. I'm really glad you came out, though."

"Me too."

The drive home was short and intimate in the dim glow from the dashboard, the open windows blowing sea-scented air through my hair, cooling my still-sweaty temples. Jason reached over again and took my hand, and I fit my fingers into the unfamiliar shape of his.

He walked me up the stairs to the front door, like a gentleman caller in a Tennessee Williams play, waited as I unlocked the door with the key Millie had given me and told me to keep. Palm trees shivered in the indigo night.

"I'm sort of thinking you'll be back," Jason said.

"I sort of am too."

"I hope it's not too long."

"So do I."

"I'm going to call you about those seminars. I wasn't kidding."

"Me either. I like the idea."

"I'm going to call you anyway. Maybe for no reason."

I laughed. "I'd like that."

This time he initiated the kiss, long and slow and heart-tripping as his tongue ran along my lips and I let it inside, meeting it with mine, his hand on the small of my back pulling me closer. It had been a long time since I'd been kissed like this—leisurely and sensually and with intent—and I felt my heart quicken, a bolt of base desire flash through me. For a moment I thought about taking the prom metaphor to its inevitable end—easing open the door, pulling him after me, tiptoeing into my bedroom, and sneaking Jason back out before Millie ever woke up.

I knew I wasn't ready for that. But the fact that I even considered it was gratifying. I was breathless when we pulled apart.

He moved his hands to either side of my face, cradling it, looking at me for a long moment that should have been uncomfortable but wasn't. "You travel safe, Grace," he said finally.

He leaned in again for one last soft kiss, and then stepped away, halfway down the steps, till he saw me safely inside and I closed the door behind me.

# Twenty-three

I knew I was in for a Gitmo-style grilling the next morning, but I didn't even mind. It came over the Belgian waffles Millie set in front of me.

"What's *that* smile all about?"

I looked up from my plate and the memory of Jason's breakfast invitation. "Come on, now. You know."

Her face broke into a smile like the sun. "Oh, thank God—I thought you might play coy and make me excavate it out of you. Tell me everything."

So I did, like we were two girlfriends at a sleepover . . . about the whole evening, including the kiss—both of them. The only thing I left out was my momentary consideration of something more—partly because she was my aunt, but mostly because she didn't need to know she'd been that right about the possibility after all. Self-confidence was not one of Millie's problems.

I braced for the full-court matchmaking press, but she surprised me.

"I'm glad you had fun. It sounds like just what you needed."

I swished the last bite of waffle in the puddle of maple syrup and melted butter on my plate, angling a look at her where she sat beside me working on her own breakfast. "You're not going to tell me why he's perfect for me? Set us up on another date? I thought that was your stock in trade."

"Are you crediting me with setting this up? Seems like this one happened all on its own."

She was right. Except for calling him to set up the punching bag, at no point in our affiliation so far could Millie have been accused of pulling the strings—I'd run into Jason organically on every other occasion, and he'd been the one to initiate our date. Something about the thought pleased me.

She didn't wait for my answer. "Sometimes people come into our lives at the right time, for a specific reason. Perhaps Jason was simply your starter pony for getting back on the horse once you go back home."

The stark reminder that this was my last day here—in paradise with my aunt Millie, who had undoubtedly come into my life at the right time for a reason—sat uneasily in my belly.

"I'll be back to visit, you know," I said, putting my fork down and facing her.

Millie just chewed contentedly, then swallowed. "Of course you will, dear. We're family."

MILLIE APPARENTLY WANTED to cram into my last day every single activity the island had to offer that we hadn't yet partaken of. After breakfast we got dressed and then she drove us across the island to a tiki hut slumped tiredly beside a tiny convenience store selling mostly sunscreen and cheap towels. She poked her head inside the store and said something to the counterman, who shuffled out a few moments later, swaying side to side like a Weeble as he made his way to the hut, jingling an enormous set of keys that I couldn't imagine he needed for this modest setup. A moment later he rolled out on two wheels like a mall security guard.

While he wordlessly went back into the hut, Millie gave me a quick tutorial in Segway operation and safety—"Because Charlie's idea of lessons is to step off the thing and hand it over," she murmured sotto voce, and I wondered whether this stout man was the Fat Charlie Jason had told me about, of Ecstasy punch fame.

When he rolled back out with another one, stepping off and pushing the handles into Millie's hands with no more than a grunt, off we went, leaning into the breeze like bowsprits.

We wheeled all over the island, everywhere the contraption's tires could navigate, and it was bizarrely fun, the Segway seeming like an extension of my body after the initial few awkward moments. It was a perfect way to see the entirety of Cypress Key closer than by car as we swung down every street, gawking at the eclectic architecture, being chased by loose dogs, buzzing down walkways at the little market, which was blessedly free of pedestrian obstacles this early in the day. At Helene's boutique we waved and leaned the machines against the front window—"they're perfectly safe here," Millie assured me—and explored some of the shops we hadn't gone into before: the Dragonfly gallery studded with pottery and tapestries and jewelry and wallpapered with colorful canvases featuring tropical images; Southern Exposure, the shop where the owner, Sheila Benton, sold hand-dyed fabrics splayed across every surface like colorful flags; the gourmet deli. We stopped for a quick lunch at Something Fishy, and Chelsea waved as I came in. "How many dozen today, Grace?" she shouted from behind the bar.

Millie lifted an eyebrow. "You're already a regular here, I see."

After sharing a plate of fries and piles of shrimp (three dozen, for the record), we mounted our Segways and wheeled back to Charlie's store, where he greeted us with another grunt and a jerk of his head toward the tiki hut and we leaned them alongside.

After that we parked at the large public beach I hadn't yet explored and walked off our big breakfast and lunch, letting the waves lap our bare feet like frisky puppies. Then it was on to rent paddleboards at Jason's hotel, where stone-faced ninja Viviana directed us to an open-air counter behind the hotel.

"Would you let Jason know we're here, if he's around when we're finished?" I said as she turned back to her keyboard at the front desk.

She glanced up, frowning, as if surprised to see we were still standing there. "I'll see if he's available. Enjoy your adventure." The perky words from the poker face were disconcerting.

"I'm not sure customer service is the right field for her," I muttered under my breath as Millie and I walked off, and I saw her smile.

"There's something going on there. I'm still figuring out what," she murmured.

Paddleboarding was basically surfing without waves, I learned as the instructor paddled out with us and showed me how to hurl myself up onto the board and find my balance. Millie, no surprise, nimbly found her feet and her "firmly planted center," as Hero, the instructor, kept exhorting me to do. ("Is that his real name?" I'd asked Millie quietly while he filled out our paperwork, and she'd lifted one shoulder. "Who knows? People come to the beach to reinvent themselves.") The woman was more than twice my age, and easily that much my fitness level. Damned if there didn't seem to be something to that whole benefits-of-an-active-lifestyle thing. I was going to have to find a way to maintain my Florida activity levels even when I was stuck inside for the long Missouri winter.

I didn't want to think about that now, though. When I finally figured out how to gain—and keep—my feet on the board, I let myself enjoy the gentle bobbing of the waves, the slosh of the cool water over my feet, and the warm sunshine on my bare shoulders, Millie paddling silently beside me paralleling the shoreline.

Jason came out just as we were pulling our boards to the sand an hour or so later, his appreciative gaze reminding me gratifyingly that I wore nothing but my one-piece bathing suit. After we toweled off and Millie and I each tied one of the bright sarongs we'd bought at Sheila's fabric store around our waists, he insisted on treating us to frozen drinks on the hotel deck overlooking the pool and the gulf beyond. While he joined us for a few minutes, I told Millie about his idea for estate planning seminars at the hotel, and she greeted the news with a nod and a Mona Lisa smile.

"What an excellent idea. No shortage of future stiffs in Florida," was all she said.

Back home a hot shower melted the fresh soreness from my muscles, and when I got out, wrapping one of Millie's plush white guest towels around my torso, I was startled by the woman in the mirror: tanned and blond tipped and glowing.

Millie cooked and I cleaned as though we'd been performing the ritual for years, and after dinner we took mugs of her thick hot chocolate to the lanai and lounged on her comfortable furniture, talking so late into the night that she finally had to lean over to nudge me to go to bed when my eyes started to droop. I hated for the day—the whole week—to end.

But I was starting to hope it might also signal a new beginning.

---

I WOKE UP early enough to watch the sky lighten outside my window, waking up the gentle gulf in a wash of pink and coral, and quickly packed. With my unprecedented shopping spree my first day I'd had to borrow an extra suitcase from Millie—"You'll bring it back on your next visit," she'd said, dismissing my protests, and I liked the warm glow of that light at the end of the tunnel of going back to Missouri . . . to the realities of a Midwest winter . . . to Brian and Angelica and my real life that had begun to seem much further away than a week and a thousand-plus miles.

But I felt like I was ready. With Millie in my life now I felt less alone in the world. Thanks to Jason I had a fresh sense of new beginnings—maybe he was a vacation "fling," maybe a rebound, but our date had shown me that there was life after Brian. Maybe not right away . . . maybe not for a while. But eventually I would get there. Even my mortification about my behavior with Brian had dissipated, absorbed into a comfortable acceptance that I'd simply been angry, furious . . . and had had a right to be.

Despite the extra suitcase, packing was a tight fit—even minus Brian's old T-shirt that I'd been sleeping in, which now lay in the trash bin in Millie's guest bath. It was time to let go of some things.

I held the box of my mother's letters for a long moment, debating whether I needed that too. I knew what they contained, and I wanted to move forward now, not look back. But they were a piece of my mom—whom I loved regardless of what I'd learned from their contents—and in the end I crammed them, box and all, into a corner of the second suitcase before flipping the lid and zipping it shut.

At my suggestion Millie and I took breakfast—a truly transformative onion-and-pepper frittata with scratch-made fluffy biscuits—down onto the dock, where we ate in our laps as the water shimmered and splashed off to the horizon.

My heart hurt at saying goodbye to this scenery. To this little island I'd run away to that had provided sanctuary in every way.

To Millie.

She had finished her breakfast, her plate atop mine on the little table between us, and now leaned back in the chaise, looking out over the water as if she saw something that I didn't. The soft morning light illuminated the wispy down of white fuzz at her temples, her blue eyes so much like mine translucent in the reflected light off the water. For all her energy, her insuppressible zest, her freakish fitness for her age, this morning my six-foot aunt looked small, as if something in her felt as diminished by my pending departure as I did. I'd finally found her at eighty-one years old. It seemed painfully unjust that I might have her in my life for only a short time.

I still had the adjustable home-care bed we'd bought to make my mother more comfortable and ease her getting in and out as her mobility deteriorated. I could so easily take care of Millie if—when—she needed it. Or before. The idea of my vibrant, colorful aunt sharing my quiet home with me made me smile. If she didn't want to live with me, I could at least settle her somewhere in Sugarberry or even Kansas City—have her close by for whatever time we had in each other's lives.

"Aunt Millie . . ." I started, searching for the right words. "What would you think about moving to Missouri?"

Her laughter burst through the peaceful morning sounds of the island waking up, as though I'd told a great joke. "Oh, honey, I spent the first act of my life trying to figure out how to get the hell out of that place and never go back. I'll be damned if I wind up there in my last act."

The foolish idea popped like a bubble—of course she wouldn't want to leave the paradise she'd created. Of course she would never want to go back to the place that had cast her away all those years ago. Millie had never really belonged in Sugarberry—I could see that so clearly even though I hadn't known the person she was in her youth. She was as much a part of Cypress Key as the knobby-kneed cypresses themselves, neither one imaginable without the other.

She must have seen something of my thoughts in my expression. "Oh, holy night. Ira used to say the filter between my mind and my mouth was missing. I'm sorry, Gracie—I only meant that this is where *my* soul belongs. I'm sure you feel the same way about Sugarberry."

Did I? I didn't thrill to my hometown, didn't feel a pull to it when I'd been away, didn't wax on about the beauty of its sprawling green fields or wide blue skies. It was just where I was . . . where I'd always been.

But I did love it. I loved the fact that Mrs. Aronson had lived in the house next door to mine for the entirety of my life—had watched me grow from a baby to the adult I (usually) was. I loved that I could greet by name nearly every person I ran into within a five-mile radius of my house. That those people knew me, cared about me, looked out for me. After my mom passed away, for weeks a steady stream of casseroles and soups and baked goods had funneled into Mom's kitchen, far more than I could eat, but they arrived with plenty of people to help me work through them: families whose estates our family firm had helped plan dropping in to visit with me, parents of kids I'd gone to school with, their children long gone to more vibrant towns. Months after most people would have forgotten the loss of someone not in their immediate family, people still stopped me in the grocery store or at the bank to tell me how much Mom was missed, to see how I was doing, to ask whether there was anything I needed. I'd been too fogged by my own grief to see it, but in a town like Sugarberry, I realized, you were never truly alone.

Millie had never experienced that side of our small town. No wonder she had none of the affection for it that I realized lived in me after all.

"Of course you wouldn't want to go back there," I said. "After everything they . . . well. I'll just miss you." Heat rose up the back of my neck. "And I'm worried about who's going to take care of you."

Millie's eyes softened. "Oh, Gracie, did you think that was why I wanted your mother to come down? Why I wanted you to?"

I hadn't consciously thought of it till that moment, but I realized it had been percolating in my mind nearly since I'd met her. I shrugged with one shoulder.

"Sweetheart . . ." She leaned forward and took my hand, then kissed the back of my fingers—tenderly, like a mother would a newborn baby. "I'm much more concerned with who is going to take care of *you*."

# Twenty-four

My mother's house looked exactly the same way I'd left it, but it felt distant to me, like a museum exhibit or an old photo unearthed from an earlier time.

I peeled off the coat I'd almost forgotten to pack, tucked away unneeded in one corner of Millie's guest closet all week, and shivered—I'd cranked up the heat the second I let myself inside—from the sixty-two I'd left it on to the balmy eighty my skin had gotten used to in Florida, hoping the high setting would chase the chill away quickly, but it would take time for the house to shake off the cold that had settled in while I'd been gone. Then before I'd even made it past the foyer I texted Millie to let her know I was home safe. It was only a little after six, but already full dark—even the lights I'd left on timer couldn't push back the gloom completely.

As if from reflex my eyes had tracked to Brian's house on my way in, the windows dark except for a single light in what I knew was his office. I saw the outline of him inside, head bent over his desk, but for the first time the arrow of pain didn't lance my heart as I drove by, just a twinge of regret. I wasn't sure for what.

I unpacked in my quiet bedroom, hanging my new clothes in the center of the closet despite the fact that I wouldn't need most of them for months, not till the temperatures crept higher than sixty. I liked looking at them, liked what they represented. This week I'd go through the rest of the closet and get rid of anything that didn't make me feel the way I did in the ones from Helene's boutique and go buy some that did. Maybe I'd ask Susie to go shopping with me—though I'd have to be careful that the shock of it didn't kill her.

I went to bed early, still on Florida time, and slept nearly ten hours. If I didn't feel quite ready to go back into the office and face Brian . . . well, at least I was well rested. I stopped at Sweet Stuff for doughnuts on my way into work, missing Millie's gourmet breakfasts, and pulled into the office, grateful for the brief reprieve when I didn't see Brian's car in the parking lot.

I cringed at the memory of what it must have looked like the morning after I'd fed the birds.

Susie was at her desk working, and when I came through the door she glanced up with a pleasant smile of greeting—then a moment later she nearly knocked over her chair standing to come around the desk.

"Grace!" she exclaimed. "I'm so happy to see you. And not just because of these." She lifted the box from my hand and set it on the raised counter of her desk before folding me into a tight squeeze I returned. I'd let myself become so isolated over the past year—even longer, really. How had I not realized that I still had family here?

"I figured I'd bring them in, since I missed Friday."

Susie pulled away but kept hold of my arms, examining me. "You look different," she said, as if it were an accusation.

I laughed. "Tan, I know. And that's with major sunscreen.

Plus . . . well, makeup." I'd needed the extra boost of confidence Millie's makeover gave me, so I'd left my hair down and put on a swipe of mascara and lip gloss.

Susie was frowning, still looking me over as if I were a prize Thoroughbred. "Nope, that's not it. Or not all of it. You look . . ." She hunted for a word. "More solid."

"Is that a nice way of saying I gained weight? Because I probably did—my aunt cooks like Anthony Bourdain."

"Your *aunt*?"

So we huddled together on the sofa in my office like gal pals while we ate doughnuts and I told her about my trip—not everything: not about Millie's past, because that wasn't my story to tell (I said she'd left the family young to travel and they didn't agree with her lifestyle); and not about Jason, because I didn't want well-intentioned Susie to make more of it than it had been in her excitement that I was "moving on," as I knew she'd been hoping I'd do for a long time now.

Susie was stunned to hear about my long-lost relative—but she'd moved here twenty-five years before with her husband to raise her kids "somewhere saner than Chicago" and didn't have the deep generations-long history with Sugarberry many in town did. For the first time I wondered whether some of the old-timers had known about Milton Bean, and why she—*he*— left for good. But I couldn't imagine nosy Marbelle Mason keeping that juicy morsel to herself all these years if she did. Maybe Milt just faded into the tapestry of Sugarberry history, another of the town's peregrines who wandered away and never came back.

"Well, the vacation did you a world of good—that's plain as daylight. You look like a different woman."

I felt like a different woman. As if my feet were planted more squarely on the ground, or I took up more space in the world. Maybe that was what Susie meant by "solid"—as if I'd been transparent before, ephemeral.

That feeling lasted right up until I heard Brian's voice in the front entryway, twenty minutes after Susie and I mopped up our crumbs and went to work, and my heart sped up like a runaway semi. It wasn't the same kind of flutter I was used to—I clutched my armrests for support and realized this adrenaline surge was made up of as much trepidation and anger as it was longing. But I took a deep breath in and forced myself to blow it slowly out, picturing the serene gulf lapping into Millie's backyard, paying attention to my stammering heartbeat until I finally felt it start to slow.

Right up until Brian appeared in my doorway with a handful of roses.

"THERE SHE IS!" he exclaimed, smiling.

The roses were orange—not romance red, but not friendship yellow either. Did they signify something in between? Were they a palliative, a peace offering after the last heated time we'd spoken . . . or did they indicate more, some sea change in his outlook that had finally brought about the realization I'd once prayed for: that he really wasn't ready to lose me?

Or did they mean anything at all?

My throat felt tight, a pulse beating in my neck so strongly I was sure he could see it.

"What's that for?" I eked out, standing as if it would help me regain my equilibrium.

He held out the cellophane-wrapped bouquet. "They're for you—kinda sad winter convenience-store roses, but it was the best I could find. I'm so glad you're home!"

I made no move to come around my desk, concentrating on my breathing, but it didn't seem to be helping.

My head shook, seemingly of its own volition. "I don't . . . I don't want those," I stammered.

His arms drooped to his sides, the cellophane cracking against his leg and leaving a wet mark on his gray pants he didn't seem to notice. "What do you mean? I got them for *you*. I was so excited you're back." He wore the bewildered, wounded expression that used to send cheerleaders swarming to comfort him after his team lost a game against one of our high school rivals, that made his mom bend the rules and give him whatever it was he'd asked for . . . that always made me forget anything at all except fixing whatever it was that had snuffed out the light of his smile.

"Okay," I said finally. "I'm sorry." I cringed inwardly to hear myself saying the words as I stepped over to where he stood.

Brian's upset cleared like a passing cloud as he held out the flowers again, the orange blooms washed out and dingy in the fluorescent overheads, their petals tipped with brown and beginning to curl.

It was as if the flowers represented every second-rate, inadequate thing I'd ever been offered, every blameless thing I'd ever apologized for, and I had a sudden vision of backhanding the sad bouquet, sending it sailing across the room, wilting orange petals flying everywhere.

*Screw it!* Millie's advice echoed in my ears.

Something wound up and ready to snap inside me abruptly let go—not with gathering spring force suddenly released into violent action, but as if the pressure building behind it had simply given way.

"Brian," I said, "why are you giving flowers to another woman when you have a girlfriend . . ." I swallowed. "A *pregnant* girlfriend at home?"

He looked as if I'd struck him. "I didn't mean it like . . . Grace, Angelica knows how close we are. I made that completely clear to her from the very beginning—I swear to you. It was a deal breaker—there was no way I was going to choose between you. She knows that a hundred percent."

I knew he was offering the information as a reassurance to me, as a kindness even, a demonstration of his affection for me. He didn't see how hurtful, how insulting his words were.

I took in another deep breath, letting it out slowly. "I don't want flowers from you," I repeated. "They are not appropriate, and they send the wrong message—not just to me, but to Angelica. Why don't you take these home to her tonight?" As he stared at me, silent and stunned, I put one hand on his upper arm, turning him around. "Now if you'll excuse me, I have a lot of catching up to do after a week away."

MY BUBBLE OF calm popped the moment I closed the door behind him.

I tried sitting on the faded Turkish rug in the sitting area, focusing on my breath, picturing the roll of gentle waves and the soothing shushing of water and palms. But I couldn't sit still, couldn't concentrate for even a moment, and I leaped back to my feet, shaking out the excess energy in my hands.

I was much too keyed up to get anything productive accomplished here. I packed up everything I'd need to work from home and told Susie she could reach me there if she needed me.

As I drove past Brian's I saw an unfamiliar car in the driveway: a sleek, shiny black sporty two-door that could only be Angelica's—it was the vehicular equivalent of her. If she knew I was back would she have risked leaving her car out, after what I'd done to Brian's? Out of habit my eyes strayed up to our old bedroom window, now blocked by new curtains. By the time I got my car into the garage my hands were shaking, my throat so tight and my heart thunking so hard it was difficult to catch a full breath.

I could not go on like this. I would literally—*literally!*—give myself a heart attack.

I dropped everything on the foyer table and headed to the hall linen closet upstairs, where ratty sheets and flattened pillows went to die because my mom couldn't bear to throw out "perfectly good bedding." Grabbing handfuls of bed linens, I threw them heedlessly to the floor: faded floral sheets softened like old paper, lumpy comforters I'd last seen when I was at eye level to them, and stacks and stacks and stacks of stained pillows.

It was this last item I was after.

I grabbed up armfuls of the pillows—it took two trips—and went down to the basement, dumping them to the concrete floor. In the garage I found lengths of rope, each looped into a figure eight and neatly tied. None were long enough for what I needed—they were scrap ends from other projects, awaiting future utility—but I connected them all together with the hitch knots Millie had shown me when we tied off the kayaks, pulled them taut, and then carried them back downstairs with a roll of duct tape.

It was a bit of a tricky prospect by myself, but I pulled up pillow after pillow and secured them to a support beam—there had to have been more than a dozen of them—so that above and below the cinched middle of the worn-out pillows was a wide-open surface.

I gave it a test punch—gingerly, in case it wasn't enough padding to protect my hands from the metal pole underneath. When all I felt was give I tried again a little harder . . . and a little harder . . . until I was beating out my fury and frustration on the pillows like a bantamweight champ on speed.

It wasn't perfect . . . but it would do.

# Twenty-five

There was no feasible way to completely avoid Brian—not when he was my business partner. Not when he was my neighbor.

So by day while we worked together I adopted . . . not armor exactly, but a protective barrier, just enough to insulate me a little from the most acute of my feelings—like slipping on an emotional condom: I'd still feel things, but *less*. It was safer.

When Brian cautiously ducked his head into my office every day to say good morning, my imaginary prophylactic allowed me to offer a pleasant smile and return his greeting. When he asked whether he could bring me anything back for lunch, it let me thank him and hold up the sack lunch I'd taken to bringing in. When every now and then he came in and sat on the edge of my desk the way he used to and tried to talk about anything even remotely personal—my vacation; a movie he thought I might like; why none of the area law firms seemed to offer flexible hours, a career conundrum I knew was that of an expectant first-time mother—I gently redirected and pleaded busyness.

A few times the troubled look in his eyes bit at me, but I kept that tucked behind the protective barrier too, just as I did the feeling of loss for the friendship we'd once had that I actually found I missed too.

It was like paddleboarding over waters I used to once immerse myself in . . . skimming across the surface, gliding over anything that lay beneath. After a while Brian seemed to understand that this would be the new world order for us, and he finally stopped making overtures of friendship, merely offering a quick smile and wave on his way in and out of the office every day, exchanging polite chitchat about safe, neutral topics—our clients, new tax laws, the weather.

But it worked. Slowly my heartbeat didn't quicken any time I caught sight of him. One night I was home and pulling into the garage before I even realized I hadn't automatically turned to look into his windows as I drove past.

"Angel" was another story. Though I was blessedly removed from seeing her by day—despite Susie's report of her touring our office, Angelica kept her distance once I came home—I lived in dread of catching indisputable evidence of the family she and Brian were creating if I happened upon her walking out to get her mail on my way home, or crouched in the garden admiring the rows of tulip bulbs I'd planted two autumns back that would soon begin to unfurl tiny green shoots. It wasn't that I envied her the pregnancy—despite the ticking of my biological clock I still somehow didn't feel an irrefutable pull to be a mother. She was simply the visceral reminder of all that I *wasn't* to Brian, all that I had never been able to be: the beautiful, polished creature who fascinated him and always had . . . the woman he raced home to get to every night or ducked out at lunch to check on . . . the mother of the children he'd so desperately wanted.

So by night I gradually learned to distract myself as well, to stay busy.

My makeshift punching bag served in a pinch when pain arrowed through me and I needed an outlet. But retreating to my unfinished basement to beat the crap out of a pile of pillows all by myself made me start to feel a little weird, like a budding serial killer, so I signed up at a martial arts studio in Marceline, just twenty minutes up the road, for a weekly beginners class in krav maga street fighting—lots of punching and kicking and throwing things to the ground that I found even more satisfying than the punching bag.

I revamped my wardrobe, trying on every single item and getting rid of anything that didn't make me feel the way the clothes Millie and Helene had helped me select did: confident, comfortable, pretty (which was most of it). And I did indeed invite Susie to go shopping with me—her buoyant personality and conversation lightened whatever mood I happened to find myself in, and several evenings our shopping excursions stretched into dinner and glasses of wine.

I started tackling some home improvement projects I'd thought about while watching HGTV in the empty evening hours over the last year but never instigated because the idea of changing three generations of my family tastes felt disloyal. But it was my home now too. So I pulled down the dated wallpaper in the living room and painted the walls a cheery seafoam green that reminded me of the shallows lapping at the mangrove roots in Cypress Key. I called the Salvation Army and set up a pickup for the decades-old living room furniture—all except for my father's butt-sprung leather chair, which I gladly offered the drivers who'd come for the donation twenty bucks to haul to the curb for garbage pickup. I picked out new furniture at a big-box store—a light-colored sofa and chairs with simple, clean lines, plush and cushy like Millie's mismatched living room pieces to invite relaxed lingering, then brightened up all the rooms with accents of sunny coral and warm teal in pillows and fluffy throws and new lamps. I ordered a few of the tropical prints I'd admired from the Dragonfly boutique at the Cypress Key market, had them framed, and hung them on the walls. The snowy gray scenery outside my window was a poor consolation for the paradise I'd left behind, but the color and warmth I'd brought into the house made it seem a little brighter.

Little by little the house started to feel like my own. My *life* started to feel like my own.

I'd also been working on the seminar Jason and I talked about. He'd called a few days after I got home to tell me he'd already had interest from several of the locals and hotel guests and to suggest dates and ideas for publicizing the first one—I liked the idea that there would be more. We wound up talking for almost two hours, a pattern that repeated every time he called for "planning sessions" I was starting to think were only an excuse.

I didn't mind.

I called Millie several times a week, the sound of her voice like an anchor holding me firm even in choppy waters, and kept her up-to-date on all my activities. In return she wove reports from the island. With the punching bag installed she'd had the bright idea to offer boxing lessons, and she now coached "one skinny adolescent with budding anger-management issues, a tiny woman who hits like Muhammad Ali, and two middle-school children who seem amazed I can still ambulate, let alone punch." Bridget had met the perfect guy—again—and broken up with him—again—and Millie was still trying to get her to let her take a hand, to Bridget's staunch refusal. One of her matches, though, had turned into a surprise success story—

Millie had gotten it in her head to pair off two of the Merry Widows, Ruth and Harold. I remembered them from that first van ride: the grumpy, taciturn man with the eyebrows and the garrulous, extroverted woman with a nose for everyone else's business. I couldn't imagine what Millie might have seen that made her think they'd be a good match, with their oil-and-water dispositions, but the two had been "thick as thieves" for the last month, she reported. "If you want to know the truth," she said, lowering her voice as if confiding classified info, "I think Ruth likes having someone she can talk to who'll just listen for hours on end—and Harold is so deaf he can't hear her anyway."

That story made me laugh. "I miss you, Aunt Millie," I said. "It's so good to hear your voice."

"I miss you too, Gracie. You make plans to come down here again soon—that key I gave you works anytime." I found myself fingering it often on my key ring, like a talisman.

My life, which had felt adrift for so long, was stabilizing, and while it didn't resemble my old life in any way, there was a lot about it that was good.

Was I happy? I didn't know, exactly. I wasn't sure anymore what happy looked like. I missed Millie, and the beach, and the sense of belonging I'd had with her from almost the very beginning.

But I was creating a sense of belonging here as well—and reminding myself of the ways I had always belonged here in Sugarberry. Susie had become a good friend, and there were two other single women from the krav maga studio I'd gone out with several times after class, sweaty and dressed down, for drinks and meandering, laughing conversations. I checked on Mrs. Aronson next door a few times a week, bringing her casseroles or soup with the excuse that "I can't quite get the hang of cooking for one" so the proud woman would accept my offerings. It turned out she'd lost her brand-new husband in World War II—they'd been married only a week before he shipped out—and we spent a few chummy evenings talking about the adjustment to being single women. It was harder then, I realized, my respect for the independent older woman swelling. She was nothing like Millie, but being with her made my missing my aunt a little less acute.

Outside my house still felt like a demilitarized zone where I had to be on alert for unwanted sightings of Angelica and her steadily growing belly, but within my four walls I'd created a little oasis. And while work still felt awkward when it was just me and Brian in the office, when I was meeting with clients I lost myself in the challenges and pleasures of helping to give them peace of mind about their estates. And I was honoring my mother's legacy—taking care of the family firm that had meant so much to her.

Every night I climbed into my solitary bed—with crisp, brand-new sheets and a thick, warm comforter I'd picked out online—and before I closed my eyes I let them wander over to the dresser, where I'd set the box of my mother's letters the day I'd unpacked and had never touched it since.

As I cleaned out the house I'd unearthed what I'd thought might offer some insight—boxes of photo albums, loose pictures, and documents tucked away in a guest room closet. But several evenings spent sifting through them had shown that the purge of Millie—Milton—from my family's history had been complete.

So nearly every night as I waited for sleep to claim me, I lay blinking in the dimness of the room at the box, turning over and over in my mind how the family-oriented mother who'd raised me with such unconditional love could have docilely accepted our family's decision to turn their backs on one of their own.

WITH THE NEW distance I'd instigated between me and Brian at the office, I realized how much of our workdays had once been spent together. Until I'd returned from Florida we'd often float between each other's offices or meet in the conference room, going over client needs and paperwork, blurring the lines on whose clients were whose and who worked on what. It was less two lawyers sharing a practice and more as if we were two facets of a single estate planner: Brian was brilliant at staying on the cusp of ever-shifting tax and inheritance and probate laws, and I was better at the personal side of things—asking the hard, uncomfortable questions and plotting out the difficult terrain of end-of-life care, family squabbles, and bequeathal minutiae. Working together we'd been more efficient, helping each other and sharing files and information rather than the totally separate functioning we'd adopted now, and I found that my workload had increased because of it—by a lot. It wasn't entirely a bad thing—keeping myself busy and my mind occupied was a big part of my MO at the moment—but sometimes I worried the new arrangement shortchanged our clients.

Like the estate I was working on now. Bob Arthur's children from his first marriage had disavowed their father entirely after their mother walked out on him because of his alcoholism, despite Mr. Arthur's consistent efforts over the years, along with his second wife, Emilia, to be part of their lives. When his consulting business had sold to Microsoft for a considerable fortune, suddenly they'd come back into the Arthurs' lives as adults. I'd been working with the couple to ascertain their wishes—Mr. Arthur was angry, adamant that his kids receive nothing, believing that they were more interested in what his business windfall meant for them than in rebuilding any kind of real relationship with their father and the woman who had loved him even in the worst of his addiction. But Mrs. Arthur thought they should give the children the benefit of the doubt.

Privately I felt Mr. Arthur might soften his position, at least a little—he was deeply in love with Emilia and spoke frequently of trying to pay back all she'd sacrificed for him through his addiction. But meanwhile, he wanted to know the possible legal ramifications of leaving his children out of the will entirely, and what rights they might have to contest it if he did.

This was Brian's field of expertise, and I couldn't in good conscience let the Arthurs suffer because of my pride. I gathered up some documents and my laptop and headed down the once-familiar path to his office.

I heard him before I rounded the corner and was turning around to wait till he was off the phone when I caught my own name, spoken low.

"You know I can't ask Grace for that. Come on."

I froze. Who was he talking to?

"I know that. . . . I *know* that. . . . Angel, I know that too."

My stomach curdled. What on earth could Angelica covet from me that she didn't already have?

"Babe . . . I'm sorry. You know how sorry I am—I hate it too. But I can't just—" Despite his low tone, I could hear he was upset. "Aw, babe . . . please don't cry. Listen, I can come home again today for lunch, okay? I'll bring you something to—I know, but you have to eat. What can you keep down? . . . Oh, Angel . . ." His voice turned from frustrated to unbearably tender, slicing into me like knives. "It kills me to hear you this unhappy. We'll find you some kind of job—don't give up on Sugarberry. Don't give up on *me*. Not after we finally found our way back to each other."

The confirmation of everything I'd feared—that it was Angelica he'd loved all along . . . that I was a runner-up, a consolation prize—made my stomach twist. Brian had never sounded with me the way I'd just heard him with her. He would have done anything I'd needed, if I'd asked—but not with the soul-deep devotion I'd just heard in his voice. It had never been mine to begin with.

The nausea was rising up the back of my throat, and I suddenly feared I might actually be sick right here in the hallway outside Brian's office, vomiting my brains out while he pleaded with the woman he loved—had always loved.

I ran back the way I'd come, not caring whether Brian heard me, clattering the laptop and papers down on Susie's desk as I raced past. She called after me, asking if I was okay.

No. I wasn't okay. How would I ever be okay?

I made it into the bathroom and locked the door, but despite the sick feeling still churning in my belly nothing came up. I crouched on the cold tile floor, breathing hard and wondering how in the world we could possibly go on like this.

# Twenty-six

I made an excuse to Susie about food poisoning before quickly gathering up my things and leaving the office. I wanted to tell her the truth, but this was where our new deeper friendship butted up against our work relationship. For all our closeness she could never truly be a confidante—it wasn't fair to Susie to put her in a position of divided loyalties. And it wasn't fair to Brian either. This was his practice too.

But I fumed all the way home about whether it had to be. Clearly there was no way we were going to be able to continue partnering together when I couldn't manage to fully separate our personal lives and history from our professional ties.

What if I were to offer to buy him out?

I could do it. If I liquidated everything I had I could probably make a fair offer tomorrow. If not, I could always finance it—our firm was a mainstay in Sugarberry and the surrounding towns and work had always been plentiful and steady. Despite the population drain of younger generations, those who remained in the area were growing even older, so I didn't see business tapering off anytime soon. If it did I could always expand—lately I'd been fascinated with the fledgling field of virtual planning: consulting with clients via videoconferencing and a secure portal to expand the firm's reach past the narrow borders of our town.

But this wasn't solely my family legacy. This firm was in Brian's blood, and he'd known long before I did that taking over the family practice wasn't just what duty required of him, but what he wanted to do. Brian loved Sugarberry—so much that he'd been willing to lose *Angel* over it years ago. Maybe that had been what she was asking of him in the call I'd overheard—"Let it go, move on, do something else." Maybe he was already planning how to do just that?

At home I went straight to the basement and started punching.

I would make that offer first thing tomorrow morning—no, tonight. March over to his house with a contract that offered fair market value for his interest in the business. Make it easy on myself. On Brian.

But it wouldn't make things easy on Brian at all, I knew. Even if it placated demanding Angelica, losing what his family—our families—had built for generations would remove a piece of his soul that nothing would replace. I wondered whether Angelica knew that. (*Smack*—my fist made a solid thunking sound as I punched into the cushion.) I wondered whether she cared. (*Smack.*)

I didn't know how long I brutalized the pile of down (such an ignominious end for its many years of service to my family), but when my shoulders started to burn and my arms grew too heavy to lift I finally had to stop, leaning against the concrete-block wall facing a wall of wire storage shelves, panting.

As I sat there letting my breathing steady, my heart rate slow to something approaching normal, I realized what I was looking at: boxes of castoff items my family had packed away for generations, meticulously labeled—*BEAN: S. canning supplies;*

*BEAN: P. school reports; ADAMS: P. and W. docs; ADAMS: G. baby clothes.*

And on the lowest shelf: *BEAN: M. personal.*

I'd always assumed that M. Bean stood for my great-grandfather, Martin. But now a tendril of excitement began to unfurl in my chest.

What if *M.* stood for *Millie?*

I yanked the box out, ignoring my screaming upper body as its weight insulted my muscles, and dropped it to the floor, clawing at the flimsy cardboard to pull back the flaps, which gave easily under tape that had long since lost its adhesive properties. My heart thudded, my hands trembling as I looked inside.

More pictures, neatly lined up in separate plastic sleeves on loose cardboard-backed pages that rested on top of one another, lumpy dried glue at the top of the pages making the pile uneven.

I eagerly thumbed through, looking for Millie, but it was just more ancient family photos of long-ago relatives. Disappointment squeezed me like a fist.

Except . . . that glue. As if the pages had been yanked from an album.

I looked again, slowly this time, and the realization sank in, so surprisingly obvious it made me laugh aloud: Millie couldn't possibly be in these pictures.

*Milton* would.

And he was—photo after photo, with eyes I should have recognized immediately, or a smile that I certainly would have if its appearance in the photos hadn't been so rare. Here was Milton standing at the fringe of a family photo, wearing an old-fashioned double-breasted suit. Holding an unnatural pose in an awkward phase that could only be a school picture. Milton with my mom: making cookies with an old-fashioned manual press; playing some kind of inexplicable game where he curled under a table while my mom sat beside him with a watering can, pretending to pour water on him; Mom on Milton's shoulders looking equal parts terrified and elated.

I laughed as I flipped through the evidence of a life I'd never heard about, cried as I watched a story unfold with a family member I'd never known existed until a few months before, Milton's appearances finally scarcer, more subdued, and even moving subtly out of frame as the years went on, as if he were being edged out of the family long before he actually was—or removing himself. Someone had kept these. I lifted the end of the box to check the label again, not realizing how hard I was praying until I confirmed what I hoped for: my mother's handwriting.

My mother had saved these. She hadn't completely erased Millie after all.

I pulled out page after page, wanting to see everything, know everything. But underneath the last page was something else—a battered mahogany-colored folder with an old-fashioned string clasp.

I pulled it out carefully, so the escaping edges of the papers inside wouldn't spill out, and set it on the floor in front of me, slowly unwrapping the string from around the little button.

Letters. Stacks of airmail envelopes with exotic stamps canceled with old-fashioned squiggly lines, each of them bearing my mother's name and this house's address in Millie's instantly recognizable spidery handwriting.

She'd kept them. My mother had kept every letter, judging by the thickness of the folder, that she'd ever received from my aunt. She hadn't let go. Not completely.

I retrieved an envelope from the back, wanting to start with the oldest ones, the way I had with my mom's—the counterparts of these, I was willing to bet, the mortar in between the replies I had already read. And then I sat there, heedless of sitting on the cold concrete floor, forgetting the pain in my shoulders and neck as I followed the magnificent life my aunt had lived once she had the courage to leave behind what no longer served her.

WHEN MY STOMACH's rumblings grew too loud and sharp to keep ignoring and my feet kept falling asleep no matter what position I moved into, I finally gathered everything back into the box, with the letters I'd read carefully stacked in reverse chronological order and set apart from the ones I had yet to finish, and lugged the whole thing upstairs.

Over dinner, the last of the nuked Amy's frozen dinners I'd vowed weeks earlier to be through with in my bid to take more time to care for myself, I kept reading.

Finally I came to the last one—but this letter bore no stamp and it wasn't addressed to my mother.

It was *from* her. This one had never been mailed.

*Dear . . . I guess I don't quite know what to call you.*

*I know the whole story now . . . well, at least as much as Mother and Father are willing to tell me. As much as they know. And I'm . . . I don't know what. I don't know anything right now, it seems—as if everything I thought was solid and steady has suddenly been torn away, or was never really real in the first place.*

A bolt of recognition struck me. That was the way I'd felt for so long—since Brian left. Since my mom died. Since I'd found out about the terrible secret my family had kept from me all my life. My mother had felt those same things. It created a strange, sad tie to her.

> *I keep trying to make sense of what simply makes no sense to me. To find out if there was something that I didn't notice or some kind of phony act you were putting on that I couldn't see through.*
>
> *I'm sorry if that hurts your feelings. I want to be honest with you. We always have been.*
>
> *I have thought about this a lot, reviewed nearly every moment we ever spent together trying to see what I overlooked. How you were somehow faking it with me. And . . . I just can't. Maybe you don't think you were ever really "you" your whole life, but I did, and I loved who you were. Who I thought you were. I can't bear to imagine that that wasn't real.*
>
> *So I'm not going to. I'm going to tuck all those memories away in a little box in my mind and I'm going to leave them there untouched, because those are some of the best times in my whole life. And I can't bear to find out they were never what I thought they were. So please don't take that away from me.*
>
> *I'm sad we'll never wander through the cabarets of Germany together, the way we talked about, or trek through a jungle . . . or pet a tortoise in the Galapagos Islands. But maybe those things were fake too, just talk, the things you say to a child. I don't want to know that either, if they were. But those are foolish and selfish dreams anyway, I realize. Family is everything—you taught me that—and mine needs me here.*
>
> *I don't hate you, if that still matters to you. I could never.*
> *Tricia*

———

I SAT WITH the letter in my hands for a long time. If only my mother had sent this one, instead of the one with that single hurtful line—*Perhaps it's best if you don't write back*. How different might Millie's life have been? That terse sentence explained nothing, shared nothing, left Millie with no insight into the painful mixed feelings my mom had been wrestling with . . . feelings that might have changed things for my aunt. Let her know that even if my mother struggled to accept her choices, she loved her no less.

The letter was undated. Had this been my mother's initial reaction to learning the truth about Millie, or had she written it after reconsideration and remorse had begun to set in? I couldn't know. And did it even matter? Millie had recovered— she was too strong not to. But what it had cost her . . . ! All those years of impotent rage and confusion and hurt. And what it must have cost my mother—the pain of hurting someone she so clearly loved, of being so desperately hurt by her, through no fault of Millie's other than following her heart. The ruthless abandonment of all my mother's dreams of seeing the world, forging her own path, out of some misplaced sense of family loyalty.

My mother had cared so much about our family legacy . . . if this was what it led to, the idea seemed comically, tragically absurd. Mom had let herself be defined by expectations, and when they left her with nothing she folded in on herself and slowly disappeared. Like me. But Millie did the opposite. When her family—our family—tried laying their expectations on her, demanding she be other than who she actually was to fit in, to be accepted and loved, she said no. And she went and lived her life her way, on her terms.

Millie had done the best she could with the hand she was dealt and her own fears and pain and anger. My mother did the best she could despite what I could see now, as an adult, was severe depression after my dad left. His abandonment must have hit directly on the raw wound Millie had inadvertently created that Mom had never let heal. Brian touched on that same wound with me—one my dad had created in me as well—but he'd done the best he could too.

So now it was down to me. I couldn't control other people's actions, their decisions. But I could control mine.

The thought swept in like a fresh breeze blowing a storm out to sea, and suddenly, after all my ruminating, I knew exactly what I wanted to do.

# Twenty-seven

It was full dark by the time I got to Brian's house, after I finished the errands I'd needed to run. When he cracked open the door he looked surprised to see me weighed down with paper sacks, grocery bags, and a large cellophane-wrapped basket.

Or maybe he was just surprised to see me, period.

"Hey," he said, his voice going up at the end in a question.

"May I come in? Just for a few minutes?" I said.

He turned his head slightly, as if checking the stairs behind him, and in the spill of light I saw his hesitation, his concern . . . and his exhaustion. Brian was worn out and I hadn't seen it till now, too busy trying to insulate myself from anything having to do with him.

"Um . . . Angelica's sleeping," he said apologetically, and for a moment anger flared at being denied entry to this house that had felt like mine all my life, at terms Angelica dictated even when she was unconscious.

But it quickly flickered out. As I'd run all over town earlier retrieving the things I'd wanted, I'd had a lot of time to think.

*She's only pretty on the outside,* Brian had said of mean Marilyn Martin when we were kids. As angry as I might be right now—as hurt—I couldn't make myself believe that he had fallen in love with a shiny, beautiful package with no substance.

And however awful it had been for me since she had come to Sugarberry, Angelica must have been miserable too—she'd moved to a strange town where everyone seemed to know everyone but no one knew her. To a tiny rural dot on a map after the excitement and energy of a big city. She was pregnant and sick and miserable, her body, clearly a fine-tuned machine she took some pride in, betraying her with its changes and hormone surges. And amid all that, her husband's former wife lived three houses away, still visibly pining for him, and he continued to befriend and defend me, going to work in close quarters with me every day in the business that had linked our families for three generations—while Angelica couldn't even find work in her field.

In a lot of ways she had it much, much worse than I did.

"Okay," I said, not letting a trace of upset into my tone. I held out the large paper sack in the crook of my left arm. "This is from Jody's Diner—plain chicken breast and boiled rice with carrots. Don't worry," I said with a wry smile. "That's for Angelica, nothing too spicy or gassy or, well, smelly, I guess, so it won't upset her stomach. For you I got chicken-fried steak with a baked potato and a salad, of course."

He looked dazed, taking the bag from me.

"That's for tonight. In here"—I hoisted the plastic bags looped around my arm—"are some things you might keep on hand: ginger ale, saltines—but also Ritzes in case that's too bland even for a pregnant woman—and some antinausea suppositories. There's no way I'd be sticking those things anywhere, but I understand that if you're nauseated enough you'll try anything. And there are a few other things I found on a pregnancy chat room that might help." I'd also thought of tucking in the recipes for the sour cream kuchen and hot chocolate, but no. Some things I was keeping for myself.

He took the bags, confusion wrinkling his face. "I . . . I thought you were mad."

I almost laughed at the understatement of my raging fury. I was coming to see that my pain was not so much from Brian not loving me as from my needing him to still love me.

"I am," I admitted. "But it's okay." I held up the basket. "This is an early baby shower gift from me. Since I won't be here. And shouldn't be invited even if I were."

He ignored my gentle upbraiding. "Where will you be?"

"I'm leaving. For a while I'll be in Florida; I don't know how long. After that . . . I'm not sure yet."

His eyebrows bunched. "But what about the firm? Our clients?"

His arms were still full and he was making no move to set the bags down, as if he'd forgotten he was still holding them. I let out a long exhale as I leaned over to set the basket on the doorstep—not a sigh so much as a release of tension.

As I'd run all over town ruminating on Brian and Angelica I'd realized something else: the thing she'd probably wanted him to ask of me in the phone call I'd overheard. The thing Brian knew was a step too far. Lawyer Angelica couldn't find a job at a law firm anywhere in town . . . and I suspected she wanted to come and work in mine.

"I'd like you to buy me out of the business," I said. "Or if that's not financially possible right now, I'm willing to stay on as a silent partner—for a time. Until you and Angelica can buy out my interest."

"What? But that's our family practice!"

I gave him a resolute smile. This was the right thing to do. For all of us. "Brian . . . we're not family anymore." I said it as gently as I could, but I could see the pain of it in his face as his arms slackened, the paper sack nearly toppling to the floor. I jerked forward to catch it, setting it down at his feet and then stepping back over the threshold again. "You and Angelica are making a family of your own . . . this is going to be *your* legacy. But it was never mine."

I thought about my mother grimly soldiering to work when her heart was shattered after my father left. It had never really been her legacy either, but she'd held on to the mantle out of an unswerving sense of family loyalty. Reading her letters made me realize that the more noble loyalty by far would have been to herself. The way Millie's had always been. If there was such a thing as loved ones looking down on you after they passed, I hoped my mother wasn't upset that I was putting the mantle down.

I thought perhaps she might understand. Might even cheer me on.

"Grace . . . you don't have to do this. I've told Angel that—"

"I'm not leaving for her," I said, cutting him off. "Or *because* of her. Or you, or my mom, or anything, really—except me. I want to go. This isn't my dream. It never was."

His mouth drooped, the shadows seeming to deepen under his eyes, and I knew I wasn't making things easier on him at the moment. "What is?"

"I don't know. But that's what I want to go find out. Meanwhile you guys need space for yours." I let myself reach forward and rest my fingers on his forearm—lightly, comfort rather than possession—then gave a reassuring squeeze and let go. "I really, really do wish you happiness."

Brian shook his head. "I'm not happy if you're going. But . . . I get it, I guess." He looked at the bags he held, as if surprised to see them still dangling from his arms, and finally set them down. "I have no idea what I'm doing, Grace," he said in a rushed whisper as he straightened. "I literally don't know if I can handle this."

I smiled, because for once that was probably actually *literally* true. "I know you pretty well—"

"Better than anyone," he cut in, and I reminded myself again—the way I would have to over and over for a while—that he didn't mean it to hurt as much as it did.

"Maybe," I said noncommittally. "But I want you to trust me when I tell you that you can handle this. This is what you've always wanted." I took a breath and closed my eyes, just for a moment, then opened them again even knowing he'd see the shine in them. "All of it. You're ready—more than ready." My throat ached, but I pushed the words out. "You're going to be a great father."

"Grace." His eyes were wet too, and he lifted his arms, making that safe haven I'd always been eager to run to, to lose myself in, to bury my face in his scent and strength and *presence*.

It took everything I had to take a step back. "Not yet. Someday. I promise."

He looked shattered and I almost reconsidered—one last hug, what was the harm? But I was saved by the sound of Angelica's wobbly voice carrying down the stairs.

"Brian? I need you. I'm literally vomiting my guts out."

I bit back a grin. Maybe they *were* actually perfect for each other.

"Go," I said. "Take care of her." I made a shooing motion and leaned in to grab the door handle when he made no move to shut it. I gave him a gentle push on the shoulder and pulled the door, then stopped just before it closed. "Brian," I said, and he stopped on the bottom stair and turned to me. "I love you," I blurted quickly, before I could change my mind. "I always have. In some ways I always will. Send me a Christmas card. I'll make sure you know where I am."

"I don't understand," he said resignedly. "This is crazy, Grace—you're just taking off with no idea where you're going, what you're going to do?"

"Nope." I lifted both hands, palms up, grinning. "Isn't it exciting?"

# Twenty-eight

The cool wash of air-conditioning that hit me as soon as I stepped off the jetway was a decoy, a false promise for the wall of warmth and humidity I knew would hit me as soon as I claimed my baggage—nobody started a new chapter in life without baggage—and exited the airport's sliding doors.

Millie said she'd be waiting for me as soon as the plane landed, and I had my mother's letters—including the last one my aunt had never gotten to read—in my carry-on to give her. I hoped they offered more comfort than pain.

She'd been delighted when I'd called to tell her my plans—inasmuch as I knew them. I was loving creating the estate planning seminar Jason had proposed, and that was where I planned to start, seeing whether it was something I might take to various towns in Florida—or to other cities, other states I'd never seen. Maybe I'd work on the virtual estate planning I'd been investigating. Do some traveling and see the world a bit until I decided what my long-range plans were, the way Millie had done, the way I'd once dreamed of doing. In between, I'd keep coming back here to see my aunt. To let the beach continue to work its magic on my soul.

I had the luxury of not having to figure out my plans right away. My inherited frugality meant that my savings accounts were comfortably funded, and I'd put the house—the house I'd inherited rather than chosen—on the market, Brian kindly offering to help oversee anything that might need immediate attention. He'd been visibly shaken to see the For Sale sign go up in the yard, but I knew firsthand that change was scary at first, until you accepted it as the new normal. He and Angelica had accepted my offer to buy out my half of the practice—that was my mom's dream. It was time for me to find my own.

I didn't know exactly what that was yet. But that was okay, I thought, my heart rate speeding up as I stepped onto the escalator and it delivered me toward where I could see Millie, Jason, and Bridget come into view, waiting for me at the bottom.

This time I was just going to enjoy the story—even if I didn't know how it was going to end.

# Acknowledgments

I always bristle at the notion that movies have long lists of credits for all the people who help make them happen, yet books don't. Please bear with me for a lengthy credits crawl—these folks deserve some screen time.

First and foremost, Michelle Stafford provided me with insight that I could never have had without her as I wrote Millie's character. Michelle's warmth, kindness, and ready willingness to share parts of her personal life with a total stranger still have me overcome with gratitude and awe. Michelle, you are as strong and fierce and gracious a lady as I've ever met, and I'm so grateful our paths have crossed. Thank you.

The beautiful, sylphlike, maddeningly-one-inch-taller-than-I-am Brooke Hardie was my go-to girl for all things estate planning. You want to see someone light up with love for what they do, schedule yourself a consultation with this woman and let her take care of all your end-of-life concerns. It's really, really not as scary or depressing as you think. Brooke, your enthusiasm for your field and for sharing it with others was a great inspiration to me, and your knowledge was invaluable—if I screwed anything up or took "artistic license," I will buy you unlimited Bloody Mary Bars at Z' Tejas by way of apology.

Tammy Shaklee, "the Gay Matchmaker" (no, I'm not making that up—Google it), was incredibly welcoming of a lookyloo author who was curious what a matchmaker did and how she did it. Watching firsthand her delight in interviewing, consulting with, and matching her H4M clients was not only edifying, but fascinating, and provided excellent insight for me into Millie. Again, all errors in the conveyance of such info are fully and entirely my own.

The real Millie bears no physical resemblance to the fictional one, though she inspired the character. My great-aunt Mildred Hlavin, a woman I scarcely knew until my mother, her favorite niece, brought her to live near us in the last years of her life, stood barely five feet tall, had electric blue eyes and a wide, ready smile, and always dressed like a fashion plate from a women's career magazine, long after her retirement. Feisty and frequently hilarious, Millie never married and was a model of living her life as she chose, social mores be damned: flirting outrageously with the men in her assisted-living apartment complex, drinking her "evening toddy" of rum right till the end, smoking till her eightieth birthday (when she abruptly quit and never looked back), and leaving a cache of surprises behind for us to discover she'd lived even freer than we imagined.

Marcie Walter's constant eagerness to read anything that fountains out of my head and onto the page is so very validating and gratifying, and I always count on her pull-no-punches feedback with my early drafts. Dr. Duana Welch, psychologist and author of the revelatory *Love, Factually* relationship books, is not only an invaluable truthometer for me in writing about relationships, but also the most supportive, positive reader and friend anyone could ask for. Stalwart friend and author Gretchen Archer told me, "I just want you to remember, forever, that I was one of the first to love Grace." I will remember, Gretchen. Forever.

An extra-grateful shout-out to Kelly Harrell, Richard LeMay, Karin Gillespie, and Laurie Frankel. You all know what you did.

I am ever thankful for the reviewers and bloggers who offer their time, passion, and support to helping connect writers to readers. And to those readers—if a book falls in the forest and there's no one to read it, does it make a difference? Thanks for being the fabulous forest creatures who make it matter.

In fact, when the creative well ran dry and I couldn't think of clever enough names for Millie's blog and website, readers came through for me with an avalanche of wonderful suggestions it was hard to choose from, and for which I am endlessly grateful. Special thanks to Eunice Douglas Durand for "Silver Linings," Stacy Kosluchar and Jessica Crawley for "New Tricks from an Old Dog," and Karyn Kash Israel for "Been There Done That." All three of those are far better than anything I came up with (as were all the suggestions that poured in)— thanks for making me look good.

My Penheads, John Jones, Amber Novak, and Kelly Harrell: What a lucky break it was that we met so many years ago and teamed up. I'm so much better thanks to you guys as part of my writing process and my life. Thank you is never enough. And for dear John, we miss you.

Agent Courtney Miller-Callihan of Handspun Lit has championed me and my books many times, not least in what turned out to be an exceptionally long and unexpectedly tortuous journey with *A Little Bit of Grace*. Thank you, Courtney, with all my heart. (And now you know firsthand the joys of gingerbread pancakes at Magnolia Café.)

Cindy Hwang, your enthusiasm and warmth significantly raised the heat index of my cockles, and after our wide-ranging, delightfully six-degrees, hour-long first phone call I knew I'd found the publishing home of my dreams at Penguin Berkley. Thanks also to editorial assistant Angela Kim, publicist Tara O'Connor, and marketing manager Bridget O'Toole, the Dream Team for any lucky author. Production and managing editors Megha Jain, Megan Elmore, and Hope Ellis made some pretty wonderful catches that kept the egg off my face, as did copy editor Sheila Moody. I'm so grateful to the whole team at Berkley for their support and enthusiasm.

Last but always first, my husband Joel (the Dogfather) good-naturedly tolerated unusual levels of neglect and neurosis with the writing of this book, and provided many dinners, kitchen cleanups, and dog walks while my head was buried in my monitor. All while pelting me with a powerful firehose of love and support and faith in me that I never, ever take for granted.

# Author's Note and Resources

It was important to me to accurately and respectfully present the experience, difficulties, and courage of a trans woman "coming into herself," especially during a time when there was so much less acceptance and understanding, and it simply could not have been done without Michelle Stafford and her generous spirit. Michelle also graciously read an early draft in record time to offer me crucial feedback. Any shortcomings or inaccuracies in Millie's experience and portrayal are entirely a result of my own inadequacies.

Brandon L. Beck and Dr. Oliver Blumer of the Transgender Education Network of Texas (www.transtexas.org) generously responded to the blind queries of a complete stranger and pointed me toward resources that proved invaluable. At a time of rampant misinformation and discrimination, it's humbling to me that so many in a marginalized, often poorly understood community were so forthcoming and welcoming to a cisgender stranger brimming with intrusive questions and asking for favors.

While researching to create the character of Millie, I was most struck by the realization that what I once thought of as

"LGBTQ+ issues" are human issues. An attack—verbal, physical, legislative, or otherwise—against any person for their appearance, gender, sexuality, lifestyle, or person is an attack on all of us, on our basic right to be who we are and feel safe in the world.

My research was by no means exhaustive, and this is a tiny, tiny fraction of the resources and reading material available on gender issues. If you're interested in learning more and broadening your understanding, any of these resources, along with many other organizations, websites, and other materials, can help.

1. The National Geographic documentary *Gender Revolution*, with Katie Couric, is a fascinating overview of the complexities of gender through research and interviews with scientists, psychologists, activists, authors, and families that will have you rethinking what you may believe about gender identity. https://katiecouric.com/gender-revolution

2. In a national study, 40 percent of transgender adults reported having made a suicide attempt, 92 percent of them before the age of twenty-five. The Trevor Project is a nonprofit organization dedicated to crisis intervention and suicide prevention among LGBTQ+ youth, and a repository of support, information, legislation, education, and other resources. www.thetrevorproject.org

3. Trans Lifeline is a nonprofit dedicated to the well-being of transgender people, running a hotline staffed by transgender people for transgender people. www.translifeline.org

4. Transgender people—particularly those of color—are far more likely to be the victims of physical violence, sexual vio-

lence, and hate crimes; each year transgender homicides continue to hit new highs. The National Coalition of Anti-Violence Programs (NCAVP) is an advocacy group that works to prevent and respond to violence against LGBTQ+ and HIV-affected people, and offers education, support, and organization. https://avp.org

5. The LGBTQ+ community is under legislative attack as never before, with a flurry of discriminatory laws being proposed and passed that assail basic civil rights. The Human Rights Campaign is the largest civil rights advocacy group protecting the rights and safety of the LGBTQ+ community, and its website offers a storehouse of information, resources, and ways you can get involved: www.hrc.org

6. The National Center for Transgender Equality provides a transgender advocacy presence in Washington, DC. https://transequality.org

7. Lambda Legal is a national legal organization whose mission is to achieve full recognition of the civil rights of lesbians, gay men, bisexuals, transgender people, and those with HIV. www.lambdalegal.org

8. One of the most affecting testimonies I saw when the Texas legislature tried to pass laws discriminating against the LGBTQ+ community was that of clinical psychologist Dr. Colt Keo-Meier, about his own path as a transgender man and his work as an expert in gender and sexuality issues. If you'd like a greater understanding of transgender issues and the trans experience, you can watch it yourself here: www.youtube.com/watch?v=vOAYIv_0K-s&feature=youtu.be. A preeminent researcher in the field of transgender health,

Keo-Meier serves on the child and adolescent specialist committee creating the next version of the World Professional Association for Transgender Health (WPATH) Standards of Care and is the cofounder of Gender Infinity, an organization dedicated to connecting gender-diverse individuals and their families with resources in the southern United States. Learn more at http://coltkeo-meier.com.

9. GLAAD, one of the most prominent media watchdog and advocacy organizations in the country for the LGBTQ+ community (www.glaad.org), offers an excellent list of further resources here: www.glaad.org/transgender/resources.

10. I'm also grateful to author Laurie Frankel, whom I contacted during the writing of this story simply as a fan of her book *Goodbye for Now*, only to learn in an astonishing instance of serendipity that her follow-up novel, which she was just about to release—the beautiful, achingly real *This Is How It Always Is*—is about a little boy who says he wants to be a girl when he grows up, and his family's lovely, loving, difficult journey to help their child be who she really is. Laurie, who has a trans daughter, was gracious enough to read an early draft of this story, and her words of encouragement and affirmation meant the world to me.

——————

# *A Little Bit of Grace*

——————

Phoebe Fox

# Discussion Questions

1. Do you believe in "the one" or do you think you can find love with more than one person throughout your life?

2. In what ways did Grace transform during her time in Florida?

3. What do you think would've happened if Grace's mom had sent the other letter to Millie?

4. Everyone struggles to be true to themselves through all stages of life. Can you think of a particular time in your life when you struggled? How did you work through it?

5. Do you think there are things that are truly unforgivable, even when it comes to family and loved ones? If so, what are some examples?

6. How do you deal with anger? Can rage ever be a force for good? How?

7. Do you think Millie's life would have been different if Grace's mom had fully accepted her and they'd stayed close? How?

8. Were Grace and Brian "right" for each other, or do you think he married her as a rebound, or a "safe" choice after heartbreak? What does either answer imply about their marriage as well as their divorce?

9. Do you agree with Grace that a friendship you may have had with an ex needs a period of dormancy after a breakup? Can you ever truly recapture the same level of friendship with someone you had a relationship with after the romance is over?

10. Grace's father would criticize Grace offhandedly when she was growing up. Did anyone ever say something thoughtless or critical to you that stayed with you and had a deep effect on your behavior or actions? Were you ever able to recognize and let go of the misbelief that created in you?

*Photo by Korey Howell*

**Phoebe Fox** has been a contributor and regular columnist for a number of national, regional, and local publications, including The Huffington Post, Elite Daily, and SheKnows. A former actor on stage and screen, Phoebe has been suspended from wires as a mall fairy; was accidentally concussed by a blank gun; and hosted a short-lived game show. She has been a relationship columnist; a movie, theater, and book reviewer; and a radio personality, and is a close observer of relationships in the wild. She lives in Austin, Texas, with her husband and two excellent dogs. *A Little Bit of Grace* is her fifth novel.

CONNECT ONLINE

PhoebeFoxAuthor.com

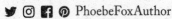 PhoebeFoxAuthor

Ready to find
your next great read?

Let us help.

**Visit prh.com/nextread**